# The Ribbon Murders

# The Ribbon Murders

## Sharon Ervin

**Five Star • Waterville, Maine**

First Edition
First Printing: March 2006

Published in 2006 in conjunction with Tekno Books.

Set in 11 pt. Plantin by Christina S. Huff.

Printed in the United States on permanent paper.

**Library of Congress Cataloging-in-Publication Data**

Ervin, Sharon.
    The ribbon murders / by Sharon Ervin.—1st ed.
        p.   cm.
    ISBN 1-59414-436-2 (hc : alk. paper)
    1. Women journalists—Fiction.   2. Serial murders—Fiction.
    3. Police—Oklahoma—Fiction.   4. Oklahoma—Fiction.
    I. Title.
    PS3605.R86R53 2006
    813'.6—dc22                                          2005029765

To Bill

# Acknowledgments

I owe special thanks to:

Tommy Graham, Oklahoma State Bureau of Investigation Agent, who laughed at my questions, but graciously shared his expertise;

Cleveland County, Oklahoma, Sheriff Bill Porter, who took me to my first homicide scene, then made me stay in the car awhile;

Store clerk Edward Long, who patiently introduced me to a variety of handguns and described the slugs they produce;

The Oklahoma Writers Federation, Inc., contest judge who awarded this one third place in the Mystery Novel Category;

Teresa Atkerson and Ronda Talley, for their excellent copy reading;

Stony Hardcastle, who insisted his creative writing class hear the entire manuscript; and

Diane Piron-Gelman, for judicious editing.

# Chapter One

*Wednesday, October 5*

I pushed open the heavy glass door to the sheriff's office on the second floor of the Bishop County Courthouse and inhaled. The air inside was a reviving sixty-five degrees. Sheriff Dudley Roundtree liked it cool. Outside, the October afternoon was a blistering ninety-four and muggy.

As I shifted my reporter's spiral notebook from one hand to the other, the wire snagged my T-shirt. I had to tug twice to pop it loose. The hole was tiny, barely noticeable. I pushed windblown hair out of my face.

Deputy Gary Spence slouched at the dispatcher's station behind the counter, absorbed in a paperback book. Lord, why did it have to be Spence? I felt relieved to see the light on in the sheriff's private office. That meant *the man* was in.

I straightened to my full five-foot-seven and spoke loudly. "Where's Patsy?"

Spence glanced up and grinned as he laid the paperback face down, flipped the radio to speaker and removed the headset. "Hey, sweetheart."

I couldn't stop the blush that burned around my shirt collar and crept upward. I usually reacted like that, even to casual endearments. I was too darn sensitive about how men, even old guys like Spence, talked to me. It was even worse when they looked at me the suggestive way Spence did.

I should have been used to it. After puberty, people—especially men—no longer complimented my astute powers of observation, my insights or my mental quickness. All evaluations stopped with my physique.

At twenty-three, I had come to appreciate any male who saw beyond my prominent physical attributes. I had some standard put-downs reserved for goons with big mouths like Spence, but I wasn't in the mood, so I gave him my long-suffering smile. "Anything I need to know?"

"Come sit on my knee, my chickadee, and I'll tell all, for a little fee." He patted his beefy thigh and sat straighter. "Did you hear that? I'm a poet. Poetry oughta get a guy a kiss, don't you think?" He turned his face, tapping his cheek with his index finger, marking the place for the imagined peck.

I felt the blush reignite. "Not on your best day, Spence. Where's Patsy?"

"She took a personal day." He arched an eyebrow and gave me his Casanova look, which actually made him resemble SpongeBob SquarePants. "I'd take one, too, if you'd go to the woods with me." He winked. "Doll, you're not foolin' anyone with that slob act."

Without intending to, I glanced down at my clothes: a corduroy jumper over a wrinkled T-shirt—with a tiny new hole—and last year's brown sandals.

Spence winked again. "Guys can visualize a D-cup, gorgeous, no matter how many layers you pile on over it."

More heat radiated from my face. Seeing my discomfort, his grin broadened. "How about it? You ready to go to the country? Let me do some hands-on investigatin'?"

"You're not my type, Spence. Besides, your wife might not like it."

"You're probably right." He stood, hitched up his gun belt and sucked in his protruding stomach. "She's pretty jealous of a hunk like me. But me and you could sneak off. . . ."

The radio speaker crackled and a man's shrill voice filled the room. Spence squinted at the machine and pressed a button. "Say again."

Sheriff Roundtree filled the doorway from his private office. The deputy glanced at him and they listened intently to the garbled message in the high-pitched squawk. It was gibberish to me, but the sheriff and deputy sobered.

"Tell Wheeler to meet me there." Roundtree turned his back on the plea in Spence's face and looked straight at me. "Do you want to go?"

Spence groaned. Whatever was happening had to be important. "Yes," I said.

"Keep up."

I spun to follow as Roundtree lunged by me, out the door, down the stairs and into the parking lot. I trotted, staying maybe two steps off the sheriff's pace as he raced out into the sweltering afternoon. I dived into the passenger seat. Roundtree started the engine and the siren. "Buckle it tight."

I cinched the seat belt snug. The car radio belched constant, excited chatter but I caught only a word here and there. I had no clue what the excitement was about.

Roundtree slowed his vehicle at the intersections in town, then opened it up as we went bawling and careening out a blacktop county road. He didn't even glance at me as he said, "When we get to the scene, you stay in the car."

I didn't know what *scene*. Questions bounced around in my mind like pinballs, but I'd never seen the sheriff this intense. I had no idea why he invited me along and then wanted me to wait in the car, but this obviously was no time to argue.

Roundtree's size and booming voice intimidated most people. Fifty-seven years old, he was retired Navy, stood six-foot-four and weighed a disciplined two hundred thirty pounds. Handsome, for an old guy, except for that knot at the bridge of his nose. He was happily married, but he and Alice had never had any kids. In the year I'd had the courthouse run, I'd learned to trust Sheriff Roundtree, even admire him. The regard was more or less mutual. He watched out for me and didn't let any news in his area slip by. I returned the favor by mentioning his name often. Guys who run for public office every four years appreciate that.

Roundtree listened intently as other voices increased the radio traffic, so I kept quiet. I watched the odometer as we drove generally north and west out of town seventeen miles before I saw traffic congestion ahead. Roundtree frowned at the cars parked helter-skelter along the road, but he didn't say anything. He seemed calm enough, so I risked a question.

"What is it?" I counted more than a dozen law enforcement cruisers. At least twenty-five people milled on the left shoulder of the road ahead.

"A homicide." He negotiated his cruiser around the cars parked at random. "The victim's naked. There'll mostly be men. It might embarrass you."

I started to object, but he held a big palm in my face like a cop stopping traffic. "I want to go first." He lowered his voice to a kindlier tone. "You stay in the car. I'll let you come after I've checked things out."

He pulled to the grassy shoulder on the right and cut the engine. A photographer was taking pictures of something in the bar ditch on the left side of the road. A grim older man, coat and tie flapping, hurried to the side of the sheriff's car.

"We can't tell who's got jurisdiction," the coat and tie said without so much as a glance at me. His words were clipped. He pulled the car door open and held it as the sheriff stepped out.

Roundtree scanned the landscape. "We're outside Bishop city limits. Still in my county, though."

The man nodded. "Cosgrove and Dominion's city limits are somewhere out here too." He shoved the car door closed, then assumed the lead as the two paced briskly toward the gathering.

Undersheriff Raymond Wheeler pulled in behind the sheriff's cruiser. He glanced at me but didn't say a word as he did a quick step to join the men. Wheeler and I were on good terms, but I didn't feel like pressing it at that particular moment.

None of the law enforcement types had barricaded the road. Of course, there wasn't much regular traffic on this old road any more with the four-lane so close. One good thing: I didn't see any other reporters around.

The sun heated the car. I cranked down a window and tried to hear snatches of the muffled conversations among the bystanders. Their voices were low but carried occasionally in the still afternoon. At times the sound was totally obliterated by the truck traffic on the interstate highway less than a mile west of us.

A patrolman came striding away from the scene. I stiffened, thinking he might be coming to get me. He nodded as he passed, but marched right on to his patrol car. I tried to relax.

The air was hot and sticky and smelled of autumn vegetation baking.

The patrolman returned carrying a blanket. He crossed the highway, through the corridor framed by law enforcement personnel, and disappeared into the bar ditch, then reemerged without the blanket.

Minutes passed. A horsefly buzzed. People at the scene seemed to move in slow motion. Heat shimmered off the blacktop. I opened the car door.

Roundtree had told me to stay in the car. I didn't see much

13

difference between staying *in* the car and *with* the car, so I stepped out.

Sources could make or break a reporter. I needed to show Riley Wedge, the wire service bureau chief, that I could cultivate people, make them trust me. Wedge and I had a deal. If I proved myself in two years on the *Clarion*, he'd promised to make me an overseas correspondent with the wire service. I had one year to go and Riley had been promoted. Now he was in an even better position to deliver on his promise.

Guys like Roundtree could make a reporter look good, so I intended to do exactly what he said—more or less. I eased the door closed and sidled forward. Standing near the front fender, I pulled out my ballpoint and notepad and jotted some of my observations: the wild ride with lights and sirens, the number of cars, the shields and faces I recognized. Roundtree had called it. There were no women.

"Who are you supposed to be with?"

The deep voice boomed right behind me. I nearly jumped out of my skin. Lurching sideways, I bumped the fender hard with my hip. He hadn't made a sound walking up.

I hissed, "Damn!" as I turned and glowered into an angry face partially concealed behind mirrored shades.

He was young, muscular, maybe six feet tall and stocky, with powerful-looking hands. "This is a murder scene, ma'am. If you're not part of the investigation, you need to leave."

His three-piece, pinstriped suit contrasted with his close-cropped hair. Some bureaucrat, a little impressed with himself.

It took heroic effort to control my voice. I did not want him to hear even a hint of nervousness. "Take a hike."

Instead of retreating, he moved a step closer. It took all my willpower not to flinch. Veins throbbed in his neck, which was constrained by a white shirt collar held fast by a somber necktie. Without meaning to, I eased back half a step, prompting a satisfied smirk that annoyed the bejeebers out of me.

He abbreviated his original question. "Who are you with?"

I pointed to the cruiser. "Sheriff Roundtree. Who are *you* with?" I sounded almost as rude as I intended.

He stood there a long moment, studying my face, before he gave a dismissive snort. "This is no place for a woman." Then he stepped around me and strode toward the cluster of investigators.

A chauvinist, probably a cop, he was one I hadn't seen before, which meant he probably wasn't from Bishop. Watching him walk, I grudgingly gave him high marks. He toed in slightly. Definitely a jock. He didn't seem observant enough to be a detective. I'd been leaning on Roundtree's car with the insignia emblazoned on its sides when the guy asked who I was with. Duh.

I massaged my hip and tried to regain my composure. I was shaking. Pinstripe had startled me. Okay, so I felt jumpy. Forgivable, surely. I was about to see my first dead person— the first unembalmed one, anyway.

"Don't be such a wuss," I whispered to my toes, which peeped from the tips of my aged sandals.

The south wind stirred, taking some of the edge off the heat and my nervousness. I turned to face the breeze, still giving myself a little pep talk when Roundtree stepped into sight. He beckoned. I took a deep breath and squared my shoulders. "This is it. Be tough."

Animated conversations among the men died as I walked into their midst. Two or three nodded responses to soft hellos, but none made eye contact—even the ones I knew pretty well. That was odd.

15

Roundtree led me down the slope into the bar ditch and indicated the body shrouded beneath a blanket.

"Is it a man?" I asked quietly. I felt reverent.

"Yes." Roundtree looked past me, studying the area.

"Was he hit by a car or shot or what?"

"He has a lump on his head, but he was strangled."

"With hands?"

"With a bootlace." He scowled. "That's off the record."

I peered up under the broad brim of his hat into Roundtree's inscrutable face. "Why off the record?"

He shot me a no-nonsense look. "Because you're here with me and I said so."

Nodding, trying to cover my embarrassment, I cleared my throat and scribbled in my notebook. I wanted to appear cool, detached, professional. "What else?"

I paid particular attention to his body language. The sheriff was a laid-back kind of man who seldom fidgeted. He picked a piece of prairie grass, hip-high, which had gone to seed. Staring beyond me, he rolled the seed pods between his palms. Chaff fluttered to the ground. His eyes shot from one thing to another.

Roundtree also was candid, a trait I admired in any politician. He might try to conceal things, but I knew he would answer truthfully if I asked the right questions. "Was he naked?"

"Uh-huh."

"Why?"

Roundtree shot me another warning glance before the look softened and his hands stilled. "He was mutilated. The killer probably stripped him so we wouldn't miss the signature."

I kept silent a moment before pushing on. "What do you mean, *mutilated?*"

He lowered his voice. "His penis was tied."

Ignoring my blush and the mental picture forming in my head, I stared at the lawman, trying to put some logical meaning to his words. "I don't understand."

He cleared his throat and peered at me as I stared into his face. Then he grimaced, took half a step closer and dropped his voice to a whisper. "Someone wound a rubber band around it. Cut off his circulation down there." He hesitated, looking at me as if his mind were somewhere else. "That damned appendage has been dead longer than he has." He paused again, as if surprised by his own words. I waited. "The murderer decorated it. Tied it with a piece of blue bow ribbon." Roundtree clenched his teeth. "The rubber band and ribbon—also off the record."

He tossed the seeds he had shucked and dusted his hands. His quick, erratic movements made me uneasy.

"You act shocked, Sheriff, but you've seen stuff like this before, right?"

Roundtree shook his head, looking through me as if he were concentrating on something else. A moment later, he nodded. "I saw atrocities in Vietnam." He seemed to be thinking out loud. "On both sides. American guys who saw too much did some pretty sick stuff."

He drew a deep breath, raising and lowering his broad shoulders. "In a war, enemies might torture a man, castrate him, but they wouldn't do something like this, this ribbon thing. I'm not what you'd call shocked, but I am surprised." He shook his head. "This is bizarre."

I gazed at the blanket, suddenly terribly curious about the person underneath it. There was a long silence. "Could a woman have done it?"

"Could have." We both stared at the covered body. "Women don't usually. . . ."

I was ready for that. "Remember Lorena Bobbitt."

Roundtree nodded again, still studying the covered body. He didn't speak.

"Maybe a homosexual?" I was selecting and voicing random thoughts carefully.

"Maybe."

The guy in the pinstripe suit had stepped close to us but remained silent, obviously eavesdropping. I made a conscious effort to ignore him. "Were there footprints?"

Roundtree pursed his lips and doubled one fist on his holstered gun, the other on his other hip. "No. The body practically made a divot when it landed, then rolled over. Thrown out of a truck, it looks like."

His words became crisp, as if he'd reached a decision. "The victim was dead quite a while before being brought out here. Not much traffic over this old road since they resurfaced the interstate. I doubt there were any disinterested witnesses. There aren't any houses within a mile. We're in the boonies."

I knew I shouldn't push too hard, but I wanted to keep him talking. "Do you know who he is?"

Roundtree glanced at Pinstripe, who shrugged. "No identification, Sheriff. No wallet. No clothes."

"How old is he? Could this be a gang thing?" I directed my questions at Roundtree, intentionally ignoring Pinstripe.

The sheriff answered. "He's about the right age, I guess, either late high school or college. There's something familiar. . . ." Roundtree frowned, as if trying to remember something.

Keeping a close eye on the sheriff's face, I said, "Could I?"

"What?"

"See him. Just his face, I mean."

18

Roundtree looked at Pinstripe, who neither moved nor spoke. "You don't think you'll pass out or anything, do you?"

"I was pre-med. I changed majors after we got to cadavers, but I didn't pass out."

Roundtree hunkered by the body and gently uncovered the man's face.

I don't know what I expected, but I'd bent close and my head jerked back as the peculiar odor of death wafted up. It seemed to surround me before it lifted into the sultry afternoon. The dead man's face was bloated and dark. He looked as if he had lain in the sun a long time. I blinked, then focused on the face. Something looked familiar about his nose and his eyebrows. His hairline. I shivered.

Pinstripe took a step forward, reaching for me with both hands as Roundtree quickly pulled the blanket back over the victim's face.

I shot a glare at Pinstripe, who lowered his hands and stopped in mid-step. Still frowning, I turned to confront the sheriff. "I thought you said you didn't know him."

Roundtree's eyes widened. "I thought he looked a little familiar. How would I know him?"

"He delivered pizza to your office during the World Series. Remember?"

The sheriff nodded. "For Colonel Jackson's? Wore the hat? Had some smart-mouthed kid with him?"

"Right. His friend made Patsy mad, shooting off his mouth, but you gave this kid the tip anyway."

"Do you know his name?"

"No. I think he's a foreign student at the university. East Indian, maybe." I flashed Pinstripe a look. His evil stare had softened to something vaguely like regard. I felt like gloating. I was contributing more around here than he was. My face is pretty transparent sometimes, and at that particular moment,

I didn't mind if he could read those thoughts. A smile twitched the ends of Pinstripe's mouth as he turned his back to me. A mind reader. Good.

Roundtree swelled to his full six-foot-four and shouted, "We may know this guy." Investigators walking the ground, bagging bits and pieces of trash in the area, looked up. "He may be a university student."

The sheriff caught my elbow and guided me up the incline to the roadway. He nudged me toward his cruiser, then turned back to Pinstripe. As soon as the sheriff released my arm, I hovered to listen.

After a quick conference with Pinstripe that I couldn't hear, Roundtree called out to the men again. "We're definitely in my jurisdiction."

I could swear I heard a collective sigh. No one objected.

"Can you bureau guys get the physical workup on him for us?" Roundtree was speaking to Pinstripe. "And get him moved?"

"Yes sir," Pinstripe said. Roundtree looked surprised. Neither man so much as glanced toward me, but I had the distinct impression they both wanted to and I wondered why.

Roundtree turned back to the gathering. "Everybody, we thank you for your help. I'll note your participation. If we need additional assistance, I'll call on you, if that's agreeable." He caught my arm and turned me toward his car again. "We'll swing by Colonel Jackson's on the way back to the office, if you've got time."

The clock in the cruiser read five. I'd made my last run to the courthouse at three-thirty. It seemed as if we had been at the murder scene only fifteen or twenty minutes. I wondered what had happened to the afternoon, but all I said was, "Sure."

20

Murder victim Charles Benunda was from Pakistan, worked for Colonel Jackson's, threw a morning newspaper route for the *Dominion Morning News,* and carried seventeen hours at the university, a math major according to the restaurant manager. The dead man tutored in his spare time, what there was of it. His English was better this year than last, and "he was a hard worker."

After a pause, the man volunteered what sounded like an odd bit of information. "The kid's not queer." He winced and shrugged. "You might think so when you find out. He marched in the gay rights demonstration on campus last spring."

Roundtree shot me a quick frown, then nodded, indicating the manager should continue.

"He went with his roommate, some guy who had been kicked out of one of the fraternities over there." The man smiled, for emphasis or maybe to show his sincerity. "Benunda isn't . . . wasn't homosexual, but he got real excited about anything that had to do with rights: human rights, constitutional freedoms, everything like that."

"What do you think?" Roundtree asked when we were back in his squad car heading toward the courthouse. His question surprised me. I checked the clock again. Six-fifty. I had a tinny taste in my mouth and felt restless, like I needed to cry or heave.

"I don't have a clue about the murder," I said, trying to get a handle on my jumbled emotions. "I can't even figure out what's happening to the time."

"The dead kid sounds like a go-getter." Roundtree spoke more to himself than to me. "No time or money for drugs or girls or pissing anyone off." He looked at me suddenly, as if he had just remembered I was there. "Sorry about that . . . the language."

I waved off the apology. He always treated me like a delicate little flower in odd ways . . . like worrying about a few cusswords after inviting me to a murder scene. He went on, still thinking out loud. "Lester and Smiley and I will take a look at his apartment, talk to his roommate. Maybe we'll turn up something."

I didn't have anything to contribute, so I kept quiet.

Roundtree glanced over at me again. "Is this too much for you?"

I gave him the best smile I could muster. "No. He just didn't seem like someone who should have been murdered."

"Oh, yeah? Exactly what kind of people do you think should be murdered?"

"No one, I guess, but you kind of expect things like that to happen to druggies. Or gang members or prostitutes. Maybe prison inmates."

"Even when you see their bodies, little girl, the toughest tough guy looks innocent and alone, like he needed a friend, or his mama."

I stared straight ahead. Women were usually the victims in sex crimes. Was this a sex crime? It certainly had all the earmarks. I squeezed my eyes closed for even thinking such a sick pun.

What had Charles Benunda done to deserve that kind of treatment? Had he offended someone with his masculinity? He hadn't seemed to me like a threatening person. But maybe he appeared that way to someone.

The sun had set by the time we got back to the courthouse. Still feeling restless, I jogged across Fourth Street to the *Clarion* parking lot. No lights burned upstairs in the news offices, so I decided to wait to transcribe my notes. I suddenly wanted to get home, to familiar surroundings and normal people and noise.

In spite of the lingering heat of the day, I shivered as I jumped into my Taurus. I was halfway home before I realized I was speeding, as if trying to outrun the mental picture of Benunda's bloated young face. It didn't work.

I felt vibrations from the music at the house when I turned the corner onto Cherry Street. Rolling up the car window offered no escape from the vibration, but it did bring protection from the night air, which suddenly had a nip. I was tired of mental pictures, tired of new, exotic experiences. Tired.

The house was a two-story Dutch, shaped like a barn. Lights burned in almost every window and the old place fairly shook with activity. It seemed to smile its welcome home, which made me smile back. I pulled into the driveway beside Ben Deuces' pickup.

Ben, Liz's boyfriend, had probably eaten my share of supper when I didn't show up on time. Housemates could vex a person's soul, but on this particular night I felt grateful for all four of mine and their grab-bag of friends.

I didn't say anything when I walked inside, as if a voice could have been heard over the din from the speakers around the sparsely furnished front room. Angela stood at the ironing board in front of the TV, jiving and pressing to the beat.

A college dropout, Angela Fires worked in the court clerk's office. A sexy, rangy blonde, she wore her hair short, played coed softball and dated jocks. She flashed me a plastic smile.

In the kitchen, Liz Pinello and Ben Deuces were up to their elbows in flour. They grinned but kept counting and kneading balls of bread dough. "Forty-seven, forty-eight. . . ." I waved as I cut through to the back stairs. The familiar sounds and smells and faces made me feel better. Here, the afternoon's events seemed remote.

Rosie Clemente came out of the upstairs bathroom, a towel wrapped around newly washed hair. "Steven called. He said he was going to the law barn at seven. You might still catch him."

"Thanks." I looked at the clock on my bedside table and kicked off my shoes. Seven twenty-five. I glanced at the phone but didn't make a move toward it.

I had found the rental house when we all decided to live together last spring: Rosie, Liz, Angie, Theresa and I. I'd taken a small bedroom on the second floor because it had two windows, one on the south, the other facing east. I liked waking up to the morning sunshine and the south breeze. At night, I could see the stars through the branches of a giant sycamore tree outside.

We didn't have many house rules. The five of us pitched in twenty-five dollars a month for cleaning supplies and paper products and we took turns doing the shopping. We didn't allow any overnight guests, male or female, except family. Occasionally we got together at Bailey's or Roper's to party, but mostly our paths went separate ways.

Rosie peeked around the partially open door. "Do you want to talk?" Tall, Italian-looking, Rosie was solidly built but she had a cherub's face.

"Sure." I pulled my jumper off over my head and tossed it on the bed. I smoothed the rumpled T-shirt, picked up a pair of grubby twill slacks from the back of the overstuffed chair, then motioned Rosie into the newly vacated spot. "What's up?"

"You first?"

"I saw a murdered guy today." I watched for Rosie's reaction.

She frowned. "Where?"

"Out on old Highway Thirty. Tossed by the side of the road like litter."

"Who was he?"

I eased down onto the side of the bed. "Do you remember the pizza delivery guy who always wore boot-cut jeans and Nikes?"

"Maybe. East Indian or something? Smiles a lot?"

"Right. Pakistani. That's who it was."

"He seemed nice. Why was he murdered?"

I could see his face in my mind. My throat got raw and I had to shrug a non-answer.

Rosie's frown deepened. "Maybe it's political, fallout from something going on in his homeland."

I tried to sound casual but I was getting the tinny taste again. "Could be, but the *high sheriff's* on it and my money's on him. He hunted 'em down twenty-three years in the Navy and to hear him tell it, he always got his man." I sounded normal.

Rosie chuckled. "As big as he is, I'll bet they gave up as soon as they heard his thundering hoof beat."

I laughed and stretched out across the bed, resting my chin on my arms.

"Was it awful?" Rosie said after a long silence.

I nodded and realized it *had* been awful. Well, most of it had. "Not all of it." I remembered Pinstripe reaching for me when he thought I was going to faint or something. That image made me smile. "There was one really great-looking guy."

Rosie's eyes rounded. "The Pakistani? He was all right, I guess, but I wouldn't call him great-looking."

"No, ninny. This was a live one. A cop, I think."

"Terrific." Rosie's voice oozed sarcasm. "What girl

wouldn't want to go around checking out dead bodies if she could meet some really buff cop?"

I sobered, remembering the dead body. "I can promise you this: if I don't see another murdered person the rest of my life, once definitely will have been enough."

Little did I know.

# Chapter Two

Ansel Benedict, public relations director at the university, telephoned at six-thirty Friday morning. His voice sounded hollow. I might want to check the university police department early, he said. "There's been an accident."

I scrubbed my face and brushed my teeth, finger-combed my hair into a ponytail, stepped into the stale twills and a mock turtleneck from the chair, slid into the scruffy sandals and darted out the door.

Ben Deuces worked the front desk at university police headquarters.

"Did you get all the flour off?" I asked.

He looked surprised. "Yeah."

"What's going on?"

He glanced at the clock on the wall, then back at me. "What're you doing here? It's not even seven. How'd you know?"

"Sources." I gave him a sincere smile. "What kind of accident?"

"A brutal one." He arched his eyebrows and lowered his voice. "Some Phi O shooting beaver at the Chi Psi Sorority House is what it looks like."

"What happened? Did they grab him and give him a swirly?"

"He's dead."

27

I sobered. "For peeking in their windows?"

"It's really strange. One of the girls found his body on the sidewalk early this morning. There was a ladder against the house. His neck was broken. The chief figures he was drunk and lost his balance, but the ladder didn't fall. And there was something else."

"What's that?" I opened my notebook.

"Well, it's kind of personal."

"Just say it, Ben. What?"

Ben looked down, studying an invisible something on his desk. "His pants were unzipped and . . . well, this little bit of ribbon was sticking out. Turned out, it was tied around his. . . ."

My eyes shot to his face. "His dick? He had a ribbon tied around his penis?"

"Yes." Ben returned my look, curiosity apparently overcoming embarrassment.

"Baby blue?" The question sounded inane.

He squinted. "How'd you know that?"

"Have you called any other law enforcement people?" I tried to keep a lid on an escalating sense of urgency.

"Not yet."

"Ben, I need to see Simp. Now."

"I can't let you go in there." He said the words but made no move to stop me. "He's got Shons and Forester in there, debriefing them. They took the call."

"Where's the body?"

"At the infirmary, I guess."

I marched to the door of University Police Chief Simpson McClellan's office. "Ben, I'll tell him you tried to keep me out, but I'm going in there."

When I opened the door to McClellan's office, three sets of eyes narrowed. I held up a hand as a sign of peace but stepped inside and closed the door behind me.

"Chief, Wednesday they found a male student's nude body out in the county by the side of Highway Thirty. He had a rubber band and a baby blue ribbon around his penis."

Shons and Forester diverted their eyes.

McClellan scowled. "It wasn't on the radio."

"The sheriff wanted the ribbon and the rubber band part kept quiet." I stepped farther into the room, staring at McClellan. "I was there. I saw the body."

The chief looked skeptical and began shaking his head.

"I don't mean I saw the *whole* body. Not the ribbon." Darn, I was getting sidetracked. "You need to call Sheriff Roundtree right now. Have you moved the body?"

"Hell, yes, we moved it. He was there in the middle of the sidewalk, a block off campus."

"Call Roundtree."

Chief McClellan's glower deepened. "Excuse us, Ms. Dewhurst," he said with a sneer, obviously thinking he could get rid of me by being rude. Fat chance. He picked up the telephone and tried again. "This is a police matter."

I didn't say a word. Nor did I move toward the door. When I'm on a story, I'm like a bulldog. It helped that Shons and Forester still couldn't look at me. I think they were embarrassed about the killer leaving such a personal signature. I, on the other hand, was getting used to it—same song, second verse.

"Sheriff Roundtree, please, University Police Chief McClellan calling." The chief's face registered surprise when the dispatcher on duty rang the sheriff's line. McClellan checked his watch, prompting me to glance at the wall clock. It was straight up seven a.m.

McClellan briefed the sheriff about the accident, omitting the part about the rubber band and the ribbon until the end.

When he added that bit of information, I heard Roundtree's rich bass voice rumble from the receiver. I couldn't understand the words, but I had a pretty good idea what he was saying.

McClellan cleared his throat, interrupting the rumble. "I wouldn't have made a connection to that at all, except Jancy Dewhurst is here. She wheedled the information out of one of my officers and busted in here. Told me to call you." He paused to listen. "No, sir, the body's been moved." McClellan shifted in his chair. "Damn it, Sheriff, I knew that, but his body was right in the middle of the sidewalk less than a block off campus." Another pause. "Yes, he was fully clothed. His pants were gapping open. He didn't have on any underwear. We were just going to cover him up. It looked like some kind of goshawful accident. . . .

"Hell, yes, I knew the boy wouldn't fix himself like that, but around here you never know. Could have been some kind of initiation ritual that got away from 'em or something. You know how crazy these college kids get."

McClellan listened intently.

"I had them take the body to Regional Hospital. You can call them before they turn him over to the funeral home, get all the tests you want. You'd better check with his folks first. Ansel Benedict with public relations can give you the information. He'll have notified Dr. Moran. You'd better be prepared. Moran'll be hot. He doesn't like stuff like this. No, sir, he doesn't. Alums don't like it either. He'll be hot."

After another brief exchange, and McClellan said goodbye, hung up the phone, took a deep breath and waved Shons and Forester out. As they left the room, the chief's eyes settled on me and he set his jaw. "Tell me about the other victim." His words were deliberate, measured. "The guy they found Wednesday."

I stared at him while I tried to think what points he would consider significant. "He was a foreign student."

"A college kid?"

I nodded, but my thoughts rambled. I wondered what other people or circumstances the two victims might have had in common.

McClellan tapped a pencil on his desk. "Was he in a fraternity?"

"No. He worked a bunch of jobs to keep himself in school. He was a math major. What about your guy?"

McClellan shrugged. "I'll know more later in the morning."

"Can you sort it out before lunch? I have a noon deadline. It's only fair we get a break on this one. Dominion beat us on the one Wednesday."

The chief pursed his lips and shook his head. "That story wasn't in until today and it isn't even on the front page. They obviously didn't hear about the ribbon business."

"Why not?"

McClellan gave me a wry smile. "I guess Roundtree forgot to mention it."

I couldn't help being pleased with Roundtree. He had saved my potential scoop. Suddenly I had that tinny taste again, and the restlessness. I pivoted and paced toward the door. "Do you think they'll let me see the body?" I was really talking more to myself than to McClellan, then decided I truly wanted his opinion and turned back to look at him. He shrugged. I prodded. "They'd let me if you called and okayed it."

"You don't need to be seein' any bodies. I've got work to do." His frown deepened. "This mess is going to take a whole lot of paperwork."

"McClellan, do me one favor." He raised his eyes and waited. "Don't tell any other reporters about the ribbons."

"They'll sniff it out somewhere else."

"Just don't let it come from you. Okay?"

McClellan flipped his hand, dismissing me as he might an annoying housefly.

On my way to the hospital, I stopped at the student union for coffee and a copy of the *Dominion Morning News*. McClellan had been right. There on page three was a two-inch wire story about an unidentified body found beside Highway Thirty on Wednesday, some twenty miles from Bishop. It looked like a rewrite of my story in Thursday's *Clarion*. So far the real story was still mine.

Feeling better, I drove to the hospital.

The information desk was manned by an older woman from the hospital auxiliary who had a hard time understanding my request at first. Finally, she started tapping keys, heaved a couple of heavy sighs and tapped more keys, but she couldn't call up the information I needed. She muttered, said she didn't often have visitors for the morgue.

"Let me help you." Before she had time to object, I slipped behind the counter. The woman looked both annoyed and relieved, but she moved to let me into her chair.

The form listed his name as Francis Speir, twenty-one, a junior economics major and member of Phi Omega Upsilon at the university. His permanent address—probably his parents' home—was in Dominion, but he lived in Bishop, in the Jessup Apartments, 213 University Drive, Apartment D. Not in the fraternity house.

I noted a few things the two victims had in common. They were both students, twenty-one years old, and lived in the same student apartment complex. Jessup had maybe two hundred units. I wrote down Speir's apartment number and put a star in the margin.

The read-out showed his body was still downstairs in the hospital morgue.

I thanked the woman at the computer and got out of there. Determined to follow up before I had time to think and wimp out, I sidestepped the elevator and jogged down the stairs near the cafeteria. I had never been in a morgue, but I felt a strong urge to get a look at this second victim. It felt like the two dead men were depending on me.

No one was in the reception room, which felt cool, no more than seventy degrees. The distinctive odors of the place reminded me of biology and zoology classes. The chill and the smell emanated from the swinging doors labeled "Lab." I paced to the door and back, mad at myself for stalling. I hated being such a chicken, but I couldn't seem to get beyond it. My heart lurched when the outside door slammed open and *Pinstripe* strolled into the office. I already felt nervous, and this man's sudden arrival sent my pulse rate up a notch.

He looked terrific in khaki slacks and a blue blazer, a crisp pale blue shirt and tie. For a split second he looked glad to see me, but then he scowled as he looked around the room. "Where's Robert?"

When I didn't answer, his dark eyes swept my way again. They didn't linger.

His holier-than-thou attitude irked me. I straightened and tried to mimic his confidence. "There's no one else around."

"What are you doing here?"

I couldn't sustain an eye lock. "I need to see someone."

"Dead or alive?"

My latent irritation mushroomed. "Dead."

"Is this a hobby with you, or what?"

"It's my job." Suddenly I felt mad enough to take him on. "Who are you and what are you doing here?"

"Wills. State Bureau of Investigation. My job. Stay here." He stepped to the swinging door, drew a deep breath and walked inside.

I was damned well not going to let some insufferable bureaucrat order me around. There is such a thing as freedom of the press and I intended to exercise it. The morgue was a public entity, and neither Wills nor my own gutlessness would keep me from tracking my story. I squared my shoulders, breathed deep and plowed right through the swinging door after him.

I stopped short when I saw two sheet-shrouded bodies on gurneys. Wills lifted the cover from the face of the nearer one. Determined not to flinch, I stepped to his side to look. It was ridiculous, but the arrogant agent and his overweening manner gave my courage a boost.

Under the sheet lay an old man, badly wrinkled, his face and hair yellow. He looked like he was napping. His lips were stretched taut to cover his teeth.

Wills looked awhile before he lowered the sheet and stepped to the second body. I was practically in his hip pocket as we moved in tandem. I couldn't help gasping as he uncovered the face.

He looked over his shoulder at me. "Do you know him?"

I could scarcely whisper. "It's Smart Mouth. He was with Benunda when they delivered pizza to the courthouse."

Wills was still holding the sheet when I bolted, through the swinging door, across the reception room and up the stairs. I had a vague sense of people around, but I charged down the hospital corridor and out without really seeing anyone or anything. My throat and eyes stung and I wanted to scream or cry or implode. Miraculously, I held all those responses in check.

The fresh air hit me like a slap. I didn't know anything, yet I had a horrible feeling I knew too much.

What did I know? Nothing. I climbed into my car and locked the doors. My hands shook as I started the engine and aimed the vehicle toward the office, back to my real life where things were normal and safe and familiar faces breathed in and out.

"There's definitely a common denominator." The sound of my own voice calmed me a little. I needed to get under control, get a handle on the panic that was knocking down bowling pins inside me. "Several. They had several things in common." I stopped for a traffic light. An annoying sound turned out to be my fingers drumming on the steering wheel. I gripped the wheel and tried to force my brain to function.

"Okay. What are they, these things in common?" I tapped an index finger against my lips. "One. They knew each other." The light changed. I peeled out. "They hung around together . . . at least that one day, they did." I swallowed twice to keep from upchucking and tapped a second finger alongside the first. "Two: they're both dead." My tongue thickened as I slowed for the stop sign a half block from the *Clarion* parking lot. I swallowed again, hard. "That's significant." I leaned forward and banged my forehead against the steering wheel.

Feeling hollow inside, I muttered at my lap. "They were so young. And they both had baby blue bows. Those awful, awful ribbons. Damn."

I forced my back ramrod straight, slammed the accelerator, whipped around the corner, shot into the parking lot and lurched to a stop.

"What's with the ribbons?" I turned off the engine. "What did these guys do . . . or see or hear . . . that got them dead?"

Fear and anger and reason all grappled for control of my

head. I released the seat belt and jumped out of the car. I had never been so eager to get into a building. I bypassed the elevator and took the stairs two at a time to the newsroom, and didn't slow down until I burst into that familiar territory. The lights blazed. I took a deep breath, relieved not to be the first one there. I didn't know how early a person had to get there to beat Ron Melchoir, the managing editor, but obviously it was before seven-forty.

Kicked back in his chair, Melchoir scanned the *Morning News*. Two other metropolitan papers awaited his attention. He glanced at me, then at the clock on the wall. Everything was normal. He picked up his coffee cup and buried his head back in his paper without saying a word. Melchoir's taking me for granted was terribly reassuring. Life beyond this place might be topsy-turvy, but here it was business as usual.

I walked straight to my desk, turned on the computer and flipped open my spiral notebook. I scribbled some margin notes, things to remind myself, then went to the bound file of recent copies of the *Clarion*.

Leafing back to our spring editions, I found the article. We had done a front page piece with pictures on the student demonstration. Picketers wanted gay rights groups included in the university's dole to student organizations.

I riffled through junk in the table drawer to locate the magnifying glass. Peering through it, I examined the picture of demonstrators on the oval in front of the administration building. Charles Benunda carried a placard near the front and was easily recognizable.

Back at my desk, I phoned Sheriff Roundtree and opened the conversation without any amenities. "I just left the morgue. I saw the second body."

"Did you know him?"

"It's 'Smart Mouth.' "

"The kid who came with pizza delivery? Benunda?"

"Yes. They both lived at Jessup."

"Roommates," Roundtree confirmed, "if his name's Speir."

"That's right."

"No wonder we couldn't find him. The SBI lab boys are at the apartment now. I'd better let 'em know."

"That Wills guy was at the morgue."

"Then the SBI already knows."

"I guess. There's something else." My words came in a rush as I tried to short-circuit my emotions. "Benunda marched up front with the leaders when the gay rights people demonstrated on campus last April."

"Like the pizza manager said. Was the roommate with him?"

"Not that I can tell from the newsprint picture, but it's grainy. I'll try to find the original cut and bring it over later to see what you come up with at the apartment." I didn't want him to think I was being crass, but I needed to remind him. "Remember, I've got a noon deadline."

"I'll look out for you as much as I can, Sis."

We hung up. I put my story in the machine, writing only what I knew, concentrating, not allowing any speculation to sneak into the copy and avoiding any mention of rubber bands or ribbons or Roundtree's off-the-record details.

"What's this, *au naturel?*"

I jumped, startled by the voice at my shoulder, and automatically hit *Save* before I looked up into Steven Carruthers' face.

The girls at the house called Steven my boyfriend, but he was too pretty for my taste. He was tall and slim and blond with fine features. The thing I liked best about Steven was that, like me, he settled for platonic. He would be easy to leave when I finished my second year on the *Clarion* and Riley Wedge called me up for the correspondent's job.

I felt completely disoriented, surprised to find myself in the newsroom, much less to find Steven there too. I shot a look at the clock. Eight forty-five. The news staff had arrived, machines hummed, the work day was underway.

Steven grinned. "You didn't call me back the other night. You were gone when I checked this morning. I figured you'd gotten out too early for breakfast. I brought you a doughnut. You look like it's Saturday morning."

In a gut reaction, I put both hands on my head to feel the ponytail I had put up without the benefit of comb or brush. Oh, Lord, Benedict had called so early, I hadn't bothered with makeup. I looked down at my clothes and nearly gagged. I had on the rumpled twills and soiled shirt. I wondered what the fastidious Agent Wills had thought when he caught me racing around the hospital looking like an unmade bed. He had been as marvelously well groomed at seven a.m. as on Wednesday afternoon. He'd looked and smelled terrific.

"Yuck." I turned my back to Steven's gaze and covered my face with both hands. "I've gotta go home."

"You look okay." Steven's expression indicated the comment was a lie. "I don't have class until ten. Want me to take you?"

I leaped up. "No, thanks. This is a major overhaul. No company."

"How about tonight?"

I couldn't even think what day it was. "What is tonight?"

"Friday."

"Oh. Okay, that's good. Come over. We'll watch TV."

"I'll bring a movie."

"I'll make supper."

He gave me a wary look. "Grilled cheese, cherry brown but not charred?"

"If you're lucky." Trying to be a little more receptive, I smiled at him over my shoulder as I hurried to the managing editor's desk. "Ron, as you can tell, I got out of the house a little early this morning. I've gotta go try again. I'll pick up the university's P.R. handouts on my way back."

Melchoir grunted, which I took as an affirmative response, before he bothered looking at me. "What have you got?"

"My first draft's on the machine."

He nodded and waved me out the door.

Steven followed me to the parking lot, opened the car door and leaned close to kiss my cheek. It was an unexpected gesture. I supposed he was just being friendly, but as he walked away, I dusted off the kiss and began thinking again about the morgue, not of the dead bodies, but of the live one that looked and smelled so good.

A random thought skipped through my mind. I wondered if Agent Wills had ever killed anyone.

# Chapter Three

*Thursday, October 13*

"Senator Crook's office." Marietta Edmunds spoke the words automatically. "No, ma'am, he won't be back in the office until Thursday evening. How rude," she said to no one, then hung up. "People ought to know the legislature's in session and he's in Dominion all week."

"I wanted to see the senator this morning." The petite middle-aged woman had been waiting forty minutes. She wore sunglasses even in the filtered light of the office, and a broad-brimmed straw hat, odd for October. Marietta assumed the cover-up indicated the woman needed to see a lawyer about a disfiguring personal injury suit.

"Yes. Mrs. Thompson, the senator's assistant, will see you next."

The visitor placed a magazine back on the lamp table. "I really must go, dear. I did not realize the senator himself would not be available. I may return tomorrow."

"He should be in the office all day Friday and Saturday, available to his constituents."

"Yes, well, I guess it will have to wait, then."

Marietta relented a little. "He does come in Thursday evenings to check his calendar and look at the mail. It's his catch-up time."

"I see." The woman offered her a thin smile, her upper lip barely visible above the scarf around her neck and chin.

Her injuries must be extensive. The poor thing probably didn't like to go out in broad daylight. Marietta returned the smile.

It was nearly twilight Thursday when Senator Robert Crook pulled his long, black Cadillac through the alley behind his office. The car glided into its usual spot under the security light beside the "No Parking on Pavement" sign.

Crook stepped from his car, took two steps into his office and shoved the door carelessly. It didn't latch.

He tossed his Stetson in a client's chair and smiled, seeing the girls had left him a fresh pot of coffee. They were trying to encourage new habits.

The office lights and the copy machine had been left on. Ignoring the mail and the stacks of files on his desk, Crook walked to the bar and poured six ounces of Black Jack Daniels into a glass. He eased into his chair, leaned back and sipped the whiskey. Eventually, he kicked off his shoes, put his feet on the desk and closed his eyes.

At seven o'clock, a diminutive woman, her face hidden by hat, scarf and sunglasses, slipped through the back door of the senator's law offices. She wore gloves. Crook started when she cleared her throat.

"Hello." He sat upright and lowered the drink to the knee hole beneath the surface of the desk. "We're closed. Everyone's gone home. Why don't you come down first thing in the morning? We'll take care of you then."

"I need to see you."

At the sound of her voice, his eyes narrowed and he regarded her more closely. "Oh, it's you. I didn't recognize you in that get-up. What do you want?"

"First, may I have a cup of coffee?"

"Okay, but let's keep this short. I've got work to do."

She disappeared toward the coffee pot, the office layout familiar territory. The senator took a quick sip and lowered his glass back to its hiding place. He rolled his head from one shoulder to the other. Reentering the room, the woman noticed.

"Do you have a headache?"

He nodded.

She unsnapped her purse and shuffled items until she produced a tin of tiny white pills.

"These will help." She offered the open tin. "You'll need four. They're terribly small."

She pushed her coffee cup toward him. He took four of the offered tablets and washed them down with her coffee. His bourbon remained in his left hand beneath the desk.

"Now, what do you want?"

She sat at the edge of a chair. "They say to wear your seat belt, but I was only going to the store for tomatoes." She turned the coffee cup round and round.

He leaned back and closed his eyes.

"Do you ever shop at Leamon's?" She prattled. "They are very reasonable. I check their ads on Wednesdays. They have good specials."

The senator squinted. He could barely focus. Her sing-song voice lulled him. He leaned, then gradually slumped sideways in his chair. He started when the glass beneath the desk slipped from his hand, but he was powerless. The woman stood. He made no effort to defend himself or to escape.

Crook Law Office opened as usual Friday morning. Marietta Edmunds told the new girl to use scented carpet cleaner on the fresh bourbon spill under the senator's desk. She peeked out back, but his car was not in its usual spot.

Marietta frowned as she collected the senator's shoes from under his chair. He'd gotten in all right, had some drinks and left without bothering to put his shoes on. He'd done stranger things before. She looked around for other telltale clutter and spied his hat. She put the shoes and the hat in a hallway closet.

When Crook had not appeared by noon, Edmunds went into her usual routine for juggling clients and disgruntled constituents and complained to her coworkers.

"It would be easier to convince people he was called away on an emergency if he were a doctor instead of a lawyer." She raised and lowered her shoulders. "But people are gullible and I've gotten to be a pretty fair liar, working for the master."

His wife called at one. Had he gotten in from the capitol yet? Marietta covered for him, as usual. She said he had an office full of people, which was true.

June Crook laughed ruefully. "He's probably sleeping it off someplace."

Crook didn't show up all day Friday. Ms. Edmunds didn't worry. It was unusual, but not unheard of.

Friday night the weather turned and a stiff north wind brought a deluge.

Sheriff Dudley Roundtree got an anonymous call at home early Saturday morning, October fifteenth.

"There's a body in a pond on the Effinger place." The voice sounded muffled and gravelly. He couldn't tell if it was a man or a woman. When the caller hung up, he used the system to call back. There was no answer at the pay phone where the call originated, two blocks from the courthouse, downtown.

Roundtree rousted deputies and called Jancy.

The Effingers had twenty ponds on their nine-hundred-acre ranch, most of them not easily accessible. Shortly after noon, searchers located a man's body face-down in the water grass at the edge of a fishing hole some fifty feet from the county road on what the Effingers called *the back side* of their property.

Searchers skirted the path to the scene, attempting to preserve any evidence that might have survived the rain. The dead man was fully clothed except for his shoes.

After checking the immediate area, Roundtree waded out and took firm hold of the victim's left arm floating in the muddy water, while Undersheriff Wheeler straightened the right arm and placed it tightly against the body. As Wheeler braced the right side, Roundtree pulled the left arm, turning the body over.

Sheriff and undersheriff stopped dead still as they recognized the man.

"Hell," Roundtree rasped and looked out over the countryside.

"He was never a friend of yours." Wheeler turned his eyes from the body to the water's edge.

Roundtree grimaced. "No, but I wouldn't wish this on my worst enemy."

The deputies stood gaping.

Roundtree set his jaw. "Call the medical examiner and the state bureau guys. Fan out. Find his car . . . and his shoes."

Wheeler looked all around, apparently puzzled. "And his hat. I've never seen the senator without his Stetson."

"Fence over here's been cut," a deputy called, indicating strands of barbed wire dangling from a post. Roundtree found fresh tire marks left by tractor treads along the shoulder of the road. The tractor had obliterated most other vehicle tracks.

They saw no footprints to or from the pond, indicating—
Roundtree told Jancy later—that the killer had placed the
body before the rain.

Despite the rainfall, bloodhounds tracked scent easily
from the pond back to the road. They could go no farther.

Pathologist Jerry Gillette called Roundtree at two o'clock
that afternoon. "The senator ingested forty milligrams of
Ambien. It knocked him out. Then someone held his head
under water at the pond. The cause of death is drowning."

Roundtree groaned.

"One other little item of note," Gillette added.

"What's that?"

"He was penilely gift-wrapped."

"What do you mean?"

The pathologist spoke softly. "A rubber band and a blue
bow ribbon."

Roundtree exploded. "Jerry, don't tell me that."

"Sorry, Sheriff. He's trussed up exactly like the students."

"Ah, hell." Roundtree banged the phone into its cradle.
He didn't caution Gillette to keep that bit of information
quiet. Gillette would, of course, unless someone asked a specific question.

"No one knows to ask that one, Sheriff," Dispatcher Patsy
Leek said, attempting to console him later.

"One does. And she'll nail it, too, because it's Saturday
and she's got time to nose around. She's got the late deadline."

Things were quiet when I walked into the sheriff's office
that afternoon. I hadn't gone out to the scene, had covered
everything pretty well by phone. I just needed a few details
from Roundtree. His door was closed. "Is he here?"

Manning the dispatcher's station, Spence appeared to be sulking as he nodded and removed the earphones.

"How about Pat? Is she around?"

"You sure ask a lot of questions." He looked like he didn't want to, but he smiled at me anyway. "She's gone to the ladies' room, *without* your permission."

"Got any new angles on the Crook murder?"

"I should be asking you," he said, clouding up again.

"Come on, what do you know?"

"You gotta wait for the high sheriff on this one, Jancy. It's sensitive stuff."

I was itching for some other information, so I tried to sound casual. "Hey, Gary, there's this guy—I think he's an SBI agent—muscular, goes around looking mean. Do you know who he is?"

"Sure do. His name's Will James, or James Wills. I can't ever remember which. I just call him old *Been There, Done That*, cause he's such a damned know-it-all."

Pretending to be indifferent, just making conversation, I picked up a magazine. "He's a cop, then. Is he any good?"

Spence's eyes narrowed. "He's okay, I guess. He's actually a lawyer. Started out with Fry and Fritch. Pace was too slow. He wanted action. Truth is, he was looking for crime."

I thought it was time to say something kind to soothe the disgruntled deputy. "You ought to like him, then. You're law enforcement." My left-handed compliment backfired, making him angry all over again.

"Sure I am. I'm out serving papers or in here dispatching for Patsy or I'm hanging out roadside guarding prisoners on trash detail. You saw what happened when we got a homicide call. Hell, the sheriff asked you to go. He never even thought of taking me. Why couldn't you have stayed here to answer our lame-o calls?"

I tried to look perplexed. "Because I don't know how to work the radio?"

"Yeah, right."

I thumbed through a *Sports Illustrated* to let him calm down a minute. "Tell me about Wills or James or whatever his name is."

Spence shrugged. "He's all right. At least he's got some pride. Stays in shape. Lawyers get soft. You know what I mean." I nodded, trying to encourage him to keep talking. He continued, warming to it. "Lawyers make their money using their big, high-dollar mouths parked on their backsides. At least *Been There* works out." He hesitated a minute, then grinned. "Man, you should see the guns on that rascal. He keeps them biceps honed." He glanced toward the window. "Other cops say he's good. They also never want to get cross-wise with him."

"Is he married?"

Gary's eyes rounded. "No, he's not, and girl, don't you be goin' there. A dragon's got a soft underbelly, but they say *Been There*'s got no tender spot. Not someone you want to go messin' with."

"Jim Wills?" Patsy strutted into the office. "Now, honey, that's a real man. A real man can be mean as dirt, then turn around and be every bit as gentle when he's with the right woman. I know a little something about that."

Barely five feet tall, Patsy Leek usually wore spike heels. A forty-plus divorcee, she wore her blonde hair long and her clothing seductive. And she could out-cuss her male cohorts. Patsy seldom complimented any man, except Sheriff Roundtree. She admired her boss.

As the sole female employee in the sheriff's office, it was Patsy's job to accompany female prisoners and to conduct their strip searches when necessary, a duty Patsy described in lurid detail to every man who asked. When things got slow, guys asked her to repeat her accounts about certain ones. She loved making men squirm. She had two kids, a girl and a boy, but she didn't talk about them much even when I inquired politely.

Gary stared at her, which surprised me. "What's that supposed to mean?"

"It means Jim Wills is no fag."

"What?"

Patsy turned on him. "We've got a whole county—a whole college—full of those wimp fags. Queers. And they're recruiting town kids every chance they get. Young kids."

I had never before seen Gary challenge anything Patsy said. "Pat, you're about half crazy. I can spot a homo a mile away. I hate those bastards. We don't ever bring none of 'em in here."

"That's what you say. We didn't used to see one gay guy through here a year. Now we're seeing 'em every week."

Gary flinched. "Name one."

"Just take my word for it."

"Nobody's hustled me."

I laughed, hoping to interrupt the conversation before it boiled over. "Well, duh."

Pat didn't smile at the gibe. Instead she slid into her chair and swiveled toward the switchboard, signaling she was through indulging in conversation with us.

As Gary started to say something else, the door to Sheriff Roundtree's office opened. He motioned me to step inside.

Grateful for the reprieve, I walked into the spartan inner office with its whitewashed walls and World War II vintage furnishings, and sat in a straight-backed oak chair across the desk from the sheriff.

"I've been on the phone all morning on this Crook thing."

He didn't mince words. Good. It was after three and I had a four o'clock deadline. "What do you need?"

"We've done the obituary and a side bar on how his death will affect the district and the state." I wanted to keep my part of the conversation brief. "We've got background. They're saving space for me on page one. All I need is a lead. Who done it and why?"

"I'm supposed to refer you to the SBI agent in charge."

I tapped my ballpoint on my notebook and didn't look at him. "Give me what you can."

"How are you coming on the other ones?"

I stopped tapping, cocked my head and stared at Roundtree, wondering about this diversion. "Do you mean Benunda and Speir?"

"Yeah."

I searched his face. He was trying to tell me something he wasn't supposed to talk about. Okay. I could play. Then I got a glimmer of understanding. "Was Crook fully clothed when you found him?"

"Yes, he was."

"Was he overdressed?"

The sheriff smiled. I was on the right track. "Yep."

"A rubber band and a bow?"

"Right."

I collapsed back in the chair and stared at the ship's clock on the wall. "I thought that was about homosexuals." I looked hard at Roundtree. "Was Crook a . . . ?"

"Not according to people who'd know."

That got me to my feet. "What the heck is going on?" My notebook lay open on the desk. I didn't need it. I folded my arms over my chest and paced to the door and back. "I don't get it."

I stopped mid-step and whipped around to confront

Roundtree. "What the heck is this about? What do the ribbons mean? Why are they significant? Are they supposed to send a message? What's the connection between a poor-as-a-church-mouse foreign student at the university, a big-mouth fraternity man, and a sixty-year-old politician?"

The sheriff spoke quietly. "I was like you. I thought the two kids might be a gay-bashing. We've been flushing folks who've assaulted or made threats against homosexuals. Crook, on the other hand, was notorious as a womanizer." The sheriff paused and shook his head. "I don't know, Sis." He leaned forward, his elbows on his desk, and ran his fingers through his hair from his forehead back, his face a study in frustration. "I just plain don't know."

I had a deadline and I had a story and I was damned well going with the whole thing. "I'm going to write it like it is, Sheriff, bands and bows, the whole enchilada. The public needs to know about this—especially men."

Roundtree stared into space a long moment before he nodded.

"I won't speculate or take any potshots." I was having a hard time breathing. I sat down and grabbed my notebook and pen. "When was he killed? Where?"

"We don't know much." Roundtree answered as I scribbled. "He died late Thursday. No visible marks on his body. We've rousted out some old political enemies, but we aren't anywhere near ready to make an arrest." He hesitated. "In your story, though, you'd probably better say an arrest is imminent."

Fifteen minutes later, as my questions got answered and my deadline approached, I leaned across the desk to pat his arm. "Thanks, Sheriff. I don't know what I'd do without you."

He attempted a smile. "That blade cuts both ways, Sis. Do me a favor?" I nodded. "Refer to me as 'a reliable source.' "

In the reception room, Patsy sat at her dispatching station and Gary leaned on the counter examining his fingernails. They both looked angry. I didn't have time to ask what was wrong.

Ron Melchoir was gone and Doug Reisener, city editor, filled Ron's chair.

"A killer left a distinctive signature when he murdered three men here . . ." My fingers flew over the keyboard. Doug networked in to read the copy on his screen as I wrote.

His shout startled me. "Dewhurst, stop."

I shot him an impatient glare. "The presses are waiting, Doug. The high-dollar guys downstairs in the shop are already on overtime. I know you can't be talking to me."

He looked ready to pop a gasket, so upset he couldn't answer. I didn't have time to indulge one of his moods. "Come on, Reisener. What's the problem?"

"You can't use the word *penis,* Dewhurst. This is a family newspaper, for crying out loud, not some yellow sheet."

Other reporters looked at me expectantly. "Okay. What word would you prefer?"

His face got redder, if that were possible. "I don't have the information to write your story for you." His voice was too loud for the distance from his desk to mine. He was flaunting his temporary authority. "Write your story but do it right."

I dropped my voice, but I was seething. "I'll write my story, Doug. You edit it however you want, then you explain to Mr. Melchoir how you had to doctor the facts to protect our readers."

"Damn it, Dewhurst." Doug jumped up and stormed over to me, but I was not intimidated. I had known three murdered guys in ten days. The public needed to know a maniac was running loose. Plus, I was on deadline. Doug getting miffed was way down on my priority list.

I turned my full attention back to the screen and pounded the keyboard, checking my notes from time to time to stay on point. Doug wandered back to Melchoir's chair and sat down. The copy editor took off toward the stairs.

Reisener complained again. He was still examining every word. "You're going to scare the hell out of everyone in town." His telephone rang, interrupting whatever else he'd planned to say, and his anger dissipated as he listened. "But, Ron, she's like a runaway horse. Someone's got to get her under control." He paused. "Yes, sir. Well, someone needs to be responsible. I am helping. No, I had no idea where you were. Okay, I'll let it come straight down, but it's rough as hell. It needs editing."

Out of the corner of my eye, I saw Doug squirm as he listened for several heartbeats. "I do understand, Ron. Sure, if you say so. But it's going to be on your head. . . . Right." After he hung up, Doug kept his eyes on the screen but he didn't say anything else to me.

I finished typing and was still polishing the story when I felt the vibration of the presses roaring to life. Someone had moved the story, questionable verbiage and all. Obviously it wasn't Doug. He hadn't touched a key or said a word since the phone call.

Ron Melchoir strolled into the newsroom, the afternoon's usual cold cigar hanging off his bottom lip. "Good job, Jance." He nodded in my direction. That was the nicest thing I had ever heard Melchoir say to any reporter.

Doug vacated Ron's chair. "We're all going to catch hell for this." He was talking to no one in particular. "Heads are gonna roll. I'm telling DeWitt I tried to stop you. I'm not taking responsibility."

"Wimp." I could barely stand to look at him. "When did you ever take responsibility for anything around here? If you're going to stay in the newspaper business, you'd better grow yourself some backbone, Dougy."

The anger boiled. I could feel it heating my face. The whole awful week seemed to culminate in that moment. Furious and frustrated and dog-tired, I didn't dare say any more. Without another word to anyone, I stomped to the exit and clattered down the stairs.

The afternoon had warmed up, the mild weather oblivious to the dire events of the last two weeks. I bypassed my car in the lot. I needed to walk. I could catch a ride back to pick up my car later.

I walked fast at first, fretting. I wondered if I had gone too far, if my job might be in jeopardy. I wasn't sure how much influence Doug had. He was always sucking up to publisher Bryce DeWitt and to the business manager, who owned a big chunk of *Clarion* stock. Doug even tried to ingratiate himself with the editor and, of course, with Ron Melchoir. I smiled. Melchoir saw Dougy boy coming a mile away, trying to slither up the corporate ladder.

The eleven blocks passed quickly. My pace slowed as I realized fall had arrived. Marigolds and mums danced in fiery defiance of the coming winter. A gentle breeze kicked up from the south and cooled my face as I walked into it. I breathed deep and dodged a wasp. "You'd better make plans, buddy. You're about to be homeless."

As usual, I felt better when the old house on Cherry Street came into view.

We didn't lock up during the day because there was so much foot traffic in and out and we didn't have much of value to entice a burglar. It didn't surprise me to find the door ajar. I jogged through the house and up the back stairs, riffled through a stack of clothes on my closet shelf to turn up a bathing suit, then ran back down and out.

I got to the indoor pool on campus by five o'clock, changed in the steamy locker room, then tromped barefoot to poolside. I didn't feel like conversation, so I avoided looking at the half-dozen people in and around the water. I walked to the edge, dived into the cool silence and relaxed as it closed around me. I surfaced, grabbed lungfuls of air and rolled under again.

In the silence, I pulled hard, knifing through the water, then surfaced just before I reached the side gasping for air. Two strokes and I grabbed the side. I felt better already. Laps would help. I swam lengthwise across the Olympic-size pool, counting crossings at first, but I didn't like concentrating on something as mundane as how many times I swam back and forth.

Finally, at the near side, I stopped to pull in more air.

"How deep is it here?" The vaguely familiar man's voice startled me. I looked up. Against the glare of fluorescent light that silhouetted him, I couldn't see his face or identify features. "Deep enough. You can dive."

"Is it eight feet or ten feet here?"

I still couldn't make out his face. "I don't know. I only use the top six or eight feet. I don't really care how much deeper it is than that."

He laughed, a casual sound I didn't recognize, and dived over my head. Seconds later, he surfaced in the middle and began a slow crawl to the far side without looking back.

His hair was dark above broad shoulders and a thick neck. His skin was olive, suntanned. I watched him for a minute, admiring the effortless movement of his body slicing through the water. His coordination soothed me. It was almost like watching a melody.

Before he reached the far side, I lifted myself onto the tile floor.

I hadn't brought a towel, a usual oversight, so I shook excess water off my arms and legs as I walked to the locker room. Without permission, my thoughts again turned to dead bodies, sexual proclivities and human conflicts. My muscles felt relaxed, my mind refreshed and all the inner turmoil assuaged, at least for the moment.

# *Chapter Four*

"Do you want to go to the show?" Steven Carruthers asked on the telephone late Saturday.

"Everybody here's going to Roper's." I waited a clock tick or two. "Do you want to go out there with us instead?"

"Not if I have to be the designated driver." His tone combined annoyance with a slight whine. "I'm sick of that. Just because I don't drink doesn't mean I want to babysit a bunch of boozers all night."

I wanted to be patient. I wanted to be polite. "Okay. I'm going with them tonight. Maybe you and I can do something tomorrow, okay?"

"Can't we have a regular date occasionally without dragging all your friends along?"

"Steven, as I explained last night, I've had a hairy week. It finished up in a row with Doug Reisener this afternoon. I don't feel like coping. I don't want to have to tiptoe around anybody else's moods. I want to relax, not get uptight trying to defend people to you."

"Jance, I don't want to argue."

"Suits me."

He waited, apparently giving me time to reconsider. I didn't. He cleared his throat. "Okay, I'll go to Roper's." He sounded dejected. "Do you want to ride with me or what?"

I didn't want to have to depend on him. "Why don't you

just meet us out there about ten?" I hoped he didn't hear the relief in my voice, but I flat didn't feel like indulging him.

He allowed a long moment of silence before he spoke. "All right, then. I'll see you at Roper's."

All four of my roommates and I had accumulated miscellaneous guys by the time Steven arrived. I was line dancing when I saw him. I waved and smiled and pointed to the table we had staked.

Although he looked like he would be a good dancer, Steven couldn't seem to relax and enjoy the music. He danced the same pattern all the time, just varied the speed. Two-stepping was a reach for his stiffly formal skills. And he acted self-conscious. His clothes, trendy on campus, looked odd among the boots and denims at Roper's. I had suggested before that he dress down for the place. He called me a closet hick.

Jancy was wearing cutoffs and boots and looked to Steven like she was releasing vexations with an exaggerated stomp. She waved off men who asked, which suited him just fine. Obviously, she wasn't looking for a partner. Her face glistened with sweat. Moisture looked as if it seeped from every pore, purging her, motivating her exaggerated movements, making her dance faster and harder until she was almost in a frenzy. When the music stopped, she stayed on the floor, talking and laughing breathlessly with people around her. When the band started, she lined up, ready to go again.

Several selections later, a tall, older gentleman asked her to two-step. Steven saw by his body language that he didn't expect her to refuse. Surprisingly, she agreed. Steven thought he knew the man but couldn't put a name to the face.

The couple moved easily around the room, Jancy chatting happily. Searching his memory, Steven sipped a soft drink and watched.

"You still toadying for the affirmative action and women's rights bunch?" Ansel Benedict baited me as we danced.

I gave him a haughty glare. "Yes, and I pay the price for it: unisex toilets. I can't tell you how much I hate being reduced to equal."

Laughing, but with a smooth move, Benedict spun me around and under his arm. "You asked for it."

"I demanded it, Benedict. Someone has to sacrifice to correct the mistakes your generation left us." I watched with satisfaction as his grin dissolved. As intended, the jab hit a sensitive chord, reminding him that he was a little old to maintain his playboy image on campus.

Benedict's precise steps deteriorated to a shuffle. "There is *not* a generation between us, Dewhurst." His smile looked forced. "I am thirty-five years old, but I happen to be the most eligible bachelor in this town."

I couldn't help a victory grin. "Gotcha!"

Benedict's taste in women had matured to graduate students, even an occasional professor. What really baffled me was why he pretended to pursue me, a female he habitually referred to as "The Mouth."

I was a college sophomore when we met. Benedict had sponsored a university news staff trip to West Texas. For long hours in the van, the bunch of us made up limericks. We were all showing off, being clever. After a while everyone else got tired of the game, but Ansel and I slogged on.

The boot-scootin' music stopped. "What do you hear from Riley Wedge?" Benedict knew how to take a jab at my most sensitive spot. It took concerted effort not to flinch.

"Not much since summer. He likes D.C."

The music began again. Ansel grabbed my hand and guided me into the circling two-steppers. "He's just stringing you along, Dewhurst. He's not seriously thinking of putting you in a bureau overseas. Your big mouth could set U.S. diplomacy back twenty years."

I arched my eyebrows, giving him fair warning, even while my feet stayed with the beat. "Like it or not, Benedict, I'm going to be an overseas news correspondent, just like I told you three years ago. Your snide remarks aren't going to change a thing. Wedge likes me. He knows I've got what it takes. Now he makes overseas assignments and I'm his very own, hand-picked protégée."

"Why'd he leave you here in Bishop, if you're such a favorite?"

"The wire service won't take me until I have two full years in the business. It's policy. The *Clarion* was Riley's choice. He's also the reason I'm in the language lab three nights a week."

"After two years and fluency, what?"

"If I do well—and I will—he'll place me with an experienced correspondent here in the States for a couple of months. Then it's *bon voyage*."

It was funny, the way Ansel's smile wavered. He looked like he'd stepped wrong or twisted something.

When the music stopped, I started back toward the table, but Ansel caught my arm, turning me around to face him. "You'll get married." He gave me a hard, accusing, curious look and waited.

I glanced down at my boots, wondering what he was thinking. Then, shrugging if off, I rose to the bait. "Ansel, marriage is for women who can't make it on their own."

He chuckled. "Eventually, she will yield to his touch." He

grinned, playfully feeding me the first line for a new limerick, a ploy we often used to communicate. He continued:

> *"Yield to kissing and hugging and such.*
> *She'll be tender and nice,*
> *Much more sugar, much less spice . . ."*

It only took me a few seconds as he waited, offering me the last line. When I had it, I returned his smile, putting the kibosh on his good humor. *"Methinks he projects way too much."*

Despite our mutual laughter, he kept watching me and he looked a little sad. *"I know a lot of gifted women who are wives."*

I wasn't going there. *"Chickens, not eagles. Not women with wings and eager to fly."*

He snickered, an intentionally annoying sound. I shot him a warning look, prompting a smile of anticipation before I spoke. "Ansel, are you sure you've got the required sensitivity to run a public relations office?"

"Maybe not, but I do possess the essentials. The main requirement is to smile and nod convincingly. As you know, I am President Moran's personal favorite staffer."

"His personal favorite yes man." I dared him to contradict me.

He pretended to be concerned. "Why are you asking about qualifications? Are you interested in my job?"

I could play that little game. "I don't know. How much does it pay?"

"A hell of a lot more than you're ever going to make on any newspaper or wire service."

"Guess not." I gave an exaggerated sigh. "Sometimes I offend people, especially people with a phony, inflated sense of themselves. The kind of people you're required to coddle."

The music started again, couples drifted back onto the dance floor and Ansel held out his arms for a schottische. I spotted Steven's morose look and declined. "I've gotta go. Steven Carruthers is waiting for me. He's the guy shooting darts at your back from right over there."

Benedict slipped his arm around my waist and nudged me toward our table. Steven stood as we approached and I reintroduced him to University "Almost Vice President, Ansel Benedict."

Steven gave Benedict his much-practiced, all-American-boy grin. "I knew I recognized you." He shook Ansel's hand heartily and I marveled. They were like two peas in a pod. As I studied them, a renegade thought streaked through my mind. Did Jim Wills dance?

Where the heck had that come from? Steven continued oozing charm all over Ansel. "You're out of uniform. Does your presence mean President F. Delano Moran will be joining us?" Steven asked.

Benedict chuckled and glanced down at his studded shirt, jeans and cowboy boots. "You can never tell. The president likes to fraternize with students." He put his arm around my shoulders and hugged me. I thought maybe he was trying to shock Steven. "We'll do it again, after I catch my breath." He looked at Steven. "Nice seeing you again, Carruthers." With that, Ansel turned and glided through the crowd toward the bar.

Steven insisted we dance. We went an obligatory round, then I dropped him off at the table and I went back to line dancing.

Steven kept a plastic smile on his face and did not object to my behavior. He even went so far as to order me a beer. I let him take me home.

"I thought we might go on a picnic tomorrow." Steven's

attitude brightened considerably in the car and I was feeling pretty mellow myself by then.

It sounded like a nice idea. "What do I bring?"

"I thought I'd get fried chicken and the fixings."

"I'll do dessert. What time?"

"What time will you be hungry?"

I mumbled, thinking out loud. "I'll go to seven-thirty church. I want to call home. I need to hear my dad's voice." Then I spoke up. "Anytime after nine-thirty."

"I'll be at your house at nine-thirty, with a breakfast biscuit to hold you. We'll go to Blackhawk Lake. It'll be good to be outside, away from school and work and, well, everybody."

By eleven-thirty a.m. Sunday, Steven and I were walking by the lake, admiring the cliffs looming on the other side. I grabbed his hand when I slipped on a craggy rock and continued holding it after I regained my footing. It seemed natural enough.

We stopped at a grassy knoll near the water, sat down and opened up the picnic sack. Oh my, the heady aroma of fried chicken smelled wonderful. I watched with anticipation as Steven spread a quilt and issued paper plates and napkins. He was always well organized.

It seemed late in the day, but the sun shone from directly overhead. A family of ducks glided across the water, leaving a quiet wake. The breeze that moved branches high overhead ruffled my hair. Death and dying seemed far away. We ate in silence, each of us deep in thought.

"Think you'll get married someday?" Steven asked as he wiped greasy fingers. We had been silent so long that I felt comfortably alone. His voice surprised me, the interruption like fingernails on a chalkboard. Odd that men kept bringing up marriage. Weren't they supposed to be skittish about the subject?

"Statistics say probably so."

"What do you think the guy will be like?"

I laughed lightly. "I don't know."

"Do you expect to fall in love across a crowded room?"

"That's supposed to have been the purest form of romantic love."

"What do you mean?" He looked perturbed.

"It's easy to be in love as long as nobody talks." I forced a smile, although I wasn't really kidding.

"Jance, I'm serious. You and I are compatible, wouldn't you say?" He flashed me one of his political grins. Steven had a radio voice, which he used when he wanted to impress people, and a whole slew of practiced facial expressions: anger, approval, grave thoughts. When he first told me about those, I thought he was kidding and laughed. It seemed so phony, preplanning your articulation and the alignment of your facial features. I studied him and wondered what in the world he was getting at. Holding up my end of the conversation, I said, "Sure we are. We have a good time together. Why?"

"I finish school in December." He flattened his practically pristine napkin, smoothed the wrinkles and folded it. "If I pass the bar, I'll be ready to launch my career. I'm going to be very successful."

"I'm sure you will be." I was still puzzling.

He squared his shoulders and gave me his seriously determined look. "I thought we might get married."

I knew him well enough to know that, while the idea seemed ludicrous to me, he meant it. I tried to keep my face impassive. I needed to stall a minute for control. I coughed and pretended to have something in my throat. Finally, when

I had a handle on my knee-jerk negative responses, I asked, "What made you think that?"

"I'm ready to begin my adult life." He sounded terse, impatient. "I like planning you in it. I could get a government job." He gazed at my face as if trying to read my thoughts. It would be brutal to let them show. "We could travel. Sooner or later we could settle someplace we both liked, buy a house, a recreational vehicle for you and our two kids and a Jag to get me to the office and back. You like politics. I want to run for public office. You could manage my early political campaigns for me."

Struggling to quell my honest reaction, I locked my arms around my knees and rocked back, looking up and smiling. I hoped he'd think I was sharing some happy secret with the sky.

Steven glared. "What's so damned funny?"

"What is it you like best about me, Steven?" I was struggling to keep my laughter bottled up or locked down, but it was beginning to seep around the edges. "Is it my cooking or my political affiliation?"

"I don't know why you think this is so damned funny." He avoided looking at me, picked a piece of grass and bit on it as he squinted at the cliffs across the water. His jaws clenched.

I lowered my voice to my most businesslike tone. "I am flattered, Steven. I'm sure you'll find someone who will appreciate being included in your grand plan for your life. But it isn't me. I've already told you, by this time next year I'll be with the wire service overseas. I've got a grand plan of my own. It doesn't include marriage, children or preconceived vehicles."

"But you're almost perfect for it." Steven regarded me urgently. "You're smart. Intuitive. Instinctive. You have good habits. We'll do something about your hair and your clothes and you'll be fine. You're loyal and observant and you have integrity. I need all those qualities in a wife."

I thought I had the laughter under control until I saw the intensity in his face. He was morbidly serious and actually thought he might talk me into his fictitious future.

Giggles spewed in spite of my best effort to squelch them. I looked to the trees overhead for help, but the wind had picked up and even the branches seemed to convulse with laughter. I didn't want to hurt his feelings and tried to guilt trip myself back to the conversation, but he was already flinging items back into the picnic sack, muttering. I couldn't distinguish his words and decided that was probably best. I didn't dare look at him, so I leaped to my feet and picked up the quilt to shake out the crumbs. Steven snatched it out of my hands and folded it. His scowl looked permanent. I had to bite my lips. The whole thing was too bizarre.

When we were in the car, he careened down the hilly blacktop road back to the four-lane. I didn't say a word until he seemed calmer. Then I tried to boost his flagging morale while giving him a clue about dealing with a woman. "Could I make a suggestion?"

"What's that?"

"Work on your presentation."

"What do you mean?" He refused to look at me.

"There are phrases a man might want to use in wooing a woman. 'I love you' is good. 'I want you,' 'I will work like the devil to make you happy,' stuff like that."

"I thought all that crap went without saying. I thought you knew I found you attractive. I naturally assumed we'd have good sex."

I laughed a little under my breath, shaking my head. For a smart guy, he was certainly . . . obtuse.

"Don't start that again," he said. His face tightened and he sulked all the rest of the way to my house.

I invited him inside. He declined without looking at me and drove away almost before I swung the car door closed.

Sunday afternoon Deputy Gary Spence got bored sitting at the silent switchboard. He paced some, stretched and leaned on the window sill to watch pigeons strutting on the courthouse walk below. He picked up a couple of pencils, tapped out a rhythm on the countertop and noticed that the cash drawer hadn't been secured.

A little curious, he opened the drawer and was surprised to see checks and currency randomly tossed. The currency was paper-clipped and had sticky notes with names. That was odd. Patsy got fussy about anything being out of place.

He stacked the bills together and put the checks in alphabetical order. In the deposit book he wrote down the receipts for the week, pleased with himself. Just because he didn't usually do a job didn't mean he couldn't do it. Patsy would probably like having the deposit already organized.

At four o'clock, Sheriff Roundtree dropped by and Gary mentioned what he'd done. The sheriff looked concerned. "Hope you're not sticking your nose into a hive of bees."

Gary chuckled, then sobered. "Boss, there's no money here from the Sims boys—neither Lesley nor Wesley."

"She probably deposited it already."

"It's not listed in the receipt book. We've got stuff here that goes back more than a week. Didn't they pay Monday?"

"Yeah, cash." Roundtree riffled through the mail that Spence had picked up at the post office on his way to work, a gesture to keep the deputy on Patsy's good side, he supposed.

"Sheriff, how much money do you suppose comes through

here in a week?" Spence asked idly as he wrapped thick rubber bands from the drawer around the tidy stacks.

Roundtree didn't look up. "I don't know. I probably should know in case anyone important ever asks." He smirked at Spence, who grinned.

"I could go over and stick this in the night depository for her."

Roundtree raised his eyebrows. "Now, boy, I warned you about that bee hive. You know she doesn't like anyone messing with her accounting system. I wrote a check for pop a couple of weeks ago and I haven't heard the last of it yet. She's afraid I won't record a check right or won't write down payments like she wants 'em written. She's awful fussy. I'm happy to leave it to her, let her pay the bills and deposit the fines. She always comes up with the money we need when we need it."

"Sheriff, I didn't mean nothin'. I had a little time on my hands. I was just tryin' to help out. The drawer was open. Should I mess 'em all up again so she won't know?"

"Nah. She probably won't thank you, but I doubt she'll chew on you too bad."

Dispatcher Patsy Leek lit into Deputy Gary Spence like a tornado tearing over the plains on Monday morning.

Highway patrol troopers, forest rangers, police officers and deputies filing reports of illegal weekend activities scurried from the office as the air turned blue with Patsy's verbal eruption.

"What's wrong with her?" Undersheriff Wheeler asked Spence when the deputy darted into the hallway, wide-eyed and flushed.

"That woman's got some bad hormones." Spence paced the outside corridor, wondering how he could get back in the office to perform his own regular Monday morning duties.

Sheriff Roundtree arrived at the courthouse to find his entire staff in the hall—all except Patsy Leek. Ordered back inside, they trailed the sheriff, using him as a shield.

Roundtree spoke softly. "Sweetheart, Gary thought he was helping."

Patsy looked past Roundtree. The deputy shuddered as her bright, angry eyes locked on him. "One more stunt like that, bozo, and you're out of here for keeps."

Roundtree had not been privy to one of Patsy's tirades before, and although he routinely concealed evidence of it, he struggled to keep a tight rein on a formidable temper of his own.

"Pat," the sheriff said, his deep voice dropping to bass. His tone got him the full attention of the dozen people in the room. "Gary Spence served as a seaman under me. This is my office. I hired him and I will decide if and when he goes. I might remind you that you are here by that same authority. Do we understand one another?"

Patsy sniffed and tossed Roundtree a hasty nod, then looked back at Spence. Her eyes glittered like sun on flint.

Roundtree cleared his throat, effectively dismissing the subject, then walked into his office. He left the door ajar.

Law enforcement people finished their business quickly. Finally, alone in the front office with Patsy, Spence made an attempt at reconciliation. "Pat, I sure am glad you don't carry a gun."

"What makes you think I don't?" She flipped open her purse. Inside was a .38-caliber Smith and Wesson Police Special.

Spence swallowed hard and gave her a shaky smile.

The atmosphere in the sheriff's office remained strained most of the morning, but no more flare-ups occurred. Things seemed normal by the time Agent Jim Wills arrived to take Roundtree and Wheeler to Dominion to brief state officials on the progress of the murder investigations. The trio had not returned by noon, when Patsy received a call about a whiteface heifer and her calf missing from the Leopolds' pasture. A deputy needed to check with one of the hands at the family's deer camp just off Scenic Route Two.

Patsy stopped Spence on his way to lunch. "Can you take a call?"

"Sure, Pat, I'd be glad to." Gary liked the idea of doing Pat a favor and making a genuine call at the same time. Finding missing livestock might be a forerunner to going after missing people.

Spence saw no reason to mention that his pickup was in the shop. He was driving his wife's VW. The ancient vehicle got good mileage and gave him no problems, as long as speed wasn't needed to do the job. Rounding up cattle required more agility than speed. He trotted down the courthouse stairs.

The deputy had just turned off the alternate route onto a dirt road, slightly more than a cattle trail, when he heard a familiar *bump, thump, bump.* He knew the feel. Flat right front tire. "Damn." He stopped in the middle of the roadway, muttering more expletives.

"I oughta be glad Linda Lee wasn't driving. Oh yeah, darlin'. It's better that it's me." He got out of the car to examine the flat, opened the trunk in the front end and lifted out the jack and the spare.

"Hate these flimsy little crank jacks." He placed it under the bumper and wound the handle. The jack base settled into the dirt before it began lifting the vehicle.

After several minutes, Gary took a break to wipe sweat from his forehead with his sleeve and look around, thinking he might spot the missing cows. He saw several of the Leopolds' Herefords, all secured in fenced pastures nearby.

Hunkering, he got the wheel up, removed the wheel bolts and wiggled the tire with both hands. As he attempted to stand with it, he staggered off-balance.

Shuffling, trying to get his feet under him, Spence slammed the tire against the fender. The little car shivered and the aged jack snapped.

Still off-balance, Gary scrambled to escape, but his right foot slipped on the uneven ground and slid under the car just as it dropped. He felt the naked steel of the wheel rim slice into his calf.

Spence yelled as the car's full weight settled on his lower right leg. He shoved the spare aside and grabbed his right thigh, half-sitting. He shuddered. The rim cut into his calf like a knife. He peered at it, but couldn't tell how bad it was. He rocked back and forth, massaging his thigh. His whole leg throbbed.

Gritting his teeth, Spence noticed the jack handle just beyond his reach.

"This hurts like hell," he shouted at the handle. He looked at his leg a long moment, at the angle of the car and back at the jack handle. He stretched as far as he could.

Almost there. Maybe if he shifted his hips.

The deputy braced his arms and lifted himself. Gritting his teeth, he shifted himself a couple of inches. Straining, he could touch the handle with the tips of two fingers. He clawed at it, inching it closer until he could get his hand around it.

Vibration! Thunder or a car? Was a car coming? There wasn't much traffic along the scenic route on a Monday in October, but Gary Spence had always been one lucky son-of-a-gun. He waited, scarcely breathing, listening.

It was a car. If it was coming from the south, the driver

should be able to see him. If it came from the north, the foliage at the turn would conceal him and the VW.

He ripped the buttons off his uniform shirt and peeled down to his T-shirt. He stuck his uniform shirt on the jack handle and then lifted the makeshift signal flag. He swung it around as much as he dared. He didn't want it to blow off.

The approaching car slowed and turned onto the cow path. Relief made Spence lightheaded, even though he couldn't see the car through the tall grass.

"What kind of a stakeout is this?" The man's voice sounded familiar.

Twisting, Spence saw Agent Wills walking toward him.

"Hell's bells." Spence wilted. "Been There, I've never been so glad to see anybody. Get me out of here."

Wills scanned the situation. "If I lift the car, can you pull yourself out?"

"Yeah." Spence sounded more certain than he felt.

Wills stepped to the front bumper, turned his back to it, stooped and slid his fingers underneath. He took firm hold, then straightened, lifting the front end of the car clear of Spence's leg.

The deputy dug both hands hard into the dirt. Using his left leg for extra power, he dragged his numb right leg from beneath the car. "Clear," he shouted.

Wills dropped the car and stepped to the deputy's side.

Spence gazed up at the agent. "I'm afraid to look. It's numb, but it's bleedin' pretty good, ain't it?"

Wills knelt beside him. Carefully he tore Spence's trouser leg and inspected the damage.

"Looks good." Wills whipped off his necktie and wound it above the injury. "Mostly it got meat. It's bleeding, but doesn't look like you have any broken bones. You'll need stitches." The agent sat back on his haunches and regarded the deputy. "Your pants are never going to be the same, but a little sewing and this leg'll be good as new. Not any prettier, of course, but fully functional."

Spence attempted a smile.

Standing, Wills bent, draped Spence's right arm over his shoulder and lifted as the deputy positioned his good leg under him. Speaking calmly, Wills walked Spence to his state police unit.

"I'll call Benny's Station, get them to send a couple of guys out to fix that tire and drive your car back to town. Does it hurt?"

"Hell, I don't know." Spence had his mind fixed on getting to the agent's car. "I'm too damned chicken to put any weight on it."

"Do you need to stop for a minute? Rest?"

Spence grunted a "yes." Taking a shaky breath, he glanced at Wills' face. "Lucky for me you showed up."

"Lucky you drive a mini-car."

Once they arrived at his cruiser, Wills lowered the deputy's hips onto the passenger seat, then pivoted the injured man to face the front. Carefully, he positioned Spence's injured right leg, then closed the door.

Both men glanced up as a long, black car slowed at the turnoff, then roared off down the highway.

Walking around the back of his car, Wills' brow furrowed as he looked at the departing vehicle. Too far away to see the plate. He veered near the VW, picked up both pieces of the broken jack and studied the ends. Looked like a clean break. He tossed them aside and quickened his pace, suddenly in a hurry to get his passenger to town.

They were halfway there before either man spoke again.

"How's the leg?" Wills asked.

Spence made a flimsy attempt to smile. He rubbed his

right thigh with both hands. "I didn't know when I was well off. I wish it still felt numb."

"We're going straight to the emergency room. Should I call someone?"

"No!" Spence's voice broke, emphasizing the single syllable. "Linda Lee worries enough without getting a call from a perfect stranger telling her I'm at the hospital."

Wills gave him a wry grin and arched his eyebrows. "Deputy, in spite of what you may have heard, I'm not perfect."

Spence returned the grin. "Come on, Wills, get serious. A wife worries about her man. It's in the job description."

Wills' expression softened. "I wouldn't know."

An hour later Agent Wills left the hospital. Spence had been treated and released and had gotten a ride home—the deputy had called his wife himself. Wills drove back out on Route Two and turned off at the cow path.

Benny hadn't gotten there yet to repair the VW.

Wills drove to the locked gate within a quarter-mile of the Leopolds' cabin, a popular deer camp. He parked, climbed over the gate and walked the rest of the way. He had an uneasy feeling about the deputy's mishap.

The rustic log cabin did not disturb nature's quiet in the area. Still, seeing it made Wills even more wary.

Instead of opening the door, he stepped to a dusty window, wiped it with the heel of his hand and peered inside.

A fireplace of natural stone took up the entire far wall. Chairs and a kitchen table stood off to one side near a doorway that opened into a primitive kitchen.

As his eyes grew accustomed to the gloom inside, Wills saw one of the straight-backed chairs oddly situated in the center of the main room, its back to the front door. He made out what appeared to be an oversized spider web threading its way from the front door to a long, thin object lying on a stack of books in the chair.

A mop? A broom, maybe? He stepped back from the window, blinked and rubbed his eyes, then looked again.

The object balanced on the stack of books was a gun—a shotgun, its barrel pointed directly at the front door, hammer cocked. The web-like threads looped through the gun's trigger.

The four-ten was a booby trap, rigged to fire at anyone entering the cabin.

"What's that about?" Wills said, looking around.

He walked back to his car, wondering. People said Gary Spence was one of those charmed kind of guys, just naturally lucky. Why would the well-blessed deputy have had what looked like an unlucky accident—a flat tire and torn-up leg? Maybe Spence's legendary good luck had run true. Maybe the flat tire had prevented his blundering into the placid little cabin and its deadly welcome.

Wills drove to the Leopolds' sprawling frame home and honked as he wound up the graveled driveway amid the commotion of baying hounds. He stepped from the car, ignoring the dogs. They quit barking as soon as his feet touched the ground, content to sniff and circle him.

Wills climbed the steps, opened the outside door and crossed the screened porch. Mrs. Leopold met him at the front door.

Mrs. Leopold and her husband, both in their sixties, were devoted to their ranch and their brood of children. Four of their five kids had married and were raising broods of their own, each in homes built within a three-mile radius of the main house. Brewer Leopold, the oldest, still lived with his parents.

"Afternoon." Mrs. Leopold straightened her glasses. Her

hair was mussed, her eyes puffy and there were pad marks on one side of her face.

"Is Eli around?"

"He's down at the barn with Brewer and some of the men, working on a tractor. Can I do something for you?"

"No, thanks, I need to talk to him." Wills sounded more abrupt than he intended, but he wanted to hurry.

Mrs. Leopold nodded as she peered at him over the rims of her glasses. Sparing her a quick smile, he went to the barn.

"Mr. Leopold, I need a little information from you."

Inside the barn, Eli and his son Brewer were kibitzing while two of the hands, covered with oil and grease, climbed in and out of the engine area of the giant machine. The elder Leopold glanced at Wills and grunted agreement. He spat brown juice at a corner before he said, "Can you stay to supper?"

"Thank you, no. I've got things I need to see about."

"Pushing too hard'll put a man in an early grave."

Wills smiled and allowed a brief silence before he spoke again. "I need to ask about your hunting cabin over by Wasp Creek."

Eli spat again.

"It's booby-trapped. There's a shotgun set to shoot anyone who opens the front door."

Eli frowned at Wills, indicating some interest. "I don't know nothin' about that."

"You don't know about the shotgun rigged to ambush someone?"

"No."

Brewer cleared his throat. "I done it, Daddy."

Eli and Wills both turned their attention to him. "We didn't give nobody permission to hunt on our place." Brewer spoke to Wills. "People keep coming in stealing. They eat up all the canned stuff and leave a mess ever' time. Coons and rats come after the leavings. It gets pretty foul. And whoever it is helped themselves to Grandpa's .22 and the binoculars. That wasn't the first time they'd been in there, but if they come back, it'll be the last time."

Eli looked at Wills as if it were the agent's turn to talk.

"Aren't Clifton's kids getting up pretty good-sized now?" Wills asked the question quietly, careful to keep any accusation out of his tone. He didn't want to put them on the defensive.

Eli scowled at his son, indicating it was Brewer's turn to talk again.

"They don't ever go up there." Brewer returned Eli's frown. "Do they?"

Eli spat again, this time all the way into the targeted corner. "You'd better go knock that deal down, son."

Brewer bobbed his head up and down several times and started out of the barn. Wills followed. "Wait up, Brewer, I'll walk with you."

Brewer grinned as he turned in his tracks. "You don't need to be afraid of them dogs. They're all bark."

Jim turned back to the family patriarch. "Thanks, Eli."

The old man wiped his hand on the front of his shirt before he shook the agent's offered hand.

"One more thing, Eli. I hear that some ranchers around here castrate calves by wrapping rubber bands around their genitals and waiting until the parts drop off by themselves. Have you ever heard of that?"

Eli nodded. "We don't do it, but some do, particularly with sheep. It's cheap. It works all right. It's hard on the animal."

"I suppose it would be. Well, thanks again."

"Good to see you. Tell your daddy hello. Come out some-time when you can stay to supper."

Wills nodded and hurried to catch up with Brewer. "Where'd you get the idea for your trap?"

"The sheriff give it to me." Brewer flashed Wills a sheepish look. "Well, not the man himself. That little blonde woman who works there, the one that talks so big and struts her stuff." He paused, apparently waiting for confirmation that Wills knew Patsy Leek. "I went in to the sheriff to report it last time them idiots broke into the cabin. She told me they'd probably never catch the fellows that done it. She's the one told me how to rig that deal."

"When was that?"

"Thursday." Brewer gazed at the sky thoughtfully. "Yep, there was a lot of excitement there that day. They done found a body out on the highway the day before and things was buzzing. They was after some queer. She 'as the only one had time to talk to me, when she could over-talk that mouthy deputy that's always hanging around in there.

"Man, he was excited, ready to cut the balls of ever' queer in the county. Said a judge that'd order it done 'ould be doing us all a favor. She told him to shut up. He did, too, but not be-fore we all knew how much he hates fags. Hell, the way he was talkin', I thought he mighta killed that guy out on the highway."

Wills regarded Brewer with amazement. "Patsy Leek told you how to rig that shotgun to shoot anyone coming through the cabin door?"

"Yeah." Brewer flashed him a matter-of-fact glance. "She didn't know 'bout Clifton's kids or none like that."

"Brewer, you've got hands working all over that place. You don't want to be shooting any of them either, do you?"

"Nah, I wasn't thinking. Grandpa built that cabin in the

thirties. He give me that old rifle on my tenth birthday. I kept it cleaned up real good. I'd been up there, left my rifle and the binoculars thinking I was going back that evenin', but I got busy and didn't get there for better'n a week. Made me mad as hell, strangers gettin' in our cabin, stealing our stuff. We're real hospitable. You know that. They was welcome to the Vienna sausages, but they had no call to take my rifle."

Wills stared into Brewer's intense face. "Right. But you know now it's important to dismantle the shotgun before some innocent person wanders in there and gets hurt."

"You bet."

As they approached the house, the dogs, sprawled in the shade of the front porch, looked up but showed no interest. The two men shook hands, then Wills got into his car and Brewer headed for his pickup.

When concentrating on a case, Wills tried to make every occurrence in the rest of the world a piece that could fit into his puzzle. He knew some things weren't connected with the killings. Still, he couldn't quell the nagging suspicion that Spence's near miss had something to do with the murders. He needed to find the connection.

There were other nettles in these cases, and one big thorn he couldn't seem to avoid. Dewhurst. He smiled wryly, thinking of her.

What a pest, everywhere, distracting him when he needed all his powers of concentration. He'd never met a woman like her—nosy, meddlesome, fiercely independent, with those big eyes, that cherub's smile and a body that'd give a monk a hard-on.

He couldn't let his guard down around her. No, sir. He needed to stay away from that one. No flirting. No kidding around. No conversation. He'd known that at first sight. She was his Kryptonite. Being around her made him weak: physically, mentally, every way he considered himself strong.

Women generally posed no threat to him. For some crazy reason, this one did.

No, sir. He couldn't afford to get mixed up with Ms. Jancy Dewhurst.

But he did need some relief from a belly full of the ribbon murders, from nightmares and crazy thoughts. He couldn't imagine the torment the victims endured before they died.

He'd swing by the university and talk Ansel Benedict into a beer, get his mind off this stuff for a while, loosen up, bounce some ideas off his old mentor. Maybe even laugh.

# Chapter Five

It was nearly three by the time I had picked up the university's daily P.R. handouts and visited with Ansel. I was on my way out when Jim Wills stepped into the reception room. As usual, Ansel had his arm draped around me. Wills looked stunned for a moment, then annoyed.

"Jimbo." Benedict greeted Wills with his usual volume, reaching to shake hands while keeping his left arm locked around my shoulders. "How's my main man?" That was a surprise; first, that these two even knew each other, much less that they were friends. Ansel was *my* friend.

Wills grinned broadly at Benedict's usual rousing good humor but his smile diminished when his gaze shifted to me. As happened every time I saw this man, my heart skipped a beat and heat swept from my collar to my hairline. In my own defense, I could not think of anything I had done to annoy him—at least not recently. I did find his exceptional good looks unnerving, which probably accounted for my physical responses to seeing him.

"Doing good." Wills answered Ansel's question while making a valiant effort to ignore me.

Ansel wasn't going to let Wills' intended slight pass. He gave my shoulder a squeeze. "Are you acquainted with Jancy Dewhurst, Bishop's own low-budget Lois Lane?"

I squirmed, wanting to put some distance between Ansel and me. He tightened his hold, so I tried to lighten the moment. "I ain't all that cheap, Benedict."

Ansel chuckled and looked to Wills for a comeback, but the agent obviously wasn't in the mood to play straight man. Instead, he gave me a strained little smile and nodded as his eyes narrowed. "We've met."

"Mostly over dead bodies," I added and fidgeted again, feeling terribly uncomfortable trapped beneath Ansel's arm.

Benedict continued to grin like a sheepdog, pretending not to notice my discomfort.

Wills' eyebrows furrowed as he finally rested his dark eyes on me. His smile looked like it had been chiseled in stone.

Self-conscious at the center of both men's attention, I glanced at Wills, then concentrated on the floor as Benedict looked from me to the agent and back. We just stood there, enduring the awkward silence that none of us attempted to fill.

Finally, Ansel ended the quiet. "How about a beer?"

The receptionist and one of his staffers glanced up, obviously interested. Ansel barked a laugh. "Not you people. Someone's got to stay on the job." His voice dropped to a falsetto whine. "It's three o'clock. Lunch was a long time ago. It's time for my break." The half-dozen employees in the office—at keyboards, filing and researching—laughed. One of the student interns blushed when they looked at her.

Wills rubbed his hands together. "I'm ready." But he lost the smile and his voice chilled when he looked my way again. "Would you care to come along?"

Benedict still had me locked beneath his protective arm. Picking up on Wills' negative vibes, I wriggled and Benedict finally released me.

Obviously, Agent Wills did not want me along. Fine. It looked like the only chance I had of cultivating him as a news source now was to stay out of his way.

I forced false cheer into my voice and pasted a smile on my face. "Maybe next time. Thanks anyway." I genuinely did not know why Wills hated me. Okay, I had been a little rude at our first meeting out on the highway. And I'd behaved oddly at our second, in the morgue. But we had been under extremely trying circumstances. Of course, I had gone around him in getting information from the sheriff on Senator Crook's death. Maybe I needed to stand clear for a while and see if his bureaucratic pride could get over it.

Ansel looked and sounded genuinely disappointed. "Come on, Jance. We'll run down to Donnie's for half an hour. A beer'll give you an afternoon boost."

I ventured another assessing glance at Wills, saw that veiled disapproval and politely declined. "It would make me want an afternoon nap, more likely. I've still got to make rounds at the courthouse. Patsy Leek's not my biggest fan. If she smells beer, she'll bounce me out of there."

At the reference to Patsy, Wills' fixed smile wavered. Only slightly, but I caught the nearly imperceptible flinch. Now what was that about? Did he and Pat have a history together? The dispatcher had implied as much, but she often dropped cryptic little hints linking herself to any man prominent in any discussion.

Ansel nudged me and the three of us walked downstairs together. Despite Ansel's continuing pleas, I excused myself at the front door of the administration building and cut toward the parking lot.

"Ride or walk?" Benedict asked Wills as they watched Jancy disappear around the side of the building.

"Let's walk." As soon as the reporter was out of sight, Wills lost his plastic smile. Ansel noticed.

"What's the problem?"

"Ah, it's this ribbon thing." Wills shrugged. "I can't get a handle on it. I've got a whole collection of isolated incidents that don't appear to have anything to do with each other. It's like a clothes dryer rolling clothes round and round. They won't mesh together and I can't figure out why I expect them to, but I have this nagging feeling they should, that there's a common thread I'm missing."

Benedict clapped him on the shoulder. "You definitely need a drink. Beer may not be enough."

Jim gave his friend a rueful smile. "Hanging out with you will probably help as much as anything."

"Jimbo, you know you're not my type." He winked and they both laughed.

In the darkness of Donnie's Tavern, strategically situated directly across from the engineering school on the campus corner, Ansel Benedict and Jim Wills argued football and politics. Gradually, subtly, they circled back to the subject at hand.

"Hell, I don't even know how many people knew about the killer's signature originally," Wills said.

"You mean before Jancy's story?"

Wills grimaced. "Right."

"Who was at the scene when they found the first body?"

"Everyone representing law enforcement in two counties and three municipalities. Multiply thirty officers on the scene times word-of-mouth to everyone they told." Wills brightened for a moment. "But the university police hadn't heard about the ribbons two days later. Not until your little girlfriend connected the dots for them."

Benedict didn't react to Wills' reference to Jancy. "I thought gay bashers usually just beat up homosexuals. Am I misinformed?"

"No, you're right, but these killings were done by someone with a serious ax to grind. We assumed homophobes might have nailed Benunda and Speir, but that theory washed when the killer iced Crook. The senator was famous for chasing women—in Dominion and more discreetly here. To complicate things, a lot of people knew all three victims. Even you, Ansel."

Benedict chuckled. "Am I a suspect? Is that why you're here?"

Wills stared into his beer until Benedict lost his smile. "Nah. You know better than that." He hesitated. "Still, you know how uptight you got last spring when the gays asked for the activities money."

"You can't be serious."

"No. I'm not." Still staring at his beer, Wills shook his head and waved off the implication.

Ansel looked annoyed. "My tolerance hit a low last spring along with my morale. Jancy has a knack for making me feel my age—insult to injury—and then she accused me of being narrow-minded. She's the one who finally convinced me to sit down with that gay rights bunch. After I did, I realized they were just kids, like all the other kids their age, floundering around, trying to find their own identities."

"Do you know Gary Spence?" Wills changed the subject abruptly.

Benedict took a sip of his beer. "Yes, why?"

"How about Robert Crook? Patsy Leek?"

The questions drew successive nods.

"Tell me what you know about them."

Benedict turned his beer glass round and round on its coaster. "Spence is a redneck. He talks big but he's harmless enough. He's pretty vocal about hating blacks, gays, college football players who sign high-dollar pro contracts, people with foreign accents and eggheads. He's married to Linda

Lee Dorsett-Spence, a perpetual university student who is a whole lot too smart for him, but doesn't know it."

"And Crook?"

"He was rare. Intelligent. Unscrupulous. Able to work a little bit of knowledge into a sizable financial war chest. Enterprising. An opportunist with no moral code to get in his way."

"Can you think of anyone who might have wanted to kill him?"

"Sure, I could make a list of at least a hundred. Former clients he'd fleeced, folks he exploited sexually, politically or financially, or all of the above."

"Can you think of anyone who'd want to call attention to his sexual habits?"

"The senator bagged a lot of women: married ones, single ones, old, young, willing, not."

Wills' voice dropped a little. "Okay, what do you know about Patsy Leek?"

"She's divorced. Has two kids: a girl, Maggie, a university student who's also a damn good dorm counselor—what we call a resident advisor—and a boy, Jason. The boy may still be in high school or he could have dropped out by now. I coached Jason in Little League. He's one of the few kids I've known who tried to get into drugs but didn't like them. I hear he drinks, but he doesn't like booze either. Other kids on the team liked him. I liked him. Before school started he began hanging with some guys from the university's drama department, older than he was, you know, guys who pat each other on the butt a lot. I asked him to come by sometime for a talk. He came to the house. We had a beer. I don't know if Pat ever knew. She doesn't like me. If you've spent time around her, you know she doesn't like most men. Classic case of penis envy."

Wills glanced up from his beer but didn't say anything.

"I can't imagine what kind of mother she is," Benedict continued. "She may have passed her personal hang-ups along to her kids."

Wills nodded. Benedict met his eyes. "You're not interested in Leek romantically, are you? She is kinda cute. Of course, you'd have to get by the age difference between you."

Wills brayed a laugh. "And I suppose you'd advise me to stay alert, what with that envy thing and all."

Benedict chuckled and shrugged. "You never can tell." He shifted to prop an elbow over the back of his chair and eyed his colleague. "If you at long last decided to get seriously interested in a woman, Jim, Jancy'd be my choice. If a man's going to sign on to support some female for the rest of his life, I think she'd come closest to making it worth his while."

Jim's grin broadened but his eyes narrowed. He leaned forward, propping his elbows on either side of his beer. "It sounds to me like Ms. Dewhurst has already bagged the granddaddy of eligible bachelors in these parts."

Benedict looked deflated. "She would have if she were interested. I'm afraid she's too rich for my blood."

"What do you mean?"

"She's smart, energetic, has a lot of savvy. She's like you, Jimbo." Ansel took a long drink of his beer, then shook his head. "To tell you the truth, Wills, I'm a coward. I want people to like me. I do whatever it takes to make that happen."

"Everyone I know does like you."

"Thanks. Anyway, it offends me when someone doesn't. That's my weakness. I'm a social coward." Benedict snorted. "Jancy sees that in me. She kids me about being a textbook yes man. She spotted it immediately. She says she doesn't blame me. She knows it's the way I am, but it annoys the hell out of her."

"She told you that, in so many words?"

"The woman's heartbreakingly honest. And that's not the worst of it. She says I'm obsessive-compulsive, just because I like things neat—the clothes hanging in my closet on hangers a certain distance apart. I like my shoes polished and books on my shelves in a certain order."

"So she's not neat?"

Benedict guffawed. "You've seen her. I don't mean she's a slob—exactly—but when most young women are preening and adjusting their clothes, she's listening and watching. She was doing a story one time when this guy behind her dropped his drink. Some of it splashed on her pant leg. She didn't blink, much less run home to change. She stayed focused.

"Now me, I can't stand for my person or my immediate surroundings to be fouled. If that drink had gotten me, I couldn't have thought about anything else until I got cleaned up.

"Those two kinds of responses come from people who would, in time, drive each other totally berserk. Unfortunately, Jancy and I have gotten close enough to realize we have a whole bunch of those kinds of differences.

"Of course, there's the age thing, too. Nearly twelve years. You, on the other hand, are what? Twenty-six?"

"Twenty-seven."

"She's twenty-three. You're an awful lot alike—same kind of energy, different kind of smart. She's more observant than you are, but you've got the wisdom to know what to do with information when you get it." He dropped his voice and raised his eyebrows. "You are also the same kind of stubborn."

"And you think we're both slobs?" Wills pretended to be offended. Benedict laughed out loud and Jim allowed a slow grin.

"No, Jim, you're fastidious, much neater than she is, you just aren't compulsive about it." Benedict grinned mischievously. "I could teach you, if you want to learn."

It was Wills' turn to laugh.

"She has an eye for detail," Benedict continued. "She hears every inflection in a voice, absorbs every nuance, like a sponge. Example. We're in an office. She notices a picture on the wall is crooked. She doesn't straighten it, but later she can describe it, in detail. If I, on the other hand, should happen to notice it's crooked, I get restless until I can straighten it. But I won't remember if it was a Remington oil or a master's degree. See what I mean?"

Wills studied Benedict with a mixture of humor and disbelief.

"And, whether you know it or not," Benedict went on, ignoring the look, "you and she have the same peculiar sense of humor. Even Roundtree mentioned it."

The waitress came with a pitcher to freshen their beer.

"You know, Jimbo, the sheriff isn't sure if he likes you or not, but he is absolutely crazy about Dewhurst, in a protective, fatherly way. There isn't anyone as good as she is, as far as he's concerned. If she likes you, he'll tolerate you. They have an enviable friendship.

"At the courthouse Christmas party, his wife told me she'd never been jealous of him, even with all those years in the military, until he started talking about Jancy. She felt better after she met Jance and saw how she and Roundtree interacted with each other, but she still pays attention to what goes on between them."

Wills smiled and gulped down the last of his beer. As expected, he felt better. Benedict's descriptions of Dewhurst had helped. No matter how much she vexed him, he couldn't seem to get her off his mind. Apparently, he wasn't the only one with that problem.

Stepping back out into the dazzling sunlight, Wills and Benedict shut their eyes against its glare. Squinting, they waited in silence for the traffic light to change.

"What do you mean, my odd sense of humor?" Wills asked as they crossed the street back onto the campus.

"Come on, you know how you are, laughing at things before other people know they're funny. You see the humor quicker. You also grasp the solemnity of a situation in a heartbeat. Jancy's like that. That quick assessing is probably what makes you a good cop and her a great reporter."

Wills nodded understanding. He liked hearing about her, liked remembering her sidling close to him in the morgue as they looked at dead bodies. And he was doubly glad she'd decided not to have a beer with them. He didn't need any more pressure right now, even the pleasant rush of a new, sexy dolly around.

Tuesday morning, Jim walked into the sheriff's office to find Spence, his splinted right leg propped up, manning the dispatcher's radio.

"Sheriff's on the telephone," Spence said, stating the obvious as Roundtree bellowed into the receiver, demanding to know what the caller meant by "poundage."

"Yeah." Wills leaned on the counter. "How do you feel?"

"On the mend."

"Where's Pat?" Wills glanced toward the magazine table.

"Another personal day."

"Is she sick?" He picked up an old *Newsweek*.

"No, it's her kid. Jason."

Wills thumbed through the magazine, appearing to give the conversation only polite attention. "What happened to him?"

"Well." Gary lowered his voice, unnecessary since he and Jim were the only people there aside from Roundtree, bellowing in the next room. "Pat and the kid have been having a standoff. When she gets home after work, she don't want to cook. Jason said he wasn't eating out every night, that she was his mom and she should fix his meals. When she got home yesterday, she found him passed out in the shower. It's a miracle he didn't drown."

The deputy shifted in his chair. Jim waited.

"It scared her half to death," Gary continued. "Turns out he's got mono. You know, the kissin' disease. The doctor told her Jason needs bed rest, wholesome meals and no stress. Ain't that a kick in the ass, when she'd just sworn she wasn't cookin'?

"Talk about your guilt trips. She's on a wild one now, mad and cussing Jason, the doctor, everyone around here one minute, next minute she's bawling."

Wills tossed the magazine back on the table, getting ready to leave as Spence continued. "She was pretty upset when she came here this morning, maybe twenty minutes, just long enough to give us our marching orders. Odd thing: she didn't even ask me about my leg. I guess she didn't notice."

Wills pursed his lips and nodded. "Guess I'll be going."

Spence glanced at the switchboard. "Sheriff's off the phone now, if you want to talk to him."

"Thanks, it'll wait. Give him time to cool down."

Because Wills seemed interested in Gary's report on Pat's kids, the deputy gave the same information to Jancy when she stopped by later in the morning. Funny thing was, she paid attention and even scribbled something in her spiral note-book. He didn't often tell her things that earned a line in that notebook.

Lincoln McMurtrey, State's Attorney General, called Roundtree's office Tuesday afternoon. The governor had appointed Agent Wills officer in charge of the Crook investigation.

Roundtree objected loudly. "He's too green. He's hardly more than a kid."

"This is straight from the governor's office, Sheriff. He knows Wills personally, thinks he's smart and a hard nose. Those other guys in the senate are adamant. There was no love lost on Crook, but they insist we honor the office. They want him to have the homage they would want if it were any of them."

"Got any hot news?" I asked as I reached the sheriff's office and slid into a chair.

Shuffling papers at the counter, Spence smiled suggestively. "I'll tell you mine, if you'll tell me yours."

"Steven Carruthers asked me to marry him."

The deputy grimaced. "Hell, yes, he did. He wants you to finish puttin' him through law school, then he'll throw you over. That's the way those guys all do. What'd you tell him?"

"I said I'd have to ask your permission."

Spence didn't blink at the sarcasm. "Then the answer is: 'No.' "

"So much for that." I pretended a deep sigh. "Your turn." Spence hobbled to the switchboard. I jumped up and was surprised to see his right leg in a brace. "What happened to you?"

"Thirty-seven stitches." Before he could say more, Agent Wills strolled into the reception room.

Wills glanced at me, prompting my usual blush. Damn, that was annoying. Before I got feverish, he turned his attention on Spence. "Is the sheriff here?"

"No, but he'll be back in forty-five minutes. If it's important, I can beep him."

"No, I'll catch him later." Wills looks directly at me again. "Hello, Ms. Dewhurst. Got any hot scoops?"

"Gary has thirty-seven stitches in his leg."

Wills nodded and looked at the deputy. Wordless, Spence stared at the floor. Wills smiled. "I heard." He shifted his smile to my face. That smile got me blushing again. He studied me for a long minute, then turned and without another word walked out the door.

I whirled on Spence. "Is it just me, or is that guy rude to everybody?"

Spence shook his head. "Right now, Jance, that man's a hero at my house."

"What?"

Spence told me about the call to the Leopolds, the flat tire, the jack breaking and the car pinning his leg. He gave me a detailed account of Wills lifting the car off him and about the rigged shotgun in the cabin that would have blown Spence's head off if he'd gotten there, because he would have "busted right in without checking things out first."

I was impressed. "He lifted a car? By himself?"

Spence shrugged. "Only a little one. A VW. Lucky for him the engine's in the back. Gave him leverage."

My eyes popped. "Lucky for someone."

Spence laid the shuffled papers aside and his voice dropped. "I've got another little news flash for you, Scoop. This afternoon the governor himself named Wills the officer in charge of the Crook investigation. Because it's part of the ribbon killings, that pretty much makes him the top law enforcement dog in the state right now. It might be smart for you to be really nice to Agent Wills."

Preoccupied with the deputy's revelations, I ambled out of the sheriff's office to finish my rounds and head back to the *Clarion.*

Why hadn't Wills said something about rescuing Spence? He was right there in the sheriff's office, face-to-face, but he hadn't mentioned it. Of course, he probably knew Gary would tell me and everybody else. Was Wills just pretending to be modest or was he the genuine article?

Back at my desk, I called the SBI offices. A secretary said Wills was not available. "Also, I should warn you, Ms. Dewhurst," the woman said, "he doesn't talk to reporters about an investigation in progress. But I will give him the message and suggest he return the call. Confidentially," the secretary added, "he hates reporters."

I rolled my eyes. "I hope that's not supposed to be classified information."

The woman didn't hang up. Instead, she said, "The best chance you have is to run into him by chance. He jogs early every morning at the Jessup Y."

"How early?"

"Six-ish."

"Why there?"

"It's close to his house."

"Thanks."

"Don't mention it." The woman gave a little chuckle. "And I mean, don't mention it."

I didn't know exactly how I could use that little tidbit of information. I checked with University Police Chief Simp McClellan. He refused to give out any information on progress in their investigation and told me to direct all my questions to Wills.

Bishop Police Chief Pete Summers told city beat reporter Cliff Renslow the same thing.

Sheriff Roundtree hadn't gotten back to his office.

"Do you know Wills with the SBI?" Melchoir asked when he sat down with Renslow and me for a story conference an hour later. We both nodded. "You need to get on his good side and stay there."

"I'll try, but the guy's a hard case." Renslow gave me a pleading look.

Talking privately with Renslow later, I was perplexed. "Cliff, I don't think Agent Wills likes women, me in particular. He's got me pegged as a feminist or a teacher's pet—you know, the way the sheriff and the D.A.'s people treat me."

Renslow shrugged. "Chief Summers and the guys in the department are high on him. The gals, of course, swoon every time he comes around. I think he's dating one of 'em. I'll talk to her, see what I can do, but you have to stay after him too."

"I will. See if you can get him on the phone. I've already tried. I couldn't get through. I'll write what we've got so far, with room for a new lead in the morning if you get anything out of him."

# *Chapter Six*

The alarm rang at five forty-five a.m. At first I couldn't imagine why. Remembering, I forced myself to get up. I didn't really mind that it was pitch black out—I liked seeing the dawn. What I didn't like was jogging. Jogging bounced body parts that were not necessarily designed for it.

Angela said it was the price I paid for having a Playmate bust.

Liz Pinello sympathized.

I put on my jogging bra and hitched it tight, then layered T-shirts for extra support. I slipped into shorts and zipped a warm-up jacket to ward off the early morning chill. I double-tied my tennis shoes and brushed and secured my hair with a banana clip.

Jogging meant sweating. No use messing with make-up. It wouldn't last long anyway. Fate intended that I simply wasn't ever to look good for this particular man.

I found Wills' address in the phone book, drove to the area near the Y, parked two blocks from his house and began running along a quiet residential street.

Honest to God, I almost didn't recognize him. I had seen him several times, but always in a coat and tie with a high sheen on his shoes. I knew he was substantially built, but I had not expected him to look quite so buff in a T-shirt and shorts. His calves and thighs were nicely formed. His brawny arms were taut, his well-cut body graceful. Muscles rippled beneath his skin like those on a big, lithe cat.

Without intending to, I slowed down, startled by the athletic rhythm of his strides. I needed to get all that admiration under control before our "chance encounter."

I had a hard time finding my voice, but finally yelled as we closed the gap between the two legs of the Jessup Y. "Hey."

He looked up, obviously surprised to see me, or maybe anyone so early on the course he habitually ran alone. When he recognized me, he didn't look as annoyed as usual.

"Hey." He didn't stop as our paths merged, but he gave me a smile and slowed to accommodate my pace. I had questions in mind, but seeing him like that, plus the smile, got me muddled.

He looked spectacular. The timing seemed wrong for blasting him with a battery of questions. Also, I needed what breath I had for running.

"Nice morning," I managed.

"Yeah." Other than settling into the slower pace, he scarcely acknowledged my presence.

We had gone nearly two blocks when I felt the vibration of a car behind us. It picked up speed. That racing engine seemed out of place in the early morning quiet.

Wills and I were on the left side of the street, facing approaching traffic, so I didn't feel concerned until the car roared, sounding as if it were directly behind us. Wills glanced back, then grabbed my upper arm and pushed, making me run faster.

I turned my head and caught a glimpse of the hood ornament on a dark-colored Cadillac. The driver's head and face were completely concealed by a broad-brimmed hat. As the car closed on us, the driver accelerated.

Wills stuck his arm in front of my face and yelled, "Tree!"

Then he was steering me over the curb toward a massive elm on the parkway.

The Cadillac leaped the curb behind us. A fan belt screeched as the car went airborne for a moment. The metal body rattled and groaned as it landed at the base of the tree. Having shoved me to the far side of the tree, Wills knocked me flat and came down on top of me. I was angry until I realized he was using his body as a shield. Spinning wheels, screaming, spat leaves, grass and mud everywhere. An earsplitting mechanical shriek echoed as the driver floor-boarded the vehicle. The car fishtailed and sideswiped the elm, but the machine was no match for the tree. Thrown into reverse, it skidded as the tires skinned the curb, then lurched forward and roared away, leaving the neighborhood in silence.

Wills lifted himself off of me, seemingly without noticing I was there. "Did you see the driver?" He stood and offered a hand, which I took, and pulled me to my feet.

I was shaking, frightened and furious.

When he finally looked at me, he put a steadying hand on my shoulder, which was okay until I realized and shrugged it off. "You're kidding, right?" Oddly enough, I had noticed more than I thought. "I did get the tag, though."

"P-B W-I-F-E," we said in unison. He had noticed it too.

"Probably stolen." Wills flicked leaves and grass off his clothing.

"Why?" I brushed at pebbles and dirt embedded in my kneecaps.

"It's June Crook's car. She's had the same tag for years on a dozen different cars."

"Was that Ms. Crook driving?"

"No. Like I said, it was probably stolen."

"Oh." Beginning to breathe steadily, I stared at him. "Who's after you? And why?"

He returned my stare. "What makes you think they were after me? Maybe it's you."

"Why either one of us?" I can be completely transparent, and I wondered at that moment if my face reflected the jumbled thoughts coming and going, rapid-fire. I had asked the question, not expecting a satisfactory answer.

Wills touched the skinned place on the tree. "Well, it looks like one of us is hitting a nerve someplace."

"Which one of us? And whose nerve?"

"I wish I knew." He glanced up, his frown a mirror of how I felt.

I stretched to my full height, determined he should do some explaining. "Agent Wills, I need to ask you some questions and I need straight answers."

"Okay." That quick, cooperative response made me suspicious. He'd yielded too easily. While I thought it over, he continued. "I have a couple for you, too."

"Oh?" That caught me completely off guard. "Like what?"

"You say you didn't know Charles Benunda or Francis Speir—either one, right?"

"I didn't know their names, but I'd seen them before. That's all."

"Did you know Senator Crook?"

"Yes."

"Personally?"

"Yes. Now it's my turn." I was brought up short for a minute, thinking before deciding to change my approach. "Did you know Crook?"

He nodded.

"All three murders are connected, aren't they?"

"You already know that."

My resolve withered as I remembered the bodies. When

Wills returned my curious stare, I turned my eyes on the ground.

"Come on," he prodded, his voice businesslike. "What else?"

"Why were you asking questions yesterday about Patsy Leek?"

"Who told you that? I never even talked to the sheriff." His face softened. "Oh. Roundtree isn't the only source you've been hustling in the sheriff's office, is he? You've been squeezing Spence too."

"Not hustling or squeezing. I take care of my people. I see that they get their names in the paper occasionally and they look out for me."

"Well, you didn't do such a hot job taking care of Crook."

"Hey, isn't that the pot calling the kettle black?" The words shot out before I had time to think, followed by instant remorse, but I didn't know how to take them back, so I punted. "I feel bad enough about what happened to Crook without you rubbing my nose in it."

Wills looked surprised. "What do you mean, you feel bad?"

"If I could have figured out what was going on, we might have caught the killer before he got to Crook."

"Swell." Wills paced in a tight circle, his hands on his hips. "Since when is protecting the public your job? I'm the officer in charge. How the hell do you think I feel?"

I shuddered. Had I ever pressed a wrong button. . . .

"Come on." Wills grabbed my arm, as if intending to turn me back to the jogging path. I jerked away from him. He frowned. "What's the matter with you?"

"I don't like people to touch me when I'm nervous . . . or mad . . . or anything."

"Or scared? The car scared you, didn't it?" I shot him a warning look, not intending to answer. "Or is it me?"

"The car, smart A. What kind of law enforcement person are you, anyway? Don't you watch TV? When you're involved in a car chase, you're supposed to be in a car, not galloping down the street trying to outrun one."

"Let's get back to your being jumpy."

I looked at the toes of my scuffed running shoes. "Some people find physical contact comforting. When I get upset, I need space. I don't even like my parents to touch me, much less strangers."

He stepped away from me and back into the street. "And you and I are strangers? I'll try to remember that."

Ignoring the barb, I fell into step as he began jogging again. "Do you think we're in for more of these upsetting little incidents?"

He didn't bother looking at me. "Maybe. Maybe not."

We ran for a block, each absorbed in our own thoughts, until a Rottweiler pup dragging a rope darted toward us. When I tried to avoid him, he snarled. The hackles on his neck bristled and he bared his teeth. I stopped, paralyzed with fear and indecision. Reflex made me look to Wills, to see if he meant to bolt. He stood there, giving me a disgusted look. Then he clenched his fists and emitted a loud, terrorizing bark. The pup and I both jumped. Wills ran at the pup, bellowing deep, awful growls and barks. Every bit as confused as I was, the dog wheeled and ran for his life, his stubby tail between his legs.

The whole thing was ridiculous. Suddenly I became aware of a gurgling, maniacal giggling. It was coming from me.

Wills was not amused. "What the hell were you afraid of?"

"He popped out of nowhere. He startled me. I thought he was going to bite."

"He was a pup."

"He's got teeth."

"You've got teeth. He doesn't have the benefit of hands. All you'd have to do, if he got too close, is grab an ear and twist it off his head. Or bite it off. He'd be away from you in a flash."

"You expect me to bite off a dog's ear? Are you nuts?"

"You need to think you can destroy an ear if you have to. They're pretty well attached. You probably couldn't, but if you thought you could, if you made the dog think so, he'd run, just like he did. That pup would have been good practice for you. Dogs don't have shoes or those long legs, either. Are you right or left-handed?"

"Right."

"You could've planted your left foot and kicked that pup into next week."

I stared at Wills. "Are you really that tough, or is this just smoke?"

He snorted. "There's a saying, Dewhurst. 'Whether you think you can or you think you can't, you're probably right.' You froze. You can't let fear paralyze you, no matter how bad things get. You've got a quick mind. When you get in a jam, use it."

He snorted again and looked annoyed, or maybe surprised, by his own words. Abruptly he turned and walked away. His steps quickened to a slow jog. Mesmerized, I caught up with him and ran alongside. This man was tough to cubbyhole. It had been my experience that guys as good-looking as Jim Wills usually had personalities like doorknobs. His occasional lectures sounded like he was taking a personal interest in me, trying to prepare me for challenges in the future. But I was none of his business. Was I? Was he interested in me? Nah. He was just one of those naturally courageous types. I'm a born coward. I chalk it up to being female, but I'm chicken even for a woman.

As we passed the Y, I was deep in thought and forgot my plan to turn back toward my car. He didn't say anything until two blocks later, when we reached his condo. I had driven past it earlier, to verify the location. It was cedar and stone on a neatly manicured lawn. Obviously, Wills liked things tidy, another argument against his being interested in me.

I was surprised when he stopped at the walkway. "Oh, I'm sorry," I said, looking around, pretending innocence. "Is this where you live?"

A grin relaxed his face. He knew. Darn it. His dark eyes twinkled, his white teeth glimmered. He had an amazing smile. "It's okay," he said. I wondered if he were patronizing me. I hate that.

I looked around some more, trying to think how to salvage my pride. "I guess I was trying too hard to sort things out and forgot to turn back toward home."

That shrewd smile flashed again. "I'll give you a lift wherever you want to go."

If he took me back to my car, he would know for certain our encounter was no coincidence. That indicated he, not I, was the target of the morning's near miss. He was the one who routinely jogged that course at that time of day. I needed to tell him, but I didn't want to embarrass myself more than I already had.

"Hellooo," he crooned, peering into my face.

"I'll . . . ah . . . just go."

He flashed a mischievous grin. "There could be another dog."

"Funny. You're a real clown, you know that?"

He lost the grin but he still looked a little smug. "Tell you what. You take my car. I drive a bureau vehicle on duty anyway. We can meet later at the snack bar in the courthouse for coffee. At ten. Can you be there?"

Melchoir's order echoed in my head: *Get close to Wills and stay there.* Wills was studying me again.

"I'll buy, if that's what's bothering you."

A quick look verified my suspicions. He was teasing me.

"Okay." To avoid his gaze, I looked around, as if getting my bearings.

He didn't invite me into his house. Instead he led me around to the garage, which opened on the alley and housed two nondescript, mid-sized cars, a gray with a standard car tag and a brown with a tax-exempt state plate.

"Do you always leave the garage door open?" I wondered again if I should tell him he definitely was the morning's target.

"No. I came out this way and forgot to put it down." He started to add something, but went inside the house instead and came back jingling keys. He tossed them to me and indicated I should take the stodgy gray Honda Civic with the civilian plate.

"If you can't make it to the snack bar at ten," he said, as if it didn't matter either way, "leave the keys with Spence when you make your morning run to the sheriff's office."

I felt weird, and definitely offended. How did he know my routine included a morning stop in Roundtree's office? And why hadn't he invited me into his house? I probably would have refused and suggested we walk around, like we had, but why hadn't he invited me? Was there a woman inside, the gal who worked in the city clerk's office?

Wordlessly I took the keys, gave him a weak smile, thanked him and got into the car.

Wills just stood there frowning as I backed out of the driveway and drove off down the street.

On my way home, I couldn't figure out my peculiar behavior. My judgment was muddled, my thoughts jumbled. Of course, three people had died. But Agent Wills seemed to be the source of my current confusion. His shifts from playful to serious had me off-balance. Circumstances probably had his moods vacillating, just like mine.

Liz Pinello was on her way out when I pulled into the driveway of the house on Cherry Street.

"Whose wheels and where are yours?" Liz piped.

"A loaner." Silently I willed her not to ask a lot of awkward questions. She raised her eyebrows, but didn't speak. "Do you have time to do me a favor?" I asked.

She checked her watch. "If it takes less than twenty minutes."

"I need you to go with me to pick up my car. You can take it to work and park it in the *Clarion* lot, if that's okay. Can Ben pick you up after work?"

"Sure. We've got a lunch date. I'll ask him then."

"By the way," Liz said as we drove to the Jessup Y, "we may have to start locking the house. It looks like someone's been coming in and rummaging around. It could be those brats next door, but we're going to start carrying our keys and locking up."

"Okay." I wasn't ready to think about any new enemies, real or imagined.

Back home in fifteen minutes, I bathed, dressed with unusual care, and applied makeup with an unsteady hand and rare concern. I knew why I was being so finicky, but didn't want to think about it. Thinking about him set butterflies swarming in my stomach.

I made a face in the mirror. "Goofy." I smiled. My smile was good. Not as striking as his, of course, but good. Sun-bleached highlights streaked my dark hair. Did he like looking at me? I laughed at my reflection. Well, I certainly liked looking at him.

Did he have a girlfriend? A live-in?

Cliff Renslow said Wills was dating someone from city hall. Had she been in his house that morning? Was a resident girlfriend the reason he hadn't invited me inside?

The idea annoyed the fire out of me.

"When did you start thinking like some drippy character in a soap?" I asked my moderately attractive reflection, then snorted in disgust. I couldn't help remembering Wills' dark eyes, his shoulders, his forearms, the way he ran, the way he walked. . . .

"The way he swam!" I said loudly. "Whoa! The silhouetted guy at the pool? I knew he sounded familiar."

I made a face at my reflection, tossed off my clothes and changed, a new blouse under the airy red jumper that emphasized my brown eyes. Wills always dressed well and looked it. I used a dirty sock to dust the new SAS loafers I had to dig out of the back of the closet. I was really putting on the dog.

About nine-thirty, I asked Ron Melchoir if we could speak privately. He preceded me into the coffee bar where we sat down alone, facing each other across the break table. He looked me over but didn't comment while I briefed him on my early morning meeting with Agent Wills, including the attempted hit-and-run.

He didn't ask how I happened to have suddenly taken up jogging and I didn't tell him why I'd been on the Jessup Y that early in the day.

Neither did I mention—or even think of—my housemates' concern that some unauthorized person or persons had been prowling through our house.

Melchoir regarded me soberly. "Why do you keep looking at the clock?"

"I didn't realize I was." I stood. "I'm supposed to meet Wills at the courthouse at ten."

Melchoir smiled broadly, leaned back in his chair, laced his fingers together and patted his stomach. "I knew you could whip that guy into shape."

I looked down at my improved clothing and wondered who was influencing whom.

Melchoir sobered. "If you need help, research, more people on the story, let me know."

I assured him I would.

Wills was not in the snack bar when I got there at nine fifty-seven. I gave the machine three hard thumps before it gave up a cup of hot chocolate. The cup toppled as it dropped from the dispenser. I fumbled but got it straightened in time to catch most of the cocoa. I sat at one of the tables, a little spooked in the deserted room in the dank courthouse base- ment. I didn't like the hollow, isolated feel of the place. As a distraction, I thumbed through my notes on the murders, which didn't make me feel any more comfortable.

Fifteen minutes later, I finished the cocoa and the note re- view and decided he wasn't coming. I slapped the notebook closed, clipped my ballpoint to the cover, and stood before I noticed him, leaning in the doorway, his arms folded across his chest, grinning like he'd been there a while.

As usual, he was impeccable, dressed in houndstooth trousers, a stiff white shirt, a tie and blazer. His teeth seemed whiter, his dark eyes clearer and his shoulders broader. I glowered at him, annoyed at myself for admiring him so bla- tantly and furious that he seemed to be aware of those private thoughts.

"How long have you been standing there?" I sounded like a shrew.

His smile broadened but he didn't answer.

"What are you grinning at?"

The smile dimmed as he shouldered himself away from the doorjamb. "Nothing. Let's get to work."

"That's what I need to do. I've been cooling my heels down here for the last twenty minutes waiting for you."

"Twenty minutes isn't long. Did you get edgy down here by yourself?"

"No. Now why did you want me to meet you here?"

He didn't answer my question. "Coffee?" he asked, digging change from his pocket for the machine, then looking to me for an answer. I shook my head, not wanting to dignify his question by answering when he had ignored mine. His cup dropped and filled perfectly. He carried it to the table, sat down and nodded for me to sit, too. Biting my lips to curb my tongue, remembering Melchoir's confidence, I did.

Wills sipped his coffee without looking at me. Nor did he bother to speak. He acted like he'd forgotten I was there, which added insult to injury and fire to my fury. Finally he laid his right hand on the table, palm up, and opened his fingers. It seemed like a vulnerable gesture for a man who had it all so together.

His fingers twitched as if daring me to touch that big, defenseless-looking hand. I glanced at his face. His dark eyes glittered and, when our gazes locked, he arched his eyebrows like he was asking an unspoken question.

My heart pounded like an Indian war drum and my breath came and went in a hurry. I had no intention of touching him. Sure, I could flirt with men like Steven and Ansel, but I would never do that with someone like this . . . this predator. This carnivore.

Wills and I stared at each other. Did he mean what I thought he meant? No. This guy had his pick of goddesses.

Frantically, I wondered what else the steady look could mean. Then he inclined his chin, removing all doubt. His movements were so blatant, so provocative, that I wanted to jump up and run. Escape. And I might have, if he hadn't closed that cunning hand and set his eyes back on the coffee cup.

When I could finally draw a full breath and regain control of my stampeding heart, I knew I was in real danger with this guy. I had withstood this first, silent siege, but I had been dangerously tempted. I could not allow myself to get too close to this man. Something about him seemed at once dangerous and nearly irresistible. No, sir, I had a grand plan for my future and this guy was not in it.

When he finally spoke, the last wisps of confusion cleared and I thought I must have imagined the threat. The atmosphere between us seemed all business-as-usual. Maybe my lapse had been a daydream.

"First," he said, his voice low, "this conversation has to be off the record, unless you get my okay on specific information." His face and demeanor were dead serious. "Do you agree?"

Meeting his eyes, I nodded, then opened my notebook and wrote the date and his name on a new page. Was his secretary mistaken? Or had he changed his policy regarding reporters? I thought awhile before allowing the next possibility. Was I special?

He sat straight. "Let's do it this way. You ask questions. I'll answer, if I can." When I looked at him, his eyes shifted to his coffee and both hands wrapped the cup.

"Did you find Crook's car?" I began.

He nodded "yes" but did not expand. I waited for more. "On the street in front of his house, three doors down," he said finally.

"Was it there all the time?"

"We don't know."

"Were the keys in it?"

"A key ring was in the front seat."

"But not the key to the ignition?"

He looked suspicious. "No. That one had been removed. Why did you ask that?"

"You sounded like you were hedging. Why wasn't the ignition key on it?"

He shrugged.

I looked through him, wondering. "Someone had to have the key to drive it," I speculated. "Maybe they took it off the key ring to open the trunk."

He shook his head. "Cadillacs have separate keys for ignition and trunk."

"Why do you think they took it?"

"I have no idea."

I was into it now, focused. "Did you find his shoes?"

Wills raised his eyes again, scrutinizing me. Again, he didn't answer immediately.

I tried to read his expressions, his body language. I waited but he continued studying me, still not speaking, so I prodded him. "The report said there were no shoes on the body."

"That wasn't in the incident report. You got hold of the investigators' workup somewhere, didn't you?"

I didn't want to get anyone in trouble, but he already knew there had been a leak.

His eyes narrowed. "You're welcome to the incident reports, but those investigators' sheets are for official use only, not for public consumption. Who gave it to you?"

I remained silent. He wasn't the only one who could play it cagey.

"Ms. Dewhurst, tell me where you got it?"

I gave him a polite smile. We were obviously back to formalities. "A reporter has to protect her sources." His face darkened. I shrugged. "You don't really care that I knew about his shoes, do you?"

His eyes became flint. "The more you know, the more you put yourself in jeopardy."

I was flattered to think he might be concerned about my safety, but I wasn't going to be distracted. "Did you find his shoes?"

"They could have been in the pond."

"They weren't, though, were they?"

He jutted his chin and shook his head.

"Where were they?" I studied him a long time. He returned my gaze, his eyes slits. Oddly, he couldn't seem to stifle the twitch at the corners of his mouth.

"Okay." He gave up a grudging smile. "The senator's secretary found a pair of shoes in his office early Friday. She tossed them in a closet. She didn't think about them again until she heard his shoes weren't with his body."

"Does that mean he was at his office Thursday night?"

"Apparently so."

"Was he killed there?"

"Maybe, maybe not. The lab people are checking."

I slumped as I exhaled. The investigation didn't seem to be moving. "How are these deaths connected? What's the common denominator? Do you have any idea at all?"

He drew a deep breath, obviously resigning himself to something. "No. But I think you may have." His tone bordered on apologetic.

"What?"

Keeping his eyes on me, he seemed to cringe. "I don't mean I think you're involved. But you were the one who put

Benunda and his friend in the sheriff's office for us. If you hadn't remembered them, we might never have associated them with town at all. They were into gay rights activities on campus. At first blush, I thought that was what got them killed."

"You thought they were homosexuals?"

"Not necessarily. But my opinion isn't the one that matters." He glanced back to the hallway before his eyes settled on me again. "Benunda, the Pakistani, was interested in constitutional rights—the right to assemble, to demonstrate, to speak freely on either side of a controversy."

I shifted position but stayed in my chair. "I heard about that, but he seemed to me like more of a smiler than a talker."

"I guess that's because you saw him delivering pizza. You didn't catch him on his soapbox. Apparently, he could be very persuasive."

Wild thoughts darted through my head. "And Crook?"

"Crook had campus connections too, which also might have misdirected us into thinking the murders were somehow linked to the university. But you came up with some pretty astute questions that got me thinking along different lines. As you probably know, the senator was a boozer. He spent a lot of money over the years covering up things he did under the influence. Everyone in law enforcement closed their eyes to it."

"Why?"

"Crook was chairman of the senate appropriations committee. State departments were funded or financially strangled on his say-so. Crook wasn't well thought of by his fellow senators. He didn't have the clout to get much legislation passed, but he could do programs damage if someone got on his bad side. Also, we happened across information indicating that, at one time, the senator was romantically linked to Patsy Leek."

It was nauseating to think of those two as a couple.

Wills continued. "The story is she dumped him. He wanted to punish her, but she took the job as sheriff's dispatcher. Even on his best day, Crook wouldn't take on Roundtree."

Surprised, I interrupted. "Crook was afraid of the sheriff? But what about the appropriations thing? Couldn't the senator control him that way?"

"Roundtree was insulated. His office gets its appropriations from a general fund for all law enforcement. Crook couldn't screw with him without taking on the whole system and he didn't dare do that because of his history with booze."

This information gave me material for some brand new theories. Maybe some homophobe on Crook's staff took matters into his own hands and Crook figured it out. Maybe a homosexual found out Benunda and Speir weren't gay and murdered them, then went after Crook for some completely unrelated reason.

Wills cleared his throat, interrupting my speculations. "A politician's strength comes from being gracious when folks cater to him. But he can't go around demanding homage. Crook got heavy-handed when he made a run at Roundtree in the election two years ago."

"But Crook and Roundtree both won."

"Crook won his race. He's always won his own race. But Sonny Desmond was his hand-picked man for sheriff. Crook promoted Desmond with pie suppers, watermelon feeds and live country music. All those functions were advertised as Democratic Party activities, but Sheriff Roundtree wasn't invited. If he showed up, they didn't let him near a microphone. Of course, Sonny and his guitar sat on the platform with the band. He was always called on to give the welcome or the benediction."

I hung on every word. "In spite of Crook's opposition, the sheriff won decisively."

Wills took a sip of his coffee and nodded. "Crook carried the county three-to-one in his senate race. Roundtree won his five-to-one. The voters let Crook know he had his job for as long as he wanted, but they would make up their own minds about other offices. Crook never had much sway in any race but his own. Dewhurst, people say you're pretty savvy about local politics. I would have thought you'd have known that."

His words piqued my pride. I hadn't realized Crook was maneuvering things right in front of my nose. Now that Wills mentioned it, I didn't know how I had been so blind. Then I got a new thought.

"Do you and Sheriff Roundtree get along?"

"Yes." Wills looked surprised. "Why?"

"I got the impression he thinks you're too green, not the right person to spearhead this investigation."

His brows became thoughtful ridges. "Professional pride, maybe. I've been with the bureau nearly four years now. I was involved in a hundred and twenty cases last year, statewide. Probably eighty percent of those were murders."

"What?" I hadn't imagined there were a hundred murders in the state in a year.

He turned his coffee cup round and round with his fingers. "The State Bureau of Investigation has almost no jurisdiction of its own. We have to be invited into a case by the law enforcement agency that has jurisdiction. We get called in by police and sheriffs' departments, district attorneys, the state attorney general, legislative committees, anyone who has subpoena powers." He glanced from his cup to my face.

I leaned forward, fascinated. My elbows on the table, I

watched him closely, eager for this new information. I had nearly forgotten Jim Wills the man, so enthralled was I with the agent's expertise. Suddenly I realized his dark eyes were fixed on my face and I was close enough to breathe the compelling scents of the man. I felt the familiar blush ooze upward from my shirt collar. At that same moment, a little smile played around his marvelous mouth.

I pulled myself up straight. His smile became more pronounced and I wondered what in the world he was thinking. Maybe I could figure it out later, this peculiar awareness that kept erupting between us, but I definitely didn't want to think about it then.

What I wanted was for him to keep talking. After a moment, his smile waned and he continued.

"Anyway, the other entities can ask us to take over the whole investigation, or they can ask for help on specific parts: lab work, interviewing a witness, fingerprinting suspects, whatever.

"If we take over the whole case—like this one—we make all the decisions and the work has to meet our standards. Roundtree's been this route before." He studied my face again. "I don't imagine he resents the way I'm running the investigation. It may be something else. Something more personal."

I leaned back in my chair, putting more distance between us in an effort to bring us back to things impersonal. "That's why they made such a big deal about whose jurisdiction it was when they found Benunda's body."

He seemed to sense my discomfort and resumed his commentary. "Right. That's also why our people were there. The Dominion P.D. called the SBI office. They wanted us at the scene. The main office called me."

"But Dominion didn't have jurisdiction."

"Right again. As it turned out, Roundtree did, and he wanted us in worse than the Dominion P.D. did."

"Why?" I was genuinely puzzled. "He's had lots of experience. Why does he need you?" I didn't realize until the words were out how tactless they sounded.

Wills chuckled, then grew serious. "The sheriff's staff has duties already. If he reassigns his people, they have to neglect their regular jobs. Besides that, deputies usually lack the expertise for a murder investigation.

"We, on the other hand, have the resources, labs, trained technicians and manpower. Generally we're called to homicides and cases of official misconduct, high-profile things that get press attention and can have repercussions for a politician when election time rolls around.

"We maintain close contact with our host law enforcement people, keep them in the loop. They usually know everything we know shortly after we have it."

"So, have you been brainstorming with Roundtree about this case?"

Wills looked at the floor. "No."

"I thought that's what you meant by keeping the host agency in the loop." I watched his body language closely. "Why aren't you giving Roundtree updates?"

"Normally, I would." He hesitated.

"You're hedging again."

"There are extenuating circumstances here."

"What do you mean? You don't think the sheriff has anything to do with the murders, do you?" I was honestly bewildered.

"Probably not." He shifted in his chair. "The pizza guy and his friend had to have been in the sheriff's office. Crook had a conflict with the sheriff. It's kind of a reach, but we do have that one little common thread."

"Roundtree can't be involved." I sounded definite but mentally I was conjuring up arguments of my own.

Wills' eyes pried into mine as if trying to read my thoughts, inviting me to share them, but all he said was, "I didn't mean to imply I thought he was." He waited, watching like a tutor encouraging a student to work through a math problem on her own. I wanted to perform well.

"Or Wheeler . . ." I said, still puzzled, "or Gary or Fletcher or . . ." I studied him intently. "You think it could be a woman. That's right, isn't it?"

He shrugged. "It's possible. I haven't ruled out anyone."

"Is it possible?" I wriggled, restless in the chair. "I wonder. She would have to be a pretty strong woman or she'd have to have a partner."

He shook his head slightly.

"Sure. She had help to transport Crook's body to the pond."

Wills kept watching me without saying a word.

I decided if I kept quiet, he might say what he was thinking. I had to bite creases in the inside of my bottom lip to keep from talking, but it worked.

"All the victims have been physically neutralized." He spoke slowly, softly. "But not one of them was overpowered by brute strength. None of them weighed more than a hundred-fifty, -sixty pounds. Hard to lift, maybe, but not all that tough to drag.

"When I start a case, Dewhurst, I look at everyone as a suspect. Guys like Spence who make a lot of noise about their racial prejudices, their intolerance for gays, topped my original list on this one. But, yeah, you're right, I have a gut feeling it is a woman."

"But what woman?" I whispered, as if the walls might be eavesdropping.

"It could be anyone." Rather than soothing me, his quiet tone only heightened my excitement. He was feeding me clues and he kept on doing it. "A disgruntled wife or secretary. A lover. I'm just saying our killer doesn't have to be someone big or strong. So far, size and strength have not been prerequisites."

"What do you mean, 'so far'? Don't you think he's . . . she's . . . done all the damage she plans to do?"

"I don't know where our perpetrator is coming from, but when someone finds out he's good at something, he's likely to continue. He," he shot me a significant look, "or she, develops a taste for it. Right now I'm looking for a common bond, every possible thing that ties the victims together."

He swigged the last of his coffee. "Motives would be nice." He adopted a thoughtful frown and tapped his cup on the table. Looking pointedly at his watch, he stood and tossed the empty cup at the trash, nailing the shot. "I've gotta go."

I jumped up and fell into lock step beside him as he started for the stairs. "How much of this can I use today?"

He stopped, pivoted and arched his brows. I could see the answer on his face. "Okay, nothing about the it-could-be-a-woman theory, right?"

He nodded.

"Better not speculate about a possible link with the sheriff's office." I glanced up to see another nod. Slowly I deflated. "Or gays on campus?"

He gave me a sad smile, but his nods continued.

My shoulders slumped. "Nothing?"

"You are good." He started up the stairs, then stopped again. "Let me ask you a question."

"Okay."

"What's your relationship with Ansel Benedict?"

At just the thought of Ansel, I brightened. "He's my friend. My champion, really."

Wills waited, so I elaborated.

"If you live long enough and you're lucky, you have maybe half a dozen champions in your life. Champions are more than friends. They're on your side, even when you're wrong. They admire you but they're careful never to say so, except behind your back. They demonstrate their regard in many other wonderful ways."

Apparently waiting for more, Wills remained silent. It was a struggle for me not to be hypnotized by those eyes when our gazes locked. I couldn't look at him and pursue rational thought at the same time.

I tried again, keeping a firm hold on my erratic emotional state. "If you have a headache, a champion gets you an aspirin. You don't have to ask. You might not even realize you need it, but he does."

Wills glanced up the stairway, then back. I met his gaze with a boldness that quickly withered. "Why? What does Ansel have to do with your murder investigation?"

Wills shrugged. "He knew all the victims, too. He tried to keep the gays from organizing on campus. I've known Ansel a long time. I'd never heard him that intolerant toward a student group. Benunda and Speir appeared to be gay rights activists. Also, Ansel worked closely with Crook hammering out budget requests for the appropriations for higher education every year. Their discussions got heated."

I suddenly felt terribly disappointed. I hated to think this was an example of Jim Wills' loyalty. I blurted out that disappointment before I thought about what I was saying. "Bottom line: you're friends but Ansel isn't above suspicion either?"

"Actually," Wills smiled sheepishly, "Ansel's been my champion, too, I guess. When I was a freshman here, I came on a football scholarship. I had no money to spend. I got a little homesick. Ansel got me grants, academic scholarships. After football, he got me on as a campus cop—two years. I worked for him in student loan administration my second year of law school. Third year, he tipped me off to a bailiff's job.

"He actually got me my first job as a lawyer, with Fry and Fritch, right out of school. My grades weren't high enough for them to even interview me."

"So you showed your gratitude by walking out?" I didn't know where that came from, except I was angry. I didn't like seeing Wills' creepy side.

His eyes practically devoured me. Before he said a word, I realized I had tapped another wrong button. "I talked to him first," Wills said testily, "when I got restless. Eight months in, I knew I didn't want to work my way out of one cubbyhole office filling in boilerplate bankruptcy pleadings to advance up the hall to the next cubbyhole doing real estate transactions.

"Ansel didn't presume to give me advice. He asked questions that helped me sort things out and come up with my own answers."

Feeling chastised, I kept quiet and let the air between us stop crackling.

Wills reflected a minute longer before he waved and hurried on up the stairs.

Not until I'd reached Roundtree's office did I remember Wills' car keys. Patsy was working the switchboard, but Gary hobbled in from the back room the minute I said hello to Pat.

"What do you need?" he asked.

I handed him the keys. "Will you give these to Agent Wills when you see him?"

Patsy turned all the way around but didn't say anything. Spence took the keys, scowling.

"You and Wills going steady now, are you?" He gave Patsy a knowing, sidelong look. She raised and lowered her eyebrows.

Seeing their exchange, I groaned a non-response and hurried out before anyone asked any more questions.

# Chapter Seven

At six-fifteen that evening, Wills' beeper piped a shrill, insistent signal. He was in transit and didn't know why they hadn't just called on his cell or the radio phone in his car. He pulled into a service station and walked to a pay telephone.

"Roundtree wants you at the college administration building NOW," the service said. Wills hung up, annoyed by the terse command. He got back in his car and drove straight to the campus.

An ambulance and two police cars blocked the oval. His curiosity spiking, Wills swung into a faculty lot and parked.

A woman sat weeping on a bench in the first-floor hallway. A medic spoke to her softly and motioned Wills up the stairs.

"What's going on?" he asked a university officer who passed him.

"You'd better talk to Roundtree or McClellan." The man scurried away.

Wills found a cluster of people gathered just outside the public relations office, among them University Police Chief McClellan and one of McClellan's men. The rest were a young woman, wide-eyed and frightened; two somber men, civilians he didn't recognize; and a third uniformed officer. Wills eased through to the reception room and spotted Roundtree.

"Sheriff?"

Roundtree crossed the outer office in three giant strides. "I preserved the scene. I called in Chief Summers and your lab crew. I beeped everyone so we wouldn't notify every nutcase in this town who has a scanner or might pick it up on a cell."

"What scene?"

People cleared a path as I burst into the anteroom. I must have looked wild-eyed and harum-scarum, though at least my jeans and sweatshirt were clean. On a mission, I ignored all the law enforcement people there. Instead, I aimed at Benedict's office like a heat-seeking missile. I didn't notice the sheriff or Wills, who are both hard to miss. Roundtree grabbed my arm. I jerked away and plunged forward. I needed to see Benedict in person to verify that the awful lie was exactly that—an awful lie.

"Dewhurst, stop." Something in Wills' command stopped my headlong rush just as I reached the threshold of Benedict's office. The door, slightly ajar, blocked my view of the interior. I recognized Wills' tone as a warning. I gulped deep breaths, but I couldn't get enough air. My condition had nothing to do with my gallop to the second floor. It felt like an asthma attack, but I don't have asthma.

Wills stepped up beside me. I stood still, something inside warning me to cherish the moment of not knowing anything for sure. I wheezed and felt paralyzed until Wills touched my arm. I jerked away from him.

"Don't touch me." I blinked hard, then reached out and tapped the door. It swung open slowly.

I gasped. The awful lie was true.

Beside me, I felt Wills stiffen and inhale.

Ansel Benedict's body slumped in his chair. His arms dangled at his sides. His eyes were closed, his mouth crookedly agape. Blood stained the front of his shirt, just below his pocket. His natty blazer lay rumpled on the floor.

Jim and I just stood there side by side, neither of us wanting to believe the macabre sight. I suppose, like me, he was recording a last memory, a mental picture we both would try repeatedly in the coming weeks to erase.

Then I saw it on the desk. I began sucking air without bothering to exhale.

The small, baby blue bow shouldn't have looked threatening, but it did.

Wills must have seen it when I did, but while I stood gasping, he moved. He dug his fingers into my upper arm. The pain jerked me out of my stupor. I turned on him, yanking to pull free, which only made him tighten his hold. "Out." There was no emotion in the word, no anger or apology, just the order. He tugged my arm as he stepped backward, removing us both from the doorway.

Back in the reception room, he released me. I glared at the carpeted floor. Then I noticed something. "What are those?"

His eyes followed mine and he stooped to hunker in the doorway, examining the carpet. Then he dropped to his hands and knees. He brushed his fingers over the plush, feeling the small, regular impressions. "I'm not sure."

"President Moran's been using a cane. Could it have left those marks?"

Wills continued studying the indentations. "Let me see the bottom of your shoes." I picked up my feet one at a time without comment, but there was nothing embedded in the soles that could have left those marks.

Roundtree stepped closer. "They ran the vacuum at five. Any marks on the carpet would have been made after that. The photographer and lab crew should be here shortly. I've made everybody stand clear until they show."

Wills nodded his approval of Roundtree's procedure, then cast a curious look at me. I met his glance, then looked away. He couldn't possibly expect me to come up with any good ideas at the moment.

His frown deepened. "It's your own damned fault, running in here like that, out of control, throwing yourself into the middle of a crime scene." His look softened. "You'll get beyond it. People do." But he sounded as if he knew seeing a murder, a sudden violent death, was a hard thing to grasp. I was discovering that it got even harder when someone you knew well was gone so abruptly. So brutally.

Wills suddenly looked grimly determined as he almost visibly cast off personal reminiscing. He was a pro, and at that moment Ansel Benedict required the services of a trained investigator, not the awful disbelief of a friend.

"Look around out there." Wills spoke so low that only I could hear. "Pay attention. Remember what you observe so you can tell me later. Do you understand?"

I glowered at him. He looked matter-of-fact, not like he was patronizing me. I nodded, swiping at the tears that pooled and trickled. I refused to turn them loose. Not now. Not yet. I was still breathing too fast and my heart pounded like it meant to break out of my chest, but I took Wills' order and surveyed the reception room.

Wills took a giant step into Benedict's office. I watched him follow the indentations in the carpet, being careful to walk well clear of the trail. Now that he'd gotten me out of his way, doing something that might even help, he could get on with his job.

When the pathologist arrived, heading up the lab crew, he ordered everyone out of the office, allowing only Wills and a police photographer to remain. Because I intentionally avoided his eyes, Wills let the crew run me off with the rest.

For once I didn't mind being forced to leave. Seeing Ansel dead had caused me more pain and nightmare material than I'd ever bargained for.

It was nearly nine o'clock when I got home. I slipped in quietly, choking back my grief until I could reach the privacy of my own room. I pulled a sticky-note message off the door and wadded it in my hand without looking at it. Closing myself away from the world, I leaned against the door for a minute before I sank to the floor, locked my arms around my knees and cried.

It was such a waste. He was such a marvelous man, so funny and bright. And now murder had squandered all the years of education and self-discipline required to get where he was. All that time learning to hold his temper in check while cajoling even the most arrogant alumnus, politician or dignitary. I cried for the loss of his smile and for his phony, self-effacing comments, ploys he devised to cut through the tough hides of the university's potential donors.

Whoever killed him couldn't have known him. People who knew him found him a charming, irreverent, gentle man, eager to please; a man who would have wanted to help, might even have counseled his assailant if the guy had given him a chance.

My sobbing ebbed as I thought of what a con artist Ansel could be. I'd told him once that the world was lucky he hadn't chosen a life of crime. I truly believed he could talk anyone into anything. If the killer had allowed any conversation, Benedict would not have died.

Why had he died? It didn't make sense. He was the kind of man who appeased his enemies and friends alike.

Suddenly I became very still. I hated the image of his body

slumped in that chair, dead. It didn't look like him at all. He would have been horrified to be seen all distorted like that.

Anger fell over me like a net, turning my consuming sorrow into fury. Who had done this incomprehensible thing? And why? Why Ansel?

Had a burglar mistakenly thought the offices were deserted?

No. There was a bow. Right there in plain sight. Left to taunt, to boast that the act had been premeditated and all the law enforcement people in the state couldn't prevent it.

The thought of the pale blue ribbon jacked my anger to rage that burned, then became ash. My mind meandered. What kind of man was Agent Wills, to survey his friend's dead body as if it were a frog in a biology class ready for dissection? And what did he mean ordering me to look around? Did he actually expect me to help solve crimes perpetrated by a madman?

To do that, I would first have to figure out the connection between Ansel and the other victims. What could it be? My head was splitting and my eyes burned. I didn't want to think about murders any more.

Looking down, I smoothed the crumpled sticky note. It was from Steven. Steven, remote from these ghastly killings. I'd like to talk to him, to anyone normal, living in the real world. Anyone *not* involved in these senseless, wasteful deaths. I could call him. And I would. Later. Maybe.

I struggled to my feet, picked up a clean sleep shirt and panties and slipped down the hall to the bathroom. I soaked a while, trying to think of home, my mom and dad and my two little brothers. I washed my hair, struggling to keep my mind on pleasant things, but it kept drifting off without permission.

As far as I could tell, all of the victims had one thing in

common. The university. Benunda and Speir as students, Crook representing the university in the legislature, and now Ansel Benedict, nearly a vice president.

I felt helpless as warm tears spilled again. Now there would be no promotion, no vice presidency that Ansel had pursued with such enthusiasm. Giving into it, I wept quietly, mourning mankind's loss, along with my own.

Later, when my grief had ebbed some, I knelt beside my bed like I had as a child. Tired of feeling powerless, I was going for help.

"Did You know?" I hesitated. Sure He did. "Sure You knew. 'Not a sparrow falls' that You don't know. Some people say You don't care, that You wind us up like clocks, set us ticking and sit back to observe us. Those people say You can't or won't intervene. I know You were there . . . at that awful moment. Why didn't You stop it?" All my impotent anger and outrage had a new target.

"This doesn't make any sense." My voice sounded peculiarly strong, like the last flicker of a dying light bulb. Yielding, I eased onto my bed, curled into a fetal position and cried softly. Sometime later, I slept.

Early Thursday, I coaxed myself out of bed, showered again and wound my hair into a topknot twist, then ironed and put on my forest green linen dress with the empire waist and scooped neck—Ansel's favorite. He always commented on how nice I looked when I wore it freshly laundered. I wanted to make a special effort to look starched and pressed and presentable as a tribute to him. I planned on going to his condo to visit his parents.

Before I left the house, Ron Melchoir phoned. "I heard about Ansel. Do you need the day off?"

An involuntary sob caught in my throat before I could assure him I was handling it. I stopped by the post office on my way downtown to check my box and spotted Patsy Leek walking into the facility as I hurried from the car. An older man entering at the same time doffed his hat and stepped back to hold the door for Pat. He stayed there, waiting for me. Patsy didn't acknowledge the gesture. I thanked the old gentleman. Pat had stopped inside, as if waiting for me.

"Good morning. How are you?" I asked.

Patsy grimaced. "Pissed."

"Why?"

"Did you see that old pervert? I started to say, 'Outta my way, bozo. This crap is not going to get you anywhere. I can get my own damn door.' "

I checked to make sure he hadn't overheard her. "He was just being nice, Patsy."

"And why do you suppose?" Her scowl deepened. "Let him be nice to his grandmother or some old dame who needs it. He ain't getting in my pants. For that price, I can damn well get my own door, thank you very much."

Patsy's comments didn't make sense, but I suddenly wanted to keep her talking to see if I could tell how deep her problem went. "How's your son?" I asked.

She turned on me. "What do you mean?"

I shrugged as if just making idle conversation. "Gary said he was sick and you'd been out of the office to take care of him. I wondered how he was."

She glowered at me a minute, evaluating, before her face and shoulders relaxed a little. "Hell, he's okay. Hardheaded, like his old man."

"Gary said your son doesn't like to eat out."

Pat's face tensed again. "So?"

"If he lived at my house, he'd dry up and blow away waiting for a meal." I chuckled at my little confession.

Pat relinquished a smile. "You live in the Doles' old place over on Cherry with a mob of girls, right?"

"There are five of us."

"Carrying tales the other way, Gary told me you don't cook much either."

"Like he would know."

The tension eased from Pat's mouth. "I've got a recipe for chicken enchiladas that'll feed an army. It's easy. You could fix it some Sunday. Surprise 'em."

A little confused, I thanked her. She neither looked nor sounded like a murderer. A little odd, but not homicidal. Wills couldn't suspect Patsy. She didn't fit the part. But what exactly did a murderer look and sound like?

Patsy fumbled in her purse. "I'll write it out and give it to you when you come by this morning."

Oh yes, the recipe. "I appreciate it. Thanks."

On our way out of the building, I went through the door first and started to hold it for Patsy, but then I thought better of it.

At my desk in the newsroom later that morning, I returned a handful of phone messages, except for two from Steven. Then, screwing up my nerve, I clicked on Ansel's obituary.

We'd written it together that past summer. It was a common practice at the *Clarion* to prepare obituaries for celebrities during their lifetimes. Ansel and I had exchanged barbs at the interview that day, laughing about a hypothetical event that seemed unlikely ever to occur.

I smiled as I recalled our banter that day. I hadn't been able to write fast enough to record all the honors and accolades Ansel recited. I had teased him about not being hobbled by false modesty, or any other kind of modesty for that matter.

Ansel enjoyed the spotlight when friends made fun of his

foibles. He claimed my mentioning his shortcomings only verified my admiration for him. I responded with laughter and noisy denials.

He'd lowered his voice and folded his hands over his chest. "After I'm gone, you must refer to me only in the most saintly terms."

I had laughed even harder . . . then. Now, here I sat, filling in details about the funeral service from the notes provided by the mortuary, listing survivors and thinking of Ansel only in the most saintly terms.

In time, I might not be able to recall the rumble of his laughter or details of his face or his demeanor when he pretended offense. Images fade. I didn't want to lose them. I had not wanted to lose him. Tears rolled down my cheeks as my fingers ran across the keyboard, freshening the obit.

"Can you do us a piece on this murder or should I get someone else?" Ron Melchoir's voice startled me. I think I jumped a foot. He stood at my shoulder, reading the copy as I typed.

I sniffled. "I'll try."

He handed me a folded tissue in silence. I appreciated both.

Regaining control, I asked a favor. "Ron, could you get someone to make the university run for a couple of days? I'll start back next week, if that's okay."

"I'll put Sandy on it."

The phone rang as I collected my pad and pen for my morning trek to the courthouse. It was Don Lockwood at the *Dominion Morning News.*

"I've been reading your stuff. Aren't you about ready to come work on a real newspaper, or are you going to keep languishing down there in Hooterville?"

I faked a laugh.

"We still miss you around here." Don referred to my student days when I did sports rewrites for the *News* on Friday and Saturday nights. Ansel had gotten me the job. "The high school coaches still ask what happened to you. You were their favorite."

This time the laugh was genuine. I had worked weekends from nine p.m. to one a.m., then went out with the guys for "burgers and bragging." Back then, Lockwood had given me a hard time about people asking specifically to talk to me when they called in their stories. He suggested I might be "too popular to be working."

"Have you seen the light yet?" he pressed.

"Don, I know you remember my plan. I'm going to sit tight for another year, then Riley Wedge is hiring me for a wire job somewhere exotic."

"Thought you might have changed your mind." He paused. "I heard about Ansel. I'm sorry, honey. I know you were close."

"Right." The word sounded curt but it was the best I could manage around a new lump in my throat.

"We may send a photographer for some art on the scene, but I figured you'd be covering and we'd use your wire story. Will you file it in time for us?"

Was he kidding? "Like Ron's going to put it on the wire in time for the competition to run our work."

He snorted. "Shoot, you know we're no competition. We don't bother to come down there anymore for the afternoon edition. You have everyone locked up. I don't know how you do it, but your sources are lined up like ducks in a row. They won't talk to anyone else. There's no use sending someone to try to out-hustle you in your own backyard."

The compliment was a much-needed warm fuzzy. "You humble me."

"I wish."

"I'll ask Ron to move it as soon as we can."

"Thanks. Hey, no kidding, you've got a job here. Just say the word."

"Thanks, Don. After the adrenaline rush, this murder stuff sure gets tiresome. I'm not ready for the metro. You guys handle a lot more of that."

"I'll be thinking of you, babe. We all liked Benedict. We're hoping for a quick solution. A piece of advice: Stay close to Wills. He's the SBI agent assigned. The head honcho. That's straight from the governor's office."

"Right."

"Do you know Wills?"

"Yes."

Don was fishing. "And he knows you?"

"Right." I wanted to plug any little hole in the dam before he came up with the bright idea of sending someone to muscle in on my territory at what he might think was a leaky spot. "Good talking to you, Don." I hung up, grabbed my notebook and headed for the courthouse.

Spence looked up and grinned when I arrived. "Patsy left this for you." He handed me the recipe for chicken enchiladas. Watching me, his grin wilted. "You look like hell."

"Thanks. I look better than I feel." He tilted his head. I took a full breath. "I may be in a weakened condition, Spence, but I can still whip you and your game gam, so watch it. Is the sheriff here?"

"Yeah, but someone's with him. What have you been crying about?"

Hating that he had noticed, I slouched into a chair. "I lost a friend."

"You've got more."

"Not like this one."

"You don't mean the old fag out at the college, do you?"

132

I sat straight up, suddenly incensed. "What are you talking about, Spence? Ansel Benedict was one of the finest men I've ever known."

"That's not what I heard. I heard he was a pervert. Invited young boys to his house, gave 'em booze and when they were soused . . . well, you know."

I leaped up, ready to do battle. "Whoever told you that is a damned liar. And you're an idiot to repeat it. Who told you that? I want to know who! Give me a name, damn it!"

Gary shrank back in his chair, shaking his head. Clearly he wanted to retract his words, but I was seething. I wasn't letting him off this hook.

"Spence, I want to know exactly who said that about Ansel Benedict. Say a name." He tried to look away but I was having none of it. "Say it!"

"Pat," Spence whispered, keeping his eyes downcast. "Patsy knew him. She's the one who told me."

"Where is she?"

He shook his head. "I don't know. I don't even know if she'll be back today."

"I'll wait." I was shaking, madder than I could ever remember being. I paced two laps around the reception room and felt totally defeated before I sank back into a chair. Then, surprising us both, I began to bawl, giant crocodile tears that splashed and rolled down my face.

Spence sat staring at the switchboard for several ticks before he set his mouth, squared his shoulders and buzzed the intercom. "Jancy's here."

A moment later Roundtree preceded Wills into the reception room. I blinked, but couldn't get it under control for a minute. The sheriff took one look at me, did a double-take and turned on Spence. "What'd you do to her?" Both fists clenched, but Roundtree kept them at his sides.

Wills stood still and stared at me. I blew my nose and turned my face to avoid his scrutiny.

Spence sounded genuinely distressed. "I didn't do nothin', Sheriff." He hesitated a moment before he lowered his voice. "It was something I said. I didn't know what I was talking about. You know how I feel about her. I wouldn't do nothin' to hurt her. No way."

Roundtree eased into the chair beside me and began patting me on the back as if burping a baby. Trying to blink fast to clear my eyes, I looked at him and couldn't subdue a sodden smile.

Wills frowned down at me. "What is your problem?"

The man knew which buttons to push to help me straighten up. "I'm really mad, Wills, and I'm tired, and I feel like I've been bawling this whole damn week."

He nodded and waited. The man obviously had some experience with overwrought females.

I mopped my nose again, my emotions too raw to be embarrassed. "Crying's good for you. It purges your psyche." I pushed strands of hair that had escaped the topknot back out of my face so I could see him better. "But it gives you one hell of a hangover. You ought to try it. You deserve it."

"The purging or the pain?"

"Both."

He nodded and stepped into the undersheriff's office where they kept the first aid kit.

Patsy walked into the reception room right then and perused us, but didn't say anything, which was probably best. She swaggered to the dispatch station and motioned Gary out of her way. After that first glance, I couldn't even bring myself to look at this woman who had such strong biases based on so little information.

Obviously concerned that I might challenge Patsy, Gary

glanced from her to me to Roundtree. Then he hobbled over to perch on the stool at the counter. He had just settled when Wills reappeared, walked over to me and held out a hand, palm up. He carried two aspirin in that one and a small paper cup of water in the other.

I looked from the offering into Wills' expressionless face and began crying all over again.

Roundtree glowered at Wills, who shrugged but didn't withdraw the aspirin. Several seconds passed. Without looking up, I took the aspirin and chased them with the water. I barely managed to whisper, "Thank you." I handed him the empty cup and dabbed my eyes with the well-used tissue. "I've got to go."

Wills stepped quickly to open and hold the door, then descended the stairs beside me in silence. He got to the outside door first and hesitated before opening it. "Where will you be about six-thirty tomorrow night?" he asked.

"Probably at work." I sniffed. "I asked off for Ansel's funeral. Saturdays we run skeleton crews." I mopped my nose again. "It's my weekend to work. I'll have to get everything done before I leave tomorrow, so I'll probably stay late. Why?"

"Just wondered."

"Nice job," Melchoir said after I edited the story and sent it to him. "I was afraid you wouldn't be able to keep the emotion out of it. You did good."

I smiled but didn't risk saying anything. He didn't praise staff people often. The comment was just one more memorable moment in a week full of them.

I started my car and braced myself for the call on Ansel's parents. I wanted to comfort them, but didn't see how I could when every time I thought of him, I started blubbering. Besides that, the green linen was badly wrinkled from a day's wear. I cruised right by his house without stopping. I still had one more day. The funeral wasn't until Saturday. Tomorrow I would look more presentable, and hopefully would have a better handle on my emotions.

But Ansel Benedict would still be dead. That thought again ignited tears.

"Mourning is allowed," I said out loud. "He was my champion. No one ever has too many of those."

Remembering the aspirin and the tiny cup, miniatures in Wills' thick, capable hands, I felt a warm rush.

There were three sticky-note messages on the door of my room, all from Steven. I didn't feel like calling him back.

# Chapter Eight

It was dark by the time I left the newsroom Friday. Melchoir had puttered around the office library for an hour. I could tell he was stalling, reluctant to leave me alone there at night.

When I finished up, he walked down the stairs with me, then he went out the back. Executives enjoyed covered parking provided behind the building. I was out front, across the street in the employees' lot.

As I waited to make sure the automatic lock engaged, Agent Wills stepped out of the shadows and onto the sidewalk. He wore an overcoat against the brisk north wind. His hands were stuffed in his pockets, his shoulders hunched against the gusts. I was surprised to see him.

"Hi," I said.

"Hi."

"What are you doing here?"

"I thought you might be ready for some supper."

"You're buying again, I suppose?"

He grinned. "I bought the coffee last time. I thought it was your turn."

"Don't play innocent with me, big boy." I scanned his marvelous face and muscular body, then laughed lightly as I tugged my purse strap over a shoulder and rubbed my hands together. "I'm going to stop by Ansel's for a few minutes to see his family. I want them to know he had friends here. People who loved him."

"And did you?"

I glanced up to find him staring at me, his expression grim. "What?"

"Did you love him?"

I shrugged and clasped my hands in front of me. "Sure I did, but I love a lot of people a lot of different ways."

"You weren't romantically involved with him, then?"

"Wills?" I met his gaze squarely. "Ansel was great, but he was old."

"Thirty-five isn't all that old." The lock on the office door clicked.

"It isn't old enough for dying, but it's old for two-stepping all night."

He chuckled into the breeze. "I see. Okay, how about this: I'll go to Ansel's with you, if you'll eat supper with me first. My car's right here." The gray sedan was parked on the street not ten steps away.

"Could we walk to Cheeries instead?"

Without answering, he turned toward the popular burger place two blocks over. I shivered as I pulled my thin suede jacket more tightly around me. It was cold out, but I wanted to walk, to feel the wind and breathe the fresh air and talk. I felt particularly comfortable right then with Wills.

"Why don't you have a date tonight?" he asked as we strolled in step, inhaling the chill air.

I shoved my hands into my jacket pockets and shivered again. "No one asked me."

"So you would have had a date if someone had asked you out?"

"No. I didn't feel like making the effort."

"What do you mean?"

"Making small talk, trying to express an interest in deer hunting or moot court competition. You know." I regarded him seriously, hoping he understood. "I'm sure guys have the same problem trying to get interested in who got new diamond earrings or which manicurist is running a special."

He nodded.

I shuffled my hands in my pockets in an effort to keep the circulation going. Wills noticed. "Give me your hand," he said. I put my right hand in his gloved left. He plunged both our hands into his warm overcoat pocket. I would have objected, except his pocket felt warmer than mine. I let my hand remain captive, unsure if we were holding hands or if it was only one friend comforting another.

We remained quietly connected like that all the way to Cheeries.

The aroma inside the diner made my mouth water at the smells of onions and meat sizzling on the grill and fresh coffee. The warmth inside steamed the windows.

Jim hung his overcoat on a rack and offered to take my jacket, but I wanted to keep it until I quit shivering.

When we sat opposite each other in a booth, I figured I should try to make conversation. "How's the investigation coming along?" I didn't know if I flushed because of Jim's solemn scrutiny or the warmth of the cafe after being out in the raw night, but I felt the heat claw up my face from my shirt collar.

I wondered if he noticed I hadn't applied new lipstick since leaving the house that morning. I pushed at my hair with both hands and hoped it wasn't standing on end. "What's wrong? Why are you looking at me like that? Am I scary?"

Wills lowered his eyes to the menu, but not quickly enough. It came as a complete surprise, but I recognized the look: the familiar intensity of an alpha male toward a female who has attracted his attention. I couldn't believe a man like

Jim Wills could find me interesting. But I responded exactly like all women probably responded to that look on his face. My breath quickened, along with my pulse and heart rates. Playing it safe, I dropped my own gaze to the menu and clasped my hands tightly in my lap.

What was happening here? I wanted this man to concentrate on solving murders. I didn't want him distracted. At the same time, I felt flattered and excited by the possibilities in that fleeting glance. I fought to keep satisfaction from showing on my face, which frequently betrayed me. The words on the menu bled together without meaning.

*He's not feeling the same rush,* I chided myself. *Grown men do not get giddy. Their hearts don't race. Their temperature doesn't climb. Somewhere along the way, mature females learn to control those involuntary responses. Why can't I?*

Suddenly I realized the awkward lull in our conversation had gone on a long time. I needed to interrupt the silence and bring us back to a safe, mind-occupying subject.

"What were you looking at on the floor in Ansel's office?"

Wills snorted a half-laugh, signaling that he recognized and maybe even approved my attempt at diversion. "Tracks. You pointed them out to me, but I didn't think you were lucid enough to realize they might mean something."

I waited for him to hold up his end of this distraction and expand the answer. He stayed quiet a moment. "There were small, regular indentations from the door directly to and around Ansel's desk."

"Were they made by Dr. Moran's cane?"

"No."

"You asked to see my shoes. The janitor had just run the sweeper. People had trampled all through the reception room, but you realized those marks in Ansel's office had to be fresh. What were they?"

"Those indentations, which I might not have noticed if you hadn't pointed them out, were left by high heels. Stilettos."

I got the picture. "Confirmation of you're a-woman-did-it theory, right?"

"Yeah, well, I suppose it could have been a cross-dresser."

I gave him my best caustic smile, but sobered quickly. "Not many women wear those any more, not in the daytime, anyway. Jim, would a woman have had the strength to strangle Benunda with that bootlace?"

"Maybe. If he was unconscious. If she had strong hands and a knee in his back."

"Where did that come from?"

Wills looked a little sheepish. "It's not my idea. It's what the autopsy indicates happened."

The waitress interrupted to take our order, but my curiosity was piqued and racing. "And Speir?" I pressed, as soon as the waitress had gone.

"Had a lump on his head. He died of suffocation—a plastic bag tied around his neck. It was removed after his death and before his body was found."

"Could a female have done in Senator Crook?"

"He had taken Ambien. It's a prescription drug for insomnia. Enough of it can put you to sleep for keeps. But our perp isn't that nice. After rendering Crook helpless, the murderer affixed the rubber band and bow, hauled him to the pond and held his face under water until he drowned. He wasn't in any condition to put up a fight."

"Could a woman have transported his body from the road to the pond by herself?"

"Sure, if she dragged him. He weighed one hundred and sixty-two pounds."

"So, she's come up with a variety of methods, but always uses the same signature."

"Very good, Dewhurst. Ansel said you were bright."

I looked to see if he was kidding, but he seemed serious, so I shrugged. "I'd like to have a recording of the conversation that produced that little gem."

Wills smiled mysteriously, but offered no further details as the waitress returned with napkins, utensils and drinks, followed quickly by our food.

"Why are you talking to me about this?" I asked, just before biting into the steaming hamburger. I wished I'd brought along my trusty notebook.

"I thought you might be able to help. Tell me what else you noticed in the P.R. office."

"I didn't see anything you didn't see. In fact, I didn't see things you did see." Wiping my mouth, I reconsidered. "I mean, I saw them, but I had no idea what they meant. Could the high heels have belonged to any of the girls in the office?"

"Nope. I looked them over carefully." He put down his burger. "I want you to take a minute and think back to being in his office. Don't frown like that. I know it's not pleasant, but try to recall every little thing you noticed before you saw the body."

I hated recalling those mental pictures of the murder scene, but I wanted to help find this lunatic and genuinely hoped to come up with something that might contribute to nailing him . . . or her. I laid my burger in the tissue-paper-lined basket, took a sip of Coke and closed my eyes to get the picture clear in my mind.

"I noticed the janitor in the hallway and the campus police outside and you guys. The computers were off. The lamps were on. I'd been there a couple of times when Ansel closed up. The staff left all the lights on in the front office and he turned them off when he left.

"The office was still warm. He liked to keep the heat on when he worked late. He punched it to 'sleep mode' when he left.

"I smelled the cedar chips they put down when they vacuum sometimes, you know, to take the musty smell out. *And,*" I opened my eyes and looked directly into his as a bolt of excitement caught me up, "I smelled *Beautiful.*"

"What?"

"The perfume. It's popular, mostly with older women. Patsy Leek wears it some." My excitement waned. "Patsy's a woman and she's got that bad attitude toward men, but she's in law enforcement. Besides that, she's tiny." His face told me something. "She's your suspect, isn't she?"

Wills didn't answer. Instead, he said, "I'm glad to know about *Beautiful.* I had a feeling you might have noticed something else that would help."

We resumed eating in silence.

Wills wiped his hands and mouth, then leaned across the table in what seemed like an intimate gesture. "Want some dessert?"

I gave him a kindly smile. "No thanks."

"Mind if I get a Cheeries cherry pie?"

"No, I don't mind." I took a deep breath and relaxed a little. "Maybe you'd better get two forks."

His dark eyes shimmered approval as he grinned and nodded.

"One more question," he said when I had a mouthful of pie. "How well do you know Steven Carruthers?"

I choked and took a drink of water, swallowing around a hard knot. "Does this have anything to do with the murders?"

He looked sheepish. "No, this is another matter altogether. You do know him, then?"

"Yes. Why?"

"Do you know anything about his associates?"

"Mostly he hangs with the law students. I know some of them."

"How about his social contacts? Who does he date?"

"I've been pretty much his primary social contact, I think, until recently."

"How recently?"

"Sunday before last." Our picnic seemed like a long time ago. Actually, it had been less than two weeks. "He thought we were ready for a permanent commitment." I met Wills' questioning gaze. "We weren't. I tried, but I didn't do a very good job of explaining why not. He got mad. I haven't seen him since. Why?"

Wills put three dollars on the table and picked up the check. I leaned back to swig the last of the milk he had ordered to go with the pie. I hated to let it go to waste. I love milk with cherry pie.

"The bureau runs security checks on people before they take the bar exam." He slid out of the booth, smiling at the empty milk glass. "Did you know that?"

I dabbed a napkin at my mouth, hoping a milk mustache wasn't making him grin. "No, I didn't."


"I'll take my car," I said when we got back to the *Clarion*. "Then you won't have to bring me all the way back."

Jim started to object, then didn't. He walked to his car, which was parked at the curb, started the engine and waited.

I crossed the street to the parking lot and had just reached the shadow of the darkened cashier's booth when I heard a wheeze. Alert and listening, I froze. One of those weird nudges a person sometimes gets held me stock-still.

Seconds ticked by as I stood there in the dark, trying to think what to do. My first hope was that Jim didn't get impatient and leave. He didn't.

"Hey," he yelled, finally. I didn't think it was safe to answer. Someone was there in the shadows, watching. Someone who didn't think I knew he was there. He might want to stay hidden for his own reasons and had no interest in me. But what if he was spying on me and planned some mischief if I made a run for my car? I decided to wait him out.

A moment later, Wills turned off his engine, got out of his car and trotted across the street, coming to check on me. He stopped at the edge of the lot and stood staring into the dark. I wondered if he felt nudges, too. When he finally spotted me, he spoke. "What's the matter?"

I flapped a hand, beckoning him to come. He walked slowly, obviously puzzled. "What is it, another Rottweiler?"

I stayed where I was, close to the cashier's booth. "I heard something."

A gunshot split the silence, ricocheting off the stucco wall between us, just over our heads. Footsteps came running closer, then stopped. Jim grabbed my arm and yanked me around the side of the booth as a second shot rang out. He shoved me to the booth's base as he scanned the area. His search stopped at a small storage building one section over.

"What are you looking for?" I whispered.

He kept his voice low. "I need a weapon."

"You have a gun, don't you?"

"Not tonight."

"Why not tonight?"

He gave me a wry grin. "I didn't consider you that much of a threat."

I clenched my teeth. "Wills, I don't want to die laughing."

He sobered. "Then let's go. Run for the storage building."

I grabbed the hand he offered and we darted across the lot. Moments later we heard footsteps following. Wills groped in the darkened doorway.

"This'll do." Triumphantly, he held up a leaf rake.

"Will do what?"

He twisted the end off the rake and looked pleased with the long, wooden handle. Gently, he pushed me behind him before he eased out of the shadows. The pole poised at his side, he crouched and ran toward the place where we had last heard footsteps. He paused and appeared to listen, then he straightened to his full height and slapped the pole hard against the cement, once, twice, and again. Echoes made the taps sound like a threat as he advanced.

Suddenly feet sounded again, running away in the darkness. Wills started to chase the sound, then turned abruptly and came back to me.

"What happened?" I was astounded that a combatant with a gun would run from one armed only with a denuded leaf rake.

"Same thing that happened with the dog. Some people and animals—our reckless driver the other morning—are bullies. Bullies are brave as long as the object of their bullying runs. But a coward won't stand if you turn on him. A bully doesn't expect to have to fight, and he knows if he holds his ground when someone who's mad or scared turns, he might get thumped." He arched his eyebrows and gave me a know-it-all grin. "I have kind of a gift. People like that—and dogs, too—can smell it. They can tell I don't mind taking a punch or getting bitten because, in the long run, if you fool with me, I'm going to get you."

My laugh sounded nervous. "Are you threatening me?"

146

His grin broadened. "Whether you think the message is for you, Dewhurst, or whether you think it isn't, you're probably right." He winked.

I giggled again, feeling giddy and more than a little uncertain.

"Now come on," he said, "let's find that slug."

I trailed him to the cashier's booth and watched quietly as he ran his hands over the stucco finish. He found the chinks he was looking for more than a foot over where our heads had been. He made a "hmmm" sound in his throat, then turned his attention to the cement lot.

I stayed close behind him. "What are you looking for?"

"A small piece of lead."

"The size of a marble?"

"Smaller."

"A BB?"

"Bigger."

"A red hot?"

"Bigger."

Was he being intentionally obtuse? "An M&M?"

He laughed but finally looked at me. "A little piece of lead, bigger than a red hot, smaller than a marble. How about if you just bring me any little pieces of lead you find laying around."

Light reflected off of a small metallic lump. I picked it up. "Is this one?"

Still carrying the rake handle, Jim took my find and me to the corner of the lot to examine the lump under the street light.

"Is that it?" I pressed, trying to read his face. "Does it help?"

"It's a slug all right, but, no, it doesn't help. You can buy a box of these for ninety-nine cents."

"How many are in a box?"

"Fifty."

"Can you tell what kind of gun it came from?"

"Just what it sounded like. A small-caliber handgun. Probably a .22."

"Why are you disappointed?"

"I kind of hoped if anybody started shooting, they'd be carrying a special."

"Is that bigger?"

He nodded, pursed his lips and looked around. "And deadlier."

"I don't get it." I didn't know why he was disappointed to be shot at with a less lethal gun. It didn't make sense. In that regard, it fit with everything else in my life these days.

Wills re-examined the chinks in the cashier's booth and shrugged. "Usually they don't keep coming like this." He tossed the rake handle, which clattered loudly as it hit the little cement guardhouse in the quiet night, then he walked me to my car. Neither of us spoke.

Marge, from Ansel Benedict's staff, greeted us as we arrived at the front door of Ansel's house at the same time.

I had met Ansel's parents before, at his office on a football game weekend, when they were joined by about two hundred other alumni and friends of the university. I shook their hands and recalled myself to the Benedicts, who seemed much older, huddling together on a large sofa in the living room with the vaulted ceiling. They seemed out of place, conversing with strangers who had worked with their son and, at least in recent years, probably had known him better than they had.

I was surprised to see those gathered had little in common—the aged, grieving parents and the lively, clever members of the sophisticated clique of which Ansel had been ringleader.

People in the house mourned in diverse ways. Wills took a bourbon and water and spoke quietly with several of Ansel's group, shaking hands and moving easily among them.

We had been there only ten or fifteen minutes when I said good-bye. I assured the Benedicts I would see them in the morning. I gave Ansel's mother my card with my home phone number and asked that they call if I could help with anything.

Working my way toward the front door, I glanced back. My visual search culminated in the depths of Jim's watchful eyes. He came quickly to join me at the front door.

"Are you leaving?"

"Yes. This factory's about to close down." I slumped to demonstrate my fatigue.

"Maybe I'd better follow you home." He looked around for a place to put his drink.

"Or not. I seem to be safe except for rare occasions when, incidentally, I happen to be with you. Then all hell breaks loose. Speeding cars, snarling dogs, sniper bullets."

He tried again. "You may need protection."

"Not when I'm not with you." Seeing his crestfallen look, I softened. I did not intend to offend this marvelous man. "Will you be at the funeral tomorrow?" I asked.

"I plan to be. Yes."

"Is there any doubt?"

"In my business, sometimes things pop up unexpectedly."

"Sometimes you act like you're trying to be mysterious or unpredictable, dodging the straight answer, implying you may or may not appear somewhere—as unpredictable as the wind."

Wills smiled, but he didn't respond.

Content to have finally had the last word, I turned and walked briskly out the door.

# Chapter Nine

There were no cars at the house and the downstairs was dark when I pulled into the driveway at nine-thirty.

"T-G-I-F," I said out loud, stepping out of my car. "All the normal people are partying, which is as it should be." I felt relieved, like I had performed a tough task by visiting the Benedicts. I had dreaded it. My dad encouraged friends to call on the bereaved. He always called it "a ministry of presence." He would be proud of me for going. I might call my parents and brag a little about my emerging maturity. And I might mention Jim Wills to my mother, not for any particular reason, except she might like knowing about him.

Thinking of him, I gathered up the books, papers and pop cans that littered my floorboards. When both hands were full, I kicked the car door closed.

I struggled up the front steps, moving cautiously in the dark. Juggling trash and purse, I just managed to turn the front door knob. Despite Liz Pinello's talk about closing up and carrying keys, my housemates had left the place unlocked. I could barely see the outlines of the sparse furnishings as I passed through our darkened living room.

In the kitchen, I put my purse on the counter, not bothering to turn on a light. Identifying the trash can by its location, I dumped the rest.

I was halfway to the back stairs when I heard a noise. For

the second time that night, I froze. A shuffling sound came from the living room.

The old house creaked oddly in the wind or when caressed by the sycamore, but that shuffling sound was not usual. I crept to the enclosed area at the bottom of the stairs and stopped again to listen.

I heard someone breathing, sensed them inching toward me in the darkness. Hairs on the back of my neck bristled.

Had I made a lot of noise coming in? Had I talked out loud to myself? Would an assailant know I was there alone, that no one else was with me or coming in behind me?

I reached around the corner, groping for the cordless wall phone.

It beeped as I punched 9-1-1. When the dispatcher answered, I laid the phone down and gave it a shove across the floor. It stopped near the leg of the kitchen table. Maybe the sliding sound, the dispatcher's bodiless voice and the muted light would distract an intruder. Or frighten him away.

What else? A weapon. I needed something to defend myself.

I had left my purse across the room on the counter. Nail file, spray perfume, out of reach. No help there.

Reaching around the corner again, I flattened my hand, seeking something I could use to ward off an attacker until help arrived. Anything.

There it was. The broom. Someone had forgotten to put it away. Bless 'em. Remembering the leaf rake, I took a firm batter's grip on the handle and waited.

The sound came again, an unfamiliar creak, shuffling footsteps. They were getting closer. Would I be able to keep him off me? I shivered.

Damn right, I'd keep him off me. I thought about Jim.

*I'm no pro. I'm not taking any punches. I'm going to hit first and I'm darn well going to knock that baby out of the park.*

I heard another sound, a stomach growling, closer than before. He was coming. I slid down to squat, my back braced against the wall. With the broom handle secure in my two fists, I lowered the far end of it to the floor and waited, scarcely breathing.

I could see a form in the darkness, a man crouching. Advancing again, then waiting. Adrenaline filled my extremities.

Could I do it? Could I slam the broom into the man's body?

Yes. I was determined to land the first blow.

He was almost on top of me when I sprang.

I yanked the end of the broom straight up as hard as I could, right between his legs. He howled and staggered backwards. I drew back and swung hard in the vicinity of his head. Reflex brought his arm up to deflect the blow, jarring my hands and arms all the way through my body to my legs. His feet slipped as he scrambled to stay upright.

I choked up on the broom handle to allow for the confines of the stairwell, assumed my best swing-away stance and swung.

He toppled sideways beneath the force of the blow. Broom straw flew, fluttering eerily in the dark as my would-be assailant's head hit the wooden floor with a resounding thud. "Jancy, stop," he rasped. "No more. Please."

Astonished at the familiar voice, I leaped over the intruder's body and darted across the room to the switch.

Light flooded the kitchen and bathed the figure writhing on the floor.

It was Steven Carruthers.

I couldn't get the crying under control as Bishop police officers answering the 911 call tried to piece together events. I knew I wasn't making sense, babbling about gunshots in the dark, rakes and brooms and biting a dog's ear off, all the while flinching and jumping if anyone got too close or tried to touch me.

"I don't know if she's doing drugs or what," one young officer confided to his partner. "She won't give up the weapon."

"It's a broom." The older officer spoke quietly. "It's not like it'll go off or anything. Let her keep it for a while. It seems to make her feel better. Talk to her. See if you can get her to stop that squalling."

Steven Carruthers at least made his explanation in complete sentences. And he wasn't crying, although his voice broke occasionally as he spoke and he kept his hands protectively over his groin.

He said I hadn't returned his calls all week. He'd read about Ansel's death. He'd come to apologize and to comfort me.

He'd been waiting for me, listening to the stereo, having a beer. He guessed he must have fallen asleep on the couch and my roommates thoughtfully turned off the lights when they left. The music had stopped automatically.

He woke when he heard someone in the kitchen in the dark. He thought it might be a prowler. The girls thought some unauthorized persons had been sneaking in when no authorized persons were home. He planned to grab the intruder or intruders, be a hero and earn his way back into my good graces.

I exhaled loudly. His explanation sounded completely plausible. The officers discussed it. Just as they decided the disturbance was a no-fault domestic misunderstanding, Sheriff Dudley Roundtree arrived at the scene in a plaid sport shirt and jeans. As he exploded through the front door, he fairly filled the room. All conversations ceased. Roundtree had heard the call on his scanner.

"Hey, Sis." Eying me, he approached cautiously. "What's going on?"

I looked at him, at the familiar crooked nose seated in the timeworn face, and felt myself relax a little before I noticed his clothes. They were wrong. I clammed up, waiting to speak until I was sure I wouldn't sound like a complete dunderhead.

Roundtree started to sit next to me. Involuntarily, I shrank from him, warning him back. I didn't want anyone too close. For sure I did not want anyone touching me. Roundtree turned away at the last minute and began talking quietly with the officers.

Deputy Spence arrived moments later, clad in T-shirt and shorts. Again, I recognized a friendly face, but his clothes made me cringe. Everyone was out of uniform, and therefore, in my uncertain state, not trustworthy.

When Steven Carruthers walked to the sofa to stand in front of me, the lawmen watched with various expressions, from the novice policeman's casual observation to Spence's obvious malice.

"I'm sorry, Jancy," Steven said. "I'm going now. I didn't know. I should have been more sensitive, should have realized the strain you'd been under. Will you forgive me?"

I looked at him, surprised by his request and relieved that he assumed responsibility for my bizarre behavior. He didn't appear to be permanently damaged. I had hit him as hard as I could, but with the bristled end of the broom. I was thankful about that.

"Sure." I didn't want to talk, nor did I make any move to walk him to the door. Instead, I just sat there clutching the broom with both hands like it was my security blanket.

Steven had almost reached the door when it opened. Agent Jim Wills stepped inside, catching the screen before it slammed behind him.

Still in his suit but without the overcoat, Wills looked hard at my face. Then his eyes swept over Steven, Spence, Roundtree and the two uniformed policemen. No one invited him in. All six of us in the room remained motionless and silent.

"Excuse me," Steven said finally, indicating he would like to get by Wills and out. Jim frowned an unspoken question at Roundtree, who nodded almost imperceptibly. At the nod, Wills stepped into the room, allowing Steven access to the door. Then he turned his full attention on me. "Do you want to go for a walk?"

I did. I really wanted to get out of there. But I didn't answer. I just unwound my legs and stood. Hanging onto the broom, I walked by Jim and straight out the door.

Spence stammered as if to object, but Roundtree waved him quiet. When I glanced back, the sheriff looked a little surprised himself.

On the front walk, Jim wrapped a hand around the broom handle. I hesitated a moment before I let him take it. He leaned it against the porch.

We walked slowly, wordlessly, crossing into the next block. He seemed content to let me break the silence when I was ready.

"What are you doing here?" I asked finally.

The darkness was broken by street lights strategically located at each intersection and a clear sky that brightened the night. The air felt as crisp as it had earlier, but the wind had died. We walked side-by-side, moving into the street when the sidewalk became uneven.

"I heard the call and recognized the address." He didn't look at me.

"How did you know it was my address?"

He grinned. "I . . . ah . . . let's see, I can't think of a way I would have known your address except the truth." He flashed me a self-conscious glance.

"Which is?" I stopped at the intersection and stared into his face.

"I looked it up in the phone book. Later, I drove by." He mumbled the confession quickly, letting the words run together.

"When?" I was not through with my interrogation, and I felt bolder, as if I had him on the ropes.

"The day we found Benunda's body by the highway and you showed up with the sheriff—the first time I saw you." He looked at me as if he were daring me.

"How'd you know my name?"

"I asked. That's why the bureau pays me the moderate bucks, to ask questions, find out who people are and what they do."

I started across the street. "And you drove by that day?" He looked embarrassed. I liked toying with him. I stepped up onto the curb and hesitated, studying his expression.

"The first time," he said, verifying.

"You've been by more than once?"

"Yeah." An embarrassed smirk stole over his face and he shuffled his feet. He looked like a kid caught with his hand in the cookie jar.

I smiled, flattered by his admissions and his chagrin. When he bowed his head, I laughed out loud.

"Big deal." His eyes shot to my face and his laugh mingled with mine. "Maybe it sounds a little warped, but I liked you. I liked the way you handled yourself out there. I liked that you

asked so many questions and most of them ones I had already
asked or planned to ask, or hadn't thought of yet and wished I
had."

"Do all nosy women affect you this way?"

"Nope."

Laughter bubbled and I felt suddenly refreshed, free from
the gloom of the whole nightmarish week. I turned and began
walking again.

He hurried to catch up. "I'm at a disadvantage here, you
know. It's your turn to say something nice about me."

My laughter became a mischievous giggle. "What if I can't
think of anything?"

"Well . . ." He cleared his throat in mock self-consciousness. "Let me help you out here. Since I'd been casing your
place, I knew what your car looked like."

My gloating laughter dissolved to a smile. I became concerned when he stepped in front of me. "When you took off
in my car the other morning," he said, "I got in the bureau's unit and took a quick run around my neighborhood.
What do you think I saw parked two blocks from the Y?
And what do you think I deduced, finding your car parked
so close to my house at that time of day and you not willing
to admit it?"

It was my turn to cringe. "I guess you probably figured I
wanted to jog in the Jessup area to see if I recognized anyone
I'd ever seen with Benunda or Speir."

"No." He let me squirm a minute. "Our secretary told me
you'd called. She told me what she'd suggested you do." He
grinned and I winced.

"Possibly I had other reasons."

"Okay. Possibly. Why didn't you return my car keys in the
snack bar? And why are you out here walking with me instead
of letting Roundtree console you? The sheriff and Spence

both showed up to take care of you, but you wouldn't let them, would you? It was me you wanted."

Caught off guard, I couldn't look at him. Instead, I smiled into the darkness, turning my head so he couldn't see my eyes or read my thoughts.

We heard a car approaching. Acting on instinct, we slipped into the shadow of a nearby live oak tree and pressed close to its trunk. After the car passed, Wills put his hand on the tree, blocking my return to the street.

"Don't get skittish," he said. "No one here's going to hurt you. You know that."

I smiled, feeling foolish. He put his free hand on the other side of me, allowing an arm's length of space between his body and mine. I studied his wonderfully symmetrical features and said, "What now?"

"You've got the smoothest, rosiest face I've ever seen." He allowed a Cheshire Cat grin. "I keep wondering if it feels as smooth as it looks."

"You want to feel my face?"

"Yeah." He crooned the word, leaning toward me, bracing himself with both hands on the tree.

I stood perfectly still and silent. He kissed my right cheek. Then, slowly brushing my nose, he moved his lips to the other side to kiss my left cheek. "Smooth. Just as I suspected."

Closing my eyes, I neither moved nor spoke.

He snorted. "It's taking every bit of willpower I've got, you know, to keep my hands on this tree."

Without looking directly at him, I placed my hands on his wrists and slid them up his forearms. I could feel his muscles strain beneath the layers of shirt and jacket. Gaining confidence, I smiled into his eyes and ran my hands over his biceps and up the broad shoulders I had admired beneath the pinstriped suit the day I saw him for the first time.

I heard the drone as a second car cruised slowly down the street. We both saw the searchlight sweeping over the lawns. He gave me a grudging smile.

"It's a black and white. Probably Roundtree or Spence looking for you."

I nodded agreement and we stepped out from beneath the tree to flag the cruiser.

It was Spence. He didn't stop when he saw us, but doused the searchlight and stepped on the gas.

"I guess he thinks you're safe." Wills arched an eyebrow like the villain in a melodrama.

"And he's right." Involuntarily, I shivered. Wills removed his suit coat and settled it around my shoulders, then took my hand. Instead of going back toward the house, he turned the other way. Obviously, he meant to walk on for a while. That was fine with me. The coat was warm from the heat of his body and smelled marvelous. Like him. We walked in silence, my hand in his, each of us entertaining private thoughts.

"Hey, Wills, do you know where your soul is?"

"What do you mean, where?"

"I mean if a surgeon was going to cut out your soul, where would he make the incision?"

"I guess I've never thought much about having my soul removed. It's probably elective surgery, in which case, my health insurance wouldn't cover it." He looked and apparently realized I was serious. "Why, where do you think your soul is?"

"I figure it's the same place they keep your personality."

"Define personality."

"Sense of humor, sympathy, courage, fear. Integrity. And shame, pride, excitement . . . all that altruistic stuff."

He nodded. "Could be, I suppose. If a man has courage, they say he has a lot of heart."

"So do you think your soul is in your chest cavity?"

"What got you started on this?"

"You did." I hesitated about going on, then plunged ahead anyway. "I've been trying to figure out why I like you."

He looked up at the sky and laughed. "Do you have to analyze it? Can't you just enjoy it?"

"But I really want to know. Why you?"

"What do you mean *why me?*" He sounded offended.

"I've been dating Steven Carruthers since last year. He's smart, ambitious, very handsome and we have a lot in common. Besides all that, my folks like him."

Wills muttered under his breath. "I don't think he's all that good-looking, really."

I laughed, but waited.

"So why did you get uptight when he talked about getting married?"

When my accusing gaze found his face, he lowered his eyes. "You do that a lot, you know," I said.

"What's that?"

"You pretend you've divulged information you shouldn't have when you actually revealed only as much as you planned to. You're not fooling anyone."

He raised his eyes and grinned. "It probably fools someone occasionally. What are we talking about now?"

"The marriage thing. The only person I mentioned that to, besides my housemate Rosie Clemente, was Spence. He is such a blabbermouth." I thought about it a minute, then added, "Be sure not to tell him anything unless you don't mind it being leaked to everyone, from the mob on down."

"The mob? You think Spence has mob connections?" He rocked his head back and laughed some more.

I shrugged and paced ahead.

"About this soul thing," he said, catching up, "what conclusions have you reached?"

He might be making fun of me, but I was genuinely curious. "When I've liked some guy, sometimes when I just ran into him, I actually felt my heart jump."

"And it happens when you see me unexpectedly?"

I pretended not to have heard him.

"And it pounds when you're excited or frightened?" he prodded.

"Right. And we say 'she loves her dog with all her heart' and 'my heart stood still . . .' And sports commentators say the racehorse or the fullback or whoever 'ran with a lot of heart.' So, where is it?"

"Probably buried in the wrinkles of our brains."

"Did you ever see an autopsy that mentioned courage wrinkles in someone's brain?"

"No, but I'll ask the pathologist for a run-down on the location of that stuff the next time I have to order an autopsy on a brain."

"Really?"

"No." He looked pained. "They'd want to scan mine. Just accept it, your heart-slash-brain has drawn a bead on me and won't be satisfied with less."

"You're pretty high on yourself."

He arched both eyebrows. "More, maybe, since I noticed that you're pretty high on me, too." He stepped in front of me, caught my face in both his hands and kissed me gently, thoroughly, right there in the middle of that quiet, residential street. When I inched forward, he gathered me closer and his lips toyed with mine.

I pushed away from him, shaken. He grinned, which annoyed me enough to say, "I hope you know we are not going to end this night romping around in somebody's bed."

His smile broadened so much that I tried to refine my statement. "You know, in the movies there's a big kiss and the next scene is clothes strewn all over the floor and the couple between the sheets."

He nodded, still grinning. "And you're telling me you're no movie buff, right?" He chuckled lightly at his own pun. "Jancy, I promise not to tell, either way."

"Better not. Roundtree would skin you."

Wills' smile faded as he feigned concern. "What have I gotten myself into?" He took my hand and started back toward the house, still in no hurry.

I took a deep breath. "I don't know why I feel so relieved. Four men are dead, including one of my favorite men in the world, and we still don't have the killer."

"Maybe you're partially relieved because tonight you found out you're not a coward."

"But tonight I was never really in danger."

"You didn't know that. Also, maybe you're a little relieved about us?"

I remembered something I had wanted to ask him about. "Was there a female at your house Wednesday?"

He gave me a slanted look. "Yes."

"Have you known her a long time?"

"Yes, I have."

"Does she live with you?"

"No."

"Will she be back?"

"Yes."

Something about the look on his face gave him away. "Is she a relative?"

162

He laughed. "My mother. Comes down from Dominion from time to time. She cooks for two or three days and stocks my freezer with homemade meals."

"But you didn't want her to meet me?"

"No. I didn't want you to meet her. If you'll remember, you and I were on shaky ground Wednesday. I didn't want her prying. There's an old legal adage: a good lawyer never asks a question in court to which he doesn't already know the answer. I sure didn't want her grilling you or me at that particular juncture." He grinned again. "She's like you. She's not big on girls' clothes strewn around my bedroom." We both laughed and he took my hand again.

"Do you have siblings?" I asked as we crossed another intersection.

"I am the third of seven kids."

"Wow! Catholic, right?"

"Hey, you are good. Have you thought of going into police work?"

"I've found my niche in life."

"Oh, yeah, what's that?"

I explained about Riley Wedge and my dream of working for the wire service overseas.

"Exactly one year to go," I said. "Next October, I'm out of here."

Jim's expression darkened. "What did Ansel think about this dream of yours?"

"He didn't say much either way, but he was happy when I got the job on the *Clarion*."

"I'll bet he was."

Theresa Graff and her date drove up just as Jim and I got back to the front porch. Ben's truck was in the driveway and music lilting from the living room indicated Ben and Liz were inside. The law enforcement vehicles that had lined the street were gone, except for Wills' car.

Inside, I felt terribly self-conscious as I introduced Jim to Theresa and Liz and their respective dates. I referred to him as "State Bureau of Investigation Agent Wills," which made him look at me with a puzzled frown.

"I guess I'd better be on my way," he said. He eyed me playfully and I cringed inside, not knowing what might be coming next. Both Liz and Theresa kept looking from my face to his. I don't think they could figure what his status was, exactly. How could I clarify things when I didn't really know myself?

"Will you come to my office in the courthouse annex Monday morning?" He looked serious enough.

"Really?"

The two other couples had stopped paying attention to each other. They seemed captivated by Jim and me.

"Yes, really. We're on the second floor. I'll look for you about ten-thirty."

"Won't you be at Ansel's funeral tomorrow morning?"

"Yes, but we'll be busy and I want you and me to powwow Monday."

"You still think I can help find the murderer?"

"That, and other things." He smiled. Seeing a suspicious glint in his eyes, I braced myself.

Jim glanced at Liz and Ben and Theresa and her date, then caught the lapel of my shirt between his thumb and index finger as he spoke to our audience.

"You people have heard of a cop making a collar?" They all nodded and the girls began twittering. "Well, this is how it works." He tugged the lapel, pulling me close. He kissed my gaping mouth, released the collar, removed his coat from around my shoulders with a tender smile for me, then he winked at Liz and left.

"Was that Steven Carruthers?" Theresa's date asked loudly as I scurried toward the back stairs. My heart hammered and I needed to get out of there. I had some thinking to do, in private. But I didn't escape fast enough.

Theresa giggled. "It didn't look like Steven."

"It didn't act like Steven," Liz chimed.

Ben drummed his fingers noisily on the arm of the sofa and chanted. "I saw Jancy sitting in a tree, K-I-S-S-I-N-G."

I took the back stairs two at a time.

Behind the closed door in my room, I remembered how Ansel Benedict had made me blush and giggle. The pall of gloom tugged again at my heart—wherever that heart was—and I thought of Ansel going for a beer with a guy he spoke admiringly of, his friend Jim Wills.

My thoughts turned to Jim: his smile, his strength, his courage, his ingenuity, his laugh.

Later, in a deep sleep, I dreamed of sweet and sour sauce, of hot fudge on cold ice cream, of leaving Bishop and working in Europe. I woke up on Saturday morning, hungry, excited, sad and strangely euphoric.

# Chapter Ten

At the funeral, Ansel's office staff insisted I sit with them in a pew directly behind the family.

Ansel's two sisters looked a lot like their brother, tall and handsome with auburn hair, fair skin and laugh lines around their eyes. They each brought a husband and an assortment of children whose antics seemed to brighten Ansel's bereft parents.

My breath caught in my throat when Jim showed up as one of the pallbearers. He looked solemn and roguishly handsome, his dark hair and eyes enhanced by the black suit, his shoes polished to their usual high sheen.

After the service, the family lined the front of the church to greet people as we filed out.

Despite the strain, Ansel's mother held her emotions in check until Jim stepped in front of her. When he shook her hand, she broke into quiet sobbing. He put his arms around her and held her for a long time, talking to her quietly as the line detoured around them. Almost overcome, I watched for a moment from the back of the church before I left. I didn't want to risk upsetting the Benedicts further with my own volatile emotions.

I went to the cemetery, but stayed back in the crowd during the graveside service. Still, I felt obligated to go to Ansel's house for the gathering afterward.

I said hello to Ansel's sisters and remarked on the little

redheaded nephew who looked so much like Ansel. I took a cup of coffee and sat uneasily on a folding chair in the living room near Mrs. Benedict. I knew Jim was around somewhere but I made no effort to locate him. Instead, I sat quietly, looking around the familiar room, remembering other gatherings with many of these same bright, witty people who shared Ansel's idea of gourmet food and cosmopolitan beverages.

"Did you know Ansel well?" Mrs. Benedict asked during a lull.

Surprised, I smiled in spite of myself. "Pretty well." My smile broadened. "I'm sorry, but when I think of Ansel, I can't help laughing. He kidded me, unmercifully sometimes, and I dished it right back when I could. He was just so . . . so totally unpredictable."

Leaning around to look at me, Ansel's dad chuckled. "I know what you mean." He turned to his wife. "Mother, remember the bird's nest in the linen closet?"

Mrs. Benedict shot her husband a dark look before she, too, yielded a grudging smile. "I still look for mites when I change the bed sheets." She shook her head at the floor. "And the time he put the kitten in his dresser drawer before we went out of town for five days. Oh, lordy."

One brother-in-law listening from across the room pulled a folding chair over near the Benedicts and said, "I know what let's do. Let's take turns telling our fondest memories of Ansel."

Other people milling nearby joined in.

One after another regaled us with recollections of Ansel's antics. Drawn by our laughter, other people drifted in to perch on the arms of chairs or settle on the floor or hearth or simply lean in doorways.

Everyone there seemed to have fond memories of Ansel's

humor, particularly his propensity for limericks. Sadly, no one seemed able to remember one. Suddenly, a woman from his staff piped up, "Jancy was his limerick sidekick. She challenged him to his best work."

Everyone turned their attention on me. "Come on, Jancy, recite one," the staffer said.

I tried to decline, but they urged me to recall a sample of Ansel's limericks. Finally, I remembered one that was less risqué than most:

> *"There was a young man name of Gunn*
> *Who enjoyed making love in the sun*
> *His buns being bare*
> *Burned to medium rare*
> *While his girlfriends kept saying, 'Well done'."*

The lines precipitated a nervous twittering that swelled to applause and sputtering, raucous laughter.

I deferred to the next person for reminiscences and glanced up into the dark, smiling gaze of Agent Wills, who was scrutinizing me from a doorway. When our eyes met, he saluted me with his drink. I smiled.

Restless that evening, I drove the one hundred thirty-five miles home to Carson's Summit to see my family. I played Scrabble with one brother and, later, chess with the other, and let them both win. Watching my efforts, my mother mentioned my new maturity.

"Mom, whatever do you mean?"

Suddenly we began giggling. We hugged each other as my dad and both brothers looked on, bewildered.

After church and lunch on Sunday, as we settled in the den, Dad asked about the murders.

I told him everything, even described the victims' bodies

in detail. He listened quietly, commenting only enough to prod me. As the story ebbed, he regarded me solemnly.

"Raw experiences like that can be dehumanizing, if you're not careful, honey."

My mother narrowed her eyes the third or fourth time I mentioned Jim Wills. Mother wasn't inclined to ask questions.

Returning to Bishop Sunday night, I felt reassured. Being at home where life was normal, where no one had died unexpectedly, put things back into perspective.

The State Bureau of Investigation offices were in the courthouse annex. A lone secretary served the four local agents whose offices were situated around the second-floor landing, a common area that doubled as reception room and secretary's office. When the secretary announced my arrival over the intercom, three doors around the common area opened.

I recognized the first two men who peered from one door as a pair who had been at the scene when they found Benunda's body. An older man in the second office I had not seen before. He smiled and nodded, then closed his door.

Emerging from the third door, Jim beamed as he introduced me to the secretary, Mrs. Teeman. She followed as he ushered me into his office and indicated I should sit in one of the two leather clients' chairs. He acted achingly polite, as if I were a stranger.

He looked great, as usual, in gray slacks, white shirt, tie and the familiar galluses. I turned all the way around to confirm that a navy blue blazer hung on the coat rack near the door.

The office, roughly fourteen by twenty feet, reflected his personality—cool and uncluttered.

"Did you put things away because I'm nosy or are you just not very busy?" I asked.

Mrs. Teeman, a sensible-looking woman in her fifties, cleared her throat as she started to pull the door closed behind her. I looked at her.

"He's a very private person," the secretary volunteered and winked at Wills. "You are definitely a first around here." Then she closed the door.

"What did she mean?" I asked. "And does everyone pop out to take a look when someone comes to see you? You haven't been talking about me behind my back, have you, Agent Wills?"

He grinned. "Investigators are by nature a curious bunch."

"I didn't know you had a real office." I stared at the certificates and degrees framed and strategically spaced on the vanity wall behind him. A computer, the screen dark, sat on the return. His desk held the usual miscellaneous accessories: a telephone, a police scanner, dictation equipment, neatly arranged stack files and a calculator.

The wall behind me, and the one to my left, were virtually hidden by bookshelves filled with sets of federal and state statutes, along with two lateral filing cabinets.

Four sparkling clean, aged, paneless windows spanned the fourth wall on my right, from the ten-foot ceiling down to the chair-rail molding that bordered the room. Centered beneath the windows was an ornate, antique library table, flanked by two chairs of similar vintage. Several books lay open on the table next to several files, closed.

Jim stood very still, watching me. "Obviously you thought I worked off an orange crate with a communication system of strings and cans." I laughed dutifully. He shook his head, as if dismissing an idea, then walked around to hunker in front of me, both hands on the arms of my chair.

"Dewhurst, I'm usually a cool, professional guy. I need objectivity in my line of work. Under normal circumstances, I would think the governor's confidence in me was well placed, but . . ." He hesitated, his eyes pleading. "I'm in real trouble here. I get reports and statements situated in front of me, the way I usually tackle a case, and the next thing you know, I'm daydreaming about you, humming some inane song. Everyone in the office is kidding me about it.

"I've liked a lot of ladies and they got a fair share of my attention when I was off-duty, but when I worked, my mind had no room for them." He interrupted himself. "Do you play tennis?"

"Yeah. I've got a nearly invisible serve."

He grinned. "I can't wait not to see it. I know you swim, of course, but only in the top six or eight feet."

"That was you? The light was behind you. I couldn't see your face, only your silhouette. Wasn't that a funny coincidence?"

"What's funny is that you thought it was coincidence. I followed you that afternoon. I saw you storm out of the newspaper office. I wanted to observe you when you got angry, which you obviously were. Do you like to dance?"

I nodded at his shotgun third-degree.

"What do you drink?" he asked next.

"Milk, tea, pop. I'm not a big boozer, but I like an occasional Bloody Mary, a gin and tonic when it's hot outside and sometimes a whiskey sour in the winter."

"Spence says you're religious. Is that true?"

"I guess." I laughed, feeling warm and giddy. "Spence got wounded when I told him to quit using 'God' and 'Jesus' as expletives. Some words are too potent for a cream puff like him."

Jim looked like he'd quit listening. Using the chair arms,

he pulled himself up over my lap and kissed me squarely on the mouth. Curious and excited, I kneaded the muscles bunching in his shoulders. He eased back.

"You don't think this is going to be one of those one-way grope things, do you? You do know I'm going to demand equal time."

I giggled, but at the same time, couldn't resist patting his cheek. He turned his face to kiss the inside of my hand and I trembled. "I really like that."

He looked pleased and a little surprised before his face softened. "Well, then, you'll really like some of the other stuff I'm going to do. If you don't, we'll work on it until you do like it."

We smiled into each other's eyes for a long moment before I squirmed, straightening upright in the chair. "I want to help you."

"All right."

"The witnesses you've already talked to. What did they say?"

Wills sat back on his heels and gave a derisive laugh.

"What's wrong?"

He laughed harder, more at himself, I supposed, than at my question. Then he stood and straightened his tie. "Nothing. Do you think you should signal before you change subjects that fast?"

"People have complained about that before. I'll try to give you warning in the future. Anyway, tell me what I'm doing here. Why did you invite me over this morning?"

He strode around and sat in the chair behind the desk, braced his elbows on the chair arms, leaned forward and frowned. "You may be a key player in this. You're sure you didn't know Benunda or Speir?" He waited.

I heaved a heavy sigh. "I told you I'd seen them. Benunda

delivered pizzas all over campus and town. We've already covered this a dozen times."

"How well did you know Crook?"

"I did a weekly interview with him on Saturday mornings. A legislative wrap-up thing for the Sunday paper."

"Were you fond of him?" Suddenly Jim sounded like an investigator again.

"When I could ignore his monumental ego, he was okay. He could be witty when he'd had something to drink. He took himself pretty seriously, considered himself a pretender to the governor's throne."

Jim was on a roll. "But he didn't ever run for governor. Why not?"

"I figure it was because he came from nothing and took failure—any kind of failure—hard. I thought he was probably a guy who'd rather not try than risk losing."

"Don't you think it's odd that you're the only person who knew all of the victims when they were alive?"

I winced at that. "I'm sure a lot of other people knew them too."

"Not all four of them."

"Actually, it's a reach to say I knew them. Like I said, I had only seen Benunda and Speir."

"Yeah, but you saw every one of them alive, within a month before they died."

I felt uneasy and defensive. "So did the sheriff and several deputies and a lot of people in and out of that office watching the game."

"How do you mean?"

"They all saw Benunda and Speir at the office when I did."

"They didn't remember them."

"That's because they were into the ball game. It was the World Series, for heaven's sake. But they did see them. And

I'm sure they all knew Senator Crook." I hesitated a minute to think. "And most of them probably knew Ansel. He knew everyone—town and gown."

Wills stood and walked over to look out the windows, tapping a pencil on the sill.

I liked the way his stiff white shirt fit snugly over his shoulders and bloused a little, despite the suspenders, over the waist of his trousers. I liked the way his trousers, pleated and cuffed, rode a little higher over his hips and lower in front. It was hard to concentrate on other things while I sat there looking at him. Minutes passed. He didn't speak.

"Is there anything else?" I asked finally, thinking I needed to leave him to his musing.

He turned and looked at me as if waking from a trance. "No." He was still frowning. "Except . . ." he added as I stood, getting ready to leave.

"What?"

"Could you guess who might be next?"

That struck a nerve. "What?"

"I told you, I don't think this killer is through."

"But why?"

"If we had the why, we might be able to figure the who. Anyway, who do you suppose might be next?"

I stared at him, dumbstruck, then sank back into the chair. "Am I a suspect? I can't believe you actually think I could murder anyone, or even that I might know who it is." I thought he liked me. How could I have been so far off the mark?

He waggled his head. "You know better than that." His eyes shimmered with what looked like genuine regard. "If it's you, I'm a dead man already."

I took that as confirmation of his regard and set my mind to the quandary at hand. "They've all been men."

He turned back to the window. "Terrific. That reduces the number of potential victims to a mere eighty-five hundred on campus and twenty-five thousand in the community, give or take."

I didn't appreciate his lack of appreciation. "Okay, it's your turn to cut the odds in half."

He pivoted toward me. "How many guys do you know?"

"Look, just because I saw all four of those men alive doesn't mean their deaths have anything to do with me."

"Could you make me a list?"

"Of all the men and boys I know in Bishop?" Did I detect a note of jealousy?

"It would be extensive, huh?"

"Wills, I went to college here. I knew fraternity guys and houseboys, men in classes, teachers, ballplayers, administrators, coaches. I work with twenty-five or thirty men at the paper. I know cops and city and county officials. I've written dozens of stories about men, from old-age pensioners to winners of high school rodeo competitions and junior livestock shows."

He nodded, obviously discouraged. "And there're probably a bunch of working stiffs like Benunda you won't even remember, until we find their bodies."

Darn him. I wanted to help. I hated for people to be obstructive when I was trying to accomplish something. I exhaled my accumulated annoyance. "If you want a list, I'll make you a list."

He shook his head.

"Wills, I thought you had a pretty good idea who the killer was."

"Oh, I've got a couple of screwball ideas rattling around in my head, but only one of my theories fits and I have no actual evidence."

"You have instincts about this kind of stuff, don't you?"

He looked defeated. "I'm supposed to have."

"Do you think they were random killings?"

"No. I think the killer believes he's eliminating a threat. I just can't figure what it is."

"You keep saying *he*. You haven't changed your mind, have you? That's an editorial *he*."

"You know it is."

"You think it's a woman because of the heel marks in Ansel's office?"

"That and a whole grab bag of other things. It just feels like a woman's work."

"And you have a specific woman in mind."

"Yes, I do, and you know perfectly well who it is."

"Then get a search warrant or something."

He winced. "The law doesn't allow me to get a warrant without evidence. I can't get one based on gut instinct. Also, I can't go around getting warrants to search the homes of every female or cross-dresser who wears spike heels. But I'm pretty sure who I'm after."

"Are you closing your mind to other possibilities?"

"Like who?"

"How about a disgruntled lover or betrayed wife or dissatisfied customer?"

"Or a temperamental journalist?"

"You honestly haven't ever thought it was me, right?"

He shook his head.

"Think of all the people you have suspected and tell me your reasons." I wanted to give him a sounding board, let him bounce his ideas out loud to hear how they played.

He seemed to understand. "Okay. I started with homophobes, people who hate gays, suspects from bashings on down to yelling matches in disturbing the peace incident reports. Like I told you, I originally thought of guys like Spence with chips on their shoulders. And guys like Ansel."

I controlled my automatic glower, but he noticed. "Obviously you didn't discuss gay-righters with him. When they marched last spring, he went completely off his rails. But I could not imagine a man using those damned ribbons. The heel prints in Ansel's office and your observation about the perfume provided some confirmation that our killer is a woman, and maybe even which woman.

"So I pursued that theory. The janitor caught a glimpse of a woman in high heels slipping out the side door of the admin building about five forty-five Wednesday evening. He noticed because she was wearing sunglasses and it was almost full dark outside. He said she had on a straw hat with a broad brim and wore a scarf around her neck.

"We did a composite sketch even though I didn't expect it to do any good, but when we showed it at Crook's law office, Mrs. Edmunds, Crook's secretary, had seen the woman that Thursday morning, right there in his office."

Intrigued, I struggled not to interrupt.

"She remembered because the woman was wearing shades and the summer straw hat and asked questions about the senator's Thursday routine. Edmunds said the woman was very insistent about seeing him."

Wills again began thrumming the pencil, this time on his desk, obviously unaware of the little habit. "The woman was supposed to return Friday. She didn't show and Crook turned up in Effinger's pond. Edmunds said the woman spoke softly; that she could have been a he in drag."

He glanced up and smiled sheepishly. "I forgot, Jancy, all this has to be off the record."

I shrugged. "I'm sort of two people with you, Wills. I'm part newshound and part . . . well, someone else."

"Who?" He perked up.

"Friend." I swallowed and avoided his gaze. "The newshound definitely wants the story. The friend is willing to wait until you give the hound a 'go.' You're safe for the moment to keep thinking out loud. Go ahead. Describe who we're looking for and why."

He paced to the windows, still carrying the pencil. "If I had to come up with a profile of the killer right now, based on the information we have and my instincts. . . ." He hesitated before turning back to me. "I'd say it's a woman who is extremely angry at men in general, not just one poor slob. Or she's angry because she isn't a man. It's likely she's in a man's job, may even supervise men. I think that partly because of the way she kills. She knows about the male anatomy and how it ties in to the male psyche. It's like she wants to destroy a man's pride, humiliate him before he dies.

"Also, women generally prefer death neat. Bloodless. Female suicides and murderers prefer poisons to guns. They don't go in much for gore. This one renders her victims defenseless, then relieves them of their manhood. She emasculates them, but she does it bloodlessly.

"She gift wraps them, uses the ribbons to make a statement that maybe only she understands. And to make sure she gets credit for the kill, of course. Sometimes I think she leaves her victims conscious enough to know what's happening to them—maybe even allows them to feel the pain, although they're helpless to stop her. Each kill may be her perverse way of getting even with some man for some atrocity perpetrated on her—punishing all males by torturing and tormenting them, especially by destroying their sexuality before she takes their lives."

He paused, frowning at something outside the window while apparently not actually seeing anything. "When she's got her vics neatly packaged, she kills them with her hands, strangling one, suffocating another, drowning the senator. But she was in a hurry with Ansel. Didn't get to give him the full treatment. Maybe she heard someone coming and had to finish him quick, with a small gun, a shot no one was close enough to hear."

"And she didn't have time to affix the ribbon."

"Yeah. The circumstances were different." Wills paced up and down the length of the library table in front of the window. "Janitors were in the building. Other people were in and out. I figure someone damn near caught her. But she risked that, delayed long enough to leave the ribbon. She wanted to make sure she got credit, even if she didn't get to enjoy his final humiliation. I'll bet that galled her. I think applying the rubber band and ribbon to her victims is significant. It gives her closure. Satisfies whatever's eating her, at least for the moment."

"Her point being?"

He shrugged. "I don't know. Control. Establishing her superiority over all males? Like Tarzan beating his chest and yodeling after he whips up on an alligator."

The clock on the wall showed it was straight-up eleven. "I've got to go," I said. "I'm supposed to be covering a medical malpractice suit in Thomas' courtroom."

"I'm going to the courthouse, too." He strode to the coat rack to retrieve his blazer. "I'll walk you over."

I wanted to provide some comic relief. I hated for him to go around burdened and feeling responsible for the murders. "You want to walk with me because you want me to protect you, right?"

"What?" My comment startled him out of his doldrums, so I decided to push it.

"If the victims are all men, I'm in no danger, so when you

179

say you want to walk along with me, I have to figure you're counting on me to protect you."

His eyes brightened as he grinned. "Yeah. I've seen you in action. You're downright inspirational."

I bit my lips to keep from laughing as I remembered my cowardice in the face of the near hit-and-run, the barking pup and the gunshot in the parking lot. "Maybe I was in a weakened condition." I reached for the doorknob.

"What do you mean?" His hand covered mine.

My heart tripped and I felt the familiar flush rising from my shirt collar. "I was emotionally overwrought."

His eyes captured mine as he sobered again. "About me?"

"Maybe."

"And now?"

I attempted to turn the knob. His hand prevented it as he held my gaze. "You like me, don't you?"

"Maybe, maybe not," I said, mimicking his standard response to my early questions. There was a long pause before he broke the quiet.

"Me too." He smiled, then bent to brush his lips over my blush-warmed cheek. "You sure smell good."

My hand trembled beneath his. He finally allowed me to turn the knob and open the door.

I blushed even more brightly as Wills put his hand on the small of my back and guided me through the reception area filled with bureau people, all of whom were grinning for no apparent reason.

Before we separated at the second floor of the courthouse, he said, "Meet me at Bailey's for supper. About six?"

My courage returned. "Am I buying?"

He looked playful. "It *is* your turn."

"If you quit seeing me. . . ."

"It'll happen when it's my turn for the check." He grinned, giving teasing confirmation to his words.

We gave each other a low-five. Our hands maintained contact longer than necessary before we parted, he going to the court clerk's office on the second floor and I climbing to the courtrooms on three.

# Chapter Eleven

Later, back in the office, something in my notes caught my attention. It was probably nothing, but someone had committed these murders. I didn't want it to be anyone I knew. But maybe it was someone close to someone I knew. Someone incensed by, say, a relative.

Okay, my theory was a long shot, but it might not hurt to check it out. No one else needed to know, unless it led somewhere. Students had pretty flexible hours. One with a grudge who was a little unbalanced might have means, motive and opportunity.

Following my hunch, I telephoned Jason Lee Trout, Patsy Leek's son, introduced myself and asked for an interview.

"I'm putting together a feature on mononucleosis among teens," I said. "I want to interview people who've had a recent experience with the disease."

He sounded receptive, eager for company. "Aren't you afraid you'll get my mono?"

"I'm not planning to kiss you."

He laughed and I took that as a yes.

"I can be there in twenty minutes, if that's okay."

He agreed.

I had second thoughts about wandering into a lion's den, but my fears were dispelled almost the minute I arrived.

Pajama-clad beneath a bathrobe, Jason Trout was tall,

gangly and polite. He offered me something to drink, which I declined, before he suggested we sit in the living room.

Jason had a fair, freckled complexion and his mother's eyes, but his strong chin and jaw obviously came from other genes.

I settled opposite him at the far end of the sofa.

"Tell me if you get tired," I began. He had dark circles under his bloodshot eyes. "This doesn't have to be a long, drawn-out session. Just call time. You won't offend me."

He said okay.

"Have any of your friends had mono?" I asked.

"Yes, several of them."

"Have you had it before?"

"Nah, and I don't think I'll be getting it again, if it's up to me."

We discussed his symptoms and the treatment. He was sharp. I would have to be careful broaching the other, more delicate subject.

"I was a close friend of Ansel Benedict's," I mentioned in passing, after Jason made a reference to the university. "You knew him too, didn't you?"

The boy's haunted expression brightened and he sat up straighter. "He was the greatest guy I ever knew." He stared intently at me, as if considering his next words before he continued. "He had a talk with me last fall that burned my tail, but he got me straightened out about a problem I thought I had."

Not wanting to look too eager, I focused on my notepad and prodded gently. "He could get pretty involved with people he liked."

"Yeah. He had a lot of friends."

"I'm afraid your mom wasn't a member of his fan club." I glanced up to see his eager expression dim to a reflective frown.

"I know. Sometimes Mom gets an idea in her head and there's no way you can convince her it's not true. The worst part of it is, it was my fault she got the wrong idea about Ansel in the first place."

I didn't move or speak, hoping my silence would induce him to continue talking. He slumped back against the sofa.

"I'd better go." I closed my notebook. "You're getting tired."

He looked at me. "Please stay. It's real nice having someone around."

I got an inspiration. A friend visiting a shut-in didn't need a search warrant. "Aren't you supposed to eat pretty often?"

He nodded, but remained motionless.

"Can I get you something?" I laid my notebook aside.

"I'd eat some chicken noodle, if someone would fix it." He gave me a languid smile.

"Okay. Where's the kitchen?"

He pointed to his right.

I made myself walk slowly into the other room. No use being overly eager to heat up a can of soup. I hoped Patsy wouldn't show up in the middle of the day. Even if she did, I had a quasi-legitimate reason for being there.

The kitchen was clean, light and well equipped, considering Patsy hated to cook. Space above the cabinets was lighted to display collections of baseball caps, fishing lures, and keys. The baseball caps advertised everything from athletic teams to: "Wormtown—offering the best worm bar in Texas." I smiled.

The fishing lures were displayed separately in printer's box cabinets, each spiny item in its own tiny compartment.

The key display was the most extensive, from a huge, highly polished brass skeleton key to a tiny one that looked like it fit a child's diary. There were dozens of car keys representing all makes and models of vehicles, many of them labeled by year.

"You're quite the collector," I called.

"They're hers," he said from the living room.

I got a saucepan from the drainer and chose a can of soup from several in the cupboard. I added water and turned on the burner, then stepped down a hall to peek into two tidy bedrooms. A third contained an unmade bed and drinking glasses collected on a bedside table. Returning to the kitchen, gaining confidence, I snooped through cabinets and drawers, not sure what I was looking for, but looking anyway.

Eventually, I retrieved saltine crackers from an upper cabinet, but had to open several packets before I found one without webs or tiny worms. Yuck.

I stirred the soup, got out a bowl and a glass and silverware, filled the glass with milk, then triumphantly took the result of my effort to the patient.

"Thanks." He looked apologetic. "I don't drink milk."

Without comment, I sat and watched as he downed the soup, drank all of the milk, and asked for more chicken noodle. He offered me a cracker. I declined. He scrutinized each one, dusted specks off with his fingers and ate them all himself.

I was curious about the problem he had discussed with Ansel but couldn't figure out how to broach the subject, so I felt relieved when he launched into an explanation without prompting.

"My problem was, I thought I was homosexual." He wiped his mouth. "I told Mom first. She had a fit and beat me up pretty good."

I tried to hide my surprise, but he noticed.

"She works out. She's real strong. Besides, I've never been

allowed to hit girls. Anyway, there's no way I'd slug Mom, no matter what she did.

"I sort of got in with this bunch of college guys who kept encouraging me to come out of the closet. They said it would make me feel better and Mom would just have to adjust. A guy on my softball team told Coach Benedict I might be coming out. Coach invited me over to his house to talk about stuff."

Jason pushed himself back on the couch and gave me a hard stare. "Now, I hadn't had any genuine homosexual experiences or anything except, you know . . . or you may not know . . . guys kind of kid around with each other sometimes when they first notice things changing with their bodies." He hesitated. "Am I embarrassing you?"

I struggled to maintain what I hoped was professional indifference. I shook my head no but couldn't continue eye contact with him. "I've got two younger brothers."

"Oh, yeah? Good, then you know what I'm talking about."

I didn't, but didn't feel the need to admit that at the moment.

"So I went over to Coach's house one Sunday night," he continued. "I didn't know what to expect. You know how he was. A neat freak and all."

I nodded and he smirked.

"He asked me if I wanted something to drink. I figured a beer might help me relax. He looked surprised when I asked for one, but he got it anyway. I only took a couple of swallows.

"We sat down and he asked me why I was hanging with guys who were so much older than I was. I told him I thought they might be my type and why I thought so.

"First thing, he said I was normal." Jason looked at me

earnestly. "You wouldn't think someone would have to tell a guy that about himself." Looking away, he shook his head in disbelief. "He said most men wonder about their sexual preferences at one time or another.

"We talked man to man. We didn't mince any words. He told me God didn't want men having sex with other men and he quoted chapter and verse.

"He said sex was more fun with girls anyway. He let me ask questions. We talked for nearly three hours.

"He got pretty clinical on me, and threw in a bunch of religious stuff. He said, bottom line: being a heterosexual man was great. The main thing I needed was for somebody, anybody, to tell me if it was morally right or wrong for a man to be gay, especially now that it's more or less optional."

I was puzzled. "Your mom didn't like what he told you?"

"She never knew. When I got home, she smelled the beer and asked where I'd been. I told her I'd been at Coach Benedict's talking about homosexuality. After that, she wouldn't listen to anything."

He eyed me speculatively. "You might not know this, but my mom hates men. The whole gender. Even me." He leaned his head back and closed his eyes.

He was tiring and I needed to leave, but I wanted to explore one last area. "Except Sheriff Roundtree."

"Roundtree?" Jason's eyes popped open and he gazed at the ceiling. "He's the biggest joke of all. She rags on him all the time, talking about how big and stupid he is. She shouldn't complain. He's good to us. He bought us our new car."

I chose my words carefully. "You mean he pays her a good salary that makes her able to buy nice cars?"

Jason frowned. "Well, yeah, I guess he pays good enough, but we make most of our big purchases in July when they start the new fiscal year and hand out the bonuses."

Roundtree grumbled long, loud and often about his tight budget and straining to make the money stretch to the end of the fiscal year in June. He never mentioned having money left over for year-end bonuses.

I put a big *X* through Number Four, next to Jason's name in my notebook. I didn't ordinarily deal with criminals, but I did know something about human nature and Jason definitely did not belong on my list of suspects. But someone else looked to be moving up.

As much as I'd admired Ansel, he'd been the first name on my list. Starting out, he was the only person I knew who had reason to be angry with the two students *and* with the senator.

I had felt just as reluctant to put Gary on my list as Number Two and Patsy as Number Three. Patsy's place had made Jason and Maggie Trout suspects Four and Five. So far, I wasn't doing very well as a detective. Indicators kept pointing to people I did not want to be the perpetrator. In spite of her diminutive size, Patsy had begun to look like my most promising suspect.

I stood and hooked my purse's shoulder strap on my arm. "Jason, I've sure enjoyed meeting you." I shook his hand. "Are you going back to bed or do you want to stay here on the couch?"

"I think I'll crash in my room for a while." He used the arm of the sofa to leverage himself to his feet. "Maybe I'll see you around the courthouse sometime."

"I hope so." I thanked him again and left.

Outside, I maintained a dignified pace to the car. Patsy's daughter was next up on my list. Before driving to the admin building, I finished and underlined the high points of my conversation with Jason in my notebook.

Intent on my quest, I walked into the admissions office on the first floor, oblivious to qualms about being in the building where someone had murdered Ansel Benedict only five days before.

Maggie Trout was a junior and a resident advisor in a freshman dorm. Records showed her in class until four o'clock. It was three-ten. I jotted down her schedule, then went to the dorm to wait.

Maggie had gotten a free cut and was one of several young women propped in front of the television in the dorm lounge with a bag of popcorn and a cola, watching a soap. She was easy to recognize, her coloring and build very like her brother's.

"Hi, I'm Jancy Dewhurst. Are you Maggie Trout?"

Maggie sat up, wiped the salt off her hand on the front of her T-shirt and offered the clean hand. I shook it.

"I read your news stories in the *Clarion* all the time." Maggie stood and beckoned to a sitting area away from the cluster watching the television. "Are you working? Is that what you're doing here?"

"Yeah. My beat includes the courthouse. County offices got their quarterly budget reports last week. I'm doing a wrap-up piece on where our tax money goes. It's been done to death, but I guess there are always a few people checking it out for the first time."

She motioned me to sit. "Sounds dull."

"Yeah. I'm trying to personalize it, you know, a dollar paid to the treasurer is budgeted to an office, becomes a salary for an employee, winds up paid to the university as tuition to educate the employee's child. Something like that. It makes for a better read."

"Good idea. Where do you come up with your ideas?"

"This time, I tried to think of something that would jazz up the county budget a little."

"I see what you mean, but I may not be your best example."

"You're a student, aren't you?"

"Yes, but I wouldn't take money from county employee Patsy Leek if I were homeless and starving."

"Patsy is your mother, then?" Casually, I curled onto the far end of the sofa. The girl nodded.

"I don't use her name for a reason. When she bounced our dad out of the house, she took back her maiden name and tried to have my brother Jason's name and mine changed, too. She made fun of the name Trout. She was willing to shed it. We weren't."

"So she refuses to pay your tuition?"

"No. I won't let her. She wants to, but she's crazy, and I mean that in the most therapeutic sense. There are too many strings attached to her giving. I tell you that from experience." Maggie set her cup and popcorn aside, dusted her hands together and shifted to sit cross-legged, putting us face to face.

As unobtrusively as possible, I pulled out my notebook and began writing. "Does your father help you, then?"

"When he can, but I have scholarships and my job here. I get by. Even if I didn't, I wouldn't ask her."

"A lot of girls and their mothers don't get along." I tossed a significant glance at the cluster of women hovering in front of the television. "Mother and daughter conflicts are common."

"My mom," Maggie said, "has a personality conflict when she's in a room all by herself. She's one of those insatiably money-motivated people. There's never enough."

"I suppose people who've had to scrimp and save in the past are especially careful."

Maggie bit her lips and shook her head. "Not Mom. Do you know why she dumped my dad?"

"No."

"She wanted more. Mom used to be fairly cute and she's very shrewd. She even got her claws into that old senator lawyer guy, the one they found in the pond."

"Robert Crook?"

"That's him. She wrote some bad checks a long time ago, then got him to represent her. He was feeling neglected at home. Mom made some moves on him. They ended up having a hot affair. It didn't last. Pretty soon they were arguing all the time, mostly over money, just like with Dad. Crook had a bunch. She wanted some. He wouldn't pay her for sleeping with him, but he would for working for him."

"She worked for him? In his law office?"

"No, at his nursing home. Sunrise Plaza. They had this little scam going. He got her hired in the sheriff's office. He and Roundtree don't get along, so he had to work it out through a friend of a friend.

"The idea was, she would route old county prisoners to the Plaza, claim the Medicaid and, when it paid, Crook would kick some back her way. She told me it was a real good deal. The government paid the freight. It didn't cost anyone anything. She said it was legal because he was a lawyer and he set it up."

I remained silent, encouraging Maggie to continue.

"I'm no genius, but I saw how this arrangement could mean trouble. Then, of course, the old guys kept dying. I don't think they fed them."

"Did Sheriff Roundtree know about the arrangement?"

"Shoot, no. Mom has the sheriff wrapped around her finger. She says, 'Jump,' and he asks, 'How high?' She doesn't let Roundtree see the financial records for his own office. Hardly lets him write a check. She does all the banking and all the check writing herself. They've got millions of dollars running through that office."

I concentrated on keeping my face expressionless. "Sounds like a gravy train to me. Why didn't you want to get on it?"

"I'm not like that. Plus, like I said, she's crazy. She's got this bad hang-up about men. She likes to screw them. I don't mean physically. I mean she likes to be in control, beat them out of stuff and one-up them. She's revised the old saw, 'youth is wasted on the young' to 'masculinity is wasted on men.' " Maggie paused to take a sip of her cola.

"I wonder where she got that?" I stretched and feigned a yawn, trying to look and sound slightly bored. "That antagonism toward men."

Maggie raised and lowered her shoulders. "She had a brother, Thom. She refers to him as 'Baby Boy Leek.' He died in a car wreck when he was sixteen. You know how it is when people die. Everyone remembers them as perfect. Grandma said the light went out of their lives when their baby boy died. Mom was fourteen.

"Mom said she did everything she could to comfort her parents, but she couldn't be Thom. She tried to make them proud of her, but they just kept grieving over him.

"She didn't remember Thom as perfect. He molested her, experimented with her. Sexually. You know. She told me once, when she'd had a couple of drinks, that she felt big relief when he died."

"Did their parents know he'd molested her?" I said quietly.

"Mom thought so, but after he died, I guess it didn't matter. Anyway, she pretty well hates men in general, especially their private parts. When she and Dad were married, she hated sex."

I tried to keep my voice calm. "Your mother's attitude doesn't include all men, does it? She has some favorites."

"There are some she sweet-talks." Maggie's frown deepened. "Those are probably the ones in the worst danger, the ones she considers worthy adversaries. Beating one of those prize guys at her little game is her favorite sport, and they don't even know they're playing."

"What kind of game?"

Maggie shrugged. "Several wound up in Sunrise Plaza hooked up to machines while she ran around with their powers of attorney and their checkbooks. She's been named sole heir in wills. You should hear the relatives howl." Maggie shifted position. "She's getting old now and her ego's kicking. Her guineas, that's what she calls her marks, are older too. Even old men want young tail. But Mom still scores one every now and then.

"It's pathetic, watching her flirt. She used to be subtle, cutting her eyes and dimpling up at everything they said. But her bait's gotten stale."

I gazed at the floor. "Was she still seeing Senator Crook when he died?"

"No. He quit her before I left home. She really hated having sex with him, said he was nasty. She did it anyway, as long as he was willing to pay her price.

"She claimed she was sacrificing herself for us, so my brother and I could have decent clothes. I told her she didn't have to do Crook for me. Just looking at that creep gave me the willies." Maggie shivered and hesitated for a long moment before she lowered her voice.

"One day Crook told Mom he was tired of her carping and squeezin' every dime and the whole nine yards. I was there at the house, getting clothes and stuff out of my closet. I couldn't believe he was giving her the heave-ho. She was always telling us how crazy he was about her.

"She screamed that she was holding him to their deal at

Sunrise Plaza. If he didn't let her keep skimming the old guys' money, she'd tell all. He didn't care. He said she could consider that scam her retirement, until she got caught, then the state would provide her room and board in her dotage."

Maggie suddenly looked up at me startled. "The bottom line of all this is, I don't think I'd be a very good subject for your story about state money being funneled from the taxpayers to a college student. Do you?"

Stunned for the moment, I studied the girl. "Are you afraid you'll get your mother in trouble telling me about the kickback scheme?" The story sounded like the unvarnished truth. Sincerity in Maggie's face confirmed for me that she'd told it just the way it was.

She shrugged. "I don't care about that. I'm completely screwed up, especially where men are concerned. She marked me for life. I think she's messed up Jason too. That's my brother. He still lives at home. She's browbeat and belittled him all his life because he's a boy. Luckily, he's an athlete. Coaches get interested in him. That helps. I imagine he's still pretty confused. I don't see how he could help it.

"Plus, I think maybe Mom's got a new financial crisis now. The 'fit could hit the shan,' as they say, any day. She called and asked if I could help her out.

"I cook on a hot plate in my dorm room. I can't even afford cafeteria food and it's cheap. A couple of bucks from me is not going to help her. When she's in a bind, she needs thousands."

Suddenly, Maggie's running commentary stopped. Intentionally, I hadn't made any move that might have inhibited her, but Maggie's conscience seemed to have kicked in. "You might be right, Ms. Dewhurst. I probably shouldn't be laying all this out for you."

I nodded solemnly and put a big *X* through Number Five on my suspect list.

"Maggie, I appreciate your candor. I won't quote you, but I may use some of the information you've given me to check out some things. If your mom gets in trouble, it won't trace back to you, at least not through me."

Maggie stared down at her own hands and began to recant. "What if I was just conning you? I watch a lot of soaps. What if I said none of what I told you is true, that I just made it up?"

I stood and fumbled in my purse to find a twenty-dollar bill, which I stuffed in Maggie's hand. "Then I'd say you tell a great story." I smiled and tried to look reassuring. "That tall tale was worth at least twenty bucks."

Late in the afternoon, Wills stuck his head in the door to the sheriff's office.

"Can I do something for you, handsome?" Patsy's smoky voice sounded huskier than usual.

"No, thanks. I'm looking for Spence."

"He ought to be right back. Why don't you come in? Take a load off. You're not afraid to be alone with me, are you, big boy?"

Before Jim could respond, he heard Spence whistling as he got off the elevator.

"Hey, Wills," Spence called as the agent turned toward him. "My man!"

Jim allowed the glass door of the office to close behind him as he stepped back out into the hall. Patsy glowered at her switchboard.

Putting his hand on Spence's shoulder, Wills turned the deputy and guided him to a wooden bench in the hallway.

"Hey, what're we doing out here, man? It's a lot more private in the office."

Wills shook his head as they sat down. "I want to pick your

brain a little, Spence. In there, we'll get interrupted. You'll end up on the phone or something."

"Okay." Spence relented, frowning, obviously not convinced, but resigned. "Shoot."

They sat on the bench facing each other.

"I want you to describe every single detail of the day the two kids delivered the pizza to your office."

"You mean just about when they came and all. You don't want anything about what happened that morning?"

Wills regarded Spence closely. "Not unless something happened that morning that pertains to their being there in the afternoon."

Spence thought. "No, nothing I know about." He settled back. "Well, they showed up just before the fifth inning. The drinks were dripping and Patsy sent me for paper towels. I got a fistful of 'em out of the men's bathroom. When I got back, Angie from down the hall took some."

"Did Patsy help mop up the mess?"

"No, she was getting the money to pay for the order. I can tell you this: she was mad as a wet hen. One kid—not the foreigner, the other one—was talking a lot and laughing real loud, you know how college kids do."

"Who was he talking to?"

"I don't know, I guess to Pat because Angie was standing there waiting for me and when I brought in the towels, she grabbed a bunch and took off."

"Who's Angie?"

"Angie, or maybe, I think . . . yeah, it's Angela, who works in the court clerk's office."

"Think now, Spence. I need you to remember the exact conversation."

Spence took a deep breath, then exhaled. "I can't remember exact words, but there was something about the money. The foreign guy was sorting through his money bag, trying to make change, I guess. I never heard him say one word except for when he was leaving and he thanked the sheriff for the tip."

"Let's go back to before the sheriff came into the room." Wills held onto his patience. "Angie took off with the paper towels and just Patsy and the two boys were there."

"And me," Spence corrected.

"And you." Wills slowed his words. "Did you see any money change hands?"

"Oh, yeah. That was the problem. The tab was twenty-two dollars. Pat gave them a hundred-dollar bill."

"Where'd she get it?"

"I don't know. It was just there, in her hand. The kid had ones and fives, but Pat didn't want those. I wondered why she didn't just open up the cash drawer. She always has money around. I didn't say nothin'. She's real touchy when you talk about the public's money around the office. She keeps that drawer locked up tight. To be real honest with you, I don't think she trusts any of us."

Wills waved a hand impatiently. "But they got the change someplace?"

"The sheriff come in and told them all to shut up. He pulled the money out of his own pocket. He handed the kid a twenty and a ten.

"The other kid started riding Roundtree about how he should give them the extra for a tip since they'd had to climb all those stairs to get up here and since they'd wasted so much time trying to get their money. The sheriff got sore. He probably meant to let the kid fish out his change, then give it back to him as a tip anyway. That's the way Roundtree is. He's generous. I'm not politicking you neither."

"Then what happened?"

"Roundtree waved off the change, just like I thought he would. The foreigner zipped up the money bag, grabbed the carrier and they left."

Wills stood, stuck his hands in his trouser pockets, paced and leaned against the wall behind the bench. They heard tapping and both glanced toward the sheriff's office. When she got their attention, Patsy beckoned Spence to come. He hopped up, but Wills called him back.

The deputy turned, looking nervous. "I've gotta get in there."

Wills grimaced. "Do me one favor?"

Spence stared at him.

"Don't tell anyone, not Sheriff Roundtree, not Patsy Leek, not anyone, about this conversation."

Spence blinked.

"I need to depend on you, Spence. I wouldn't ask if I didn't think it was important."

The deputy lowered his voice. "You can count on me, Wills. That's for sure."

Patsy wanted Spence to finish loading the staplers, complaining that he'd left in the middle of a job. He sighed his relief.

She seemed to be in a good mood, smiling and pleasant. She even asked if his leg was bothering him. She seldom cared about anything he had to say, so he welcomed her attention.

"What was Agent Wills being so secretive about?" she asked idly.

"He wanted us to sit out there in the hall. I guess he was watching for somebody or something."

"What'd he have to say?"

Spence shrugged and started filling another stapler. "Not much."

"Did he say how his murder investigation is going?"

"Nah. He just asked how my leg was and stuff like that. I really don't know that he wanted anything, except maybe some company."

When she didn't speak, Spence ventured a look. Pat stared at him, eyes narrowed. She looked annoyed. He turned his attention back to the staplers.

Ten minutes later, he looked through the glass door to see Agent Wills still seated on the bench, writing in a small, black notebook.

Angela Fires hurried to the counter in the court clerk's office when Jim Wills entered. Two other deputy clerks who had started forward glared at her. Angela had grown curious about the eligible Mr. Wills after her housemates' reports of his sudden appearance and surprising behavior at their house on Friday night.

"Can I help you?"

"Are you Angela?"

She smiled. "Yes, I am. What can I do for you?"

"I'm Jim Wills, with the . . ."

"I know who you are," she blurted, then looked surprised and bit her lip.

He leaned toward her over the counter. "Do you remember watching the World Series in the sheriff's office back in September?"

She lowered her voice to match his. "I went over as much as I could every single day. Are you wanting to know about the day the dead guys came in? I mean, the guys who are dead now but weren't then, of course." She twittered.

"Yes." Instead of smiling at her coquetry, Wills looked deadly serious and a little intimidating.

Angela sobered and fingered the charm on the chain

around her neck, sliding it back and forth. "Yeah, I was there when they brought the pizza."

"Tell me exactly what you remember."

"Well, I was in the sheriff's inner office watching the ball game with everybody else."

"Everybody?"

"Yes. Well, except Patsy. She had to get their deposit ready."

"How do you know that?"

"She was counting money out of the drawer and putting it in neat little stacks."

"On the counter?"

"Well, no. She put it in stacks on her desk, then put rubber bands around each stack. When one was ready, she'd stick it in her purse."

"You didn't see a bank bag?"

"No. Sometimes bank bags invite trouble, you know. A lot of women who have stores downtown carry their deposits in their purses."

Wills' brows furrowed. "And when the boys made the pizza delivery, were you still there?"

"Yes. The kid from Pakistan was real cute but kind of shy, you know. He looked at me and smiled but he was bashful. He put the pizza carrier on the counter and gave Pat the ticket. She took a twenty out of the drawer to pay him, but it was the only one she had. When it wasn't enough, she accidentally put the twenty in her purse and pulled a hundred-dollar bill out and locked the cash drawer. That's when the other one, the one the newspaper called Speir, started kidding her about pocketing office money.

"He was trying to be funny, you know, but nobody laughed, so he got louder. You could tell he was making her really mad.

"The madder she got, the louder and more obnoxious he got, trying to kid her out of it." Angie shook her head. "I've been in those situations myself. Believe me, talking just makes them worse."

Wills nodded. "What did he say?"

"Oh, you know, kidding her about pilfering, putting office money in her purse. About how she was giving herself better tips in the sheriff's office than they got delivering pizzas. How they could do a lot better if they got to tap the till for their own tips like she did. That kind of stuff.

"He said he bet she drove a big, fine car while they ran around on three cylinders. You know, just talk. He should have shut up." She paused to study Jim before she continued. "Mr. Wills, you know Patsy, don't you?"

"Yes."

"You know how she dresses, trying to look all young, like a college kid or something?"

He nodded.

"Well, when he couldn't get her to smile one way, he tried another. He started saying how cute she was and how he bet a lot of old guys hung around there just to get an eyeful of her.

"I could see her steaming. The 'old guy' crack struck a nerve.

"The drink cups were sweating all over the counter. Pat yelled, then the sheriff yelled, and I just wanted to get out of there. That's when Gary showed up with the paper towels. I took a bunch and carried some of the drinks back to where we were watching the game."

Wills' face relaxed and he almost smiled. "Could I have your address and phone number in case I need to contact you later?"

"You already have it." She paused for dramatic emphasis. "I'm one of Jancy Dewhurst's housemates."

She watched carefully but the man showed no reaction except for another nod. "Yes, I have it then. Thank you for your time, Ms. Fires. I'd like to ask that you keep our conversation confidential." His face softened and he looked into her eyes. "Will you do that for me?"

She gazed back at him. "Yes, Mr. Wills. I'm more than happy to cooperate with you any way I can."

# Chapter Twelve

Bailey's was crowded with the Monday night football throng getting oiled for action when I got there at six o'clock straight-up. I squeezed through to the bar where a guy let me step in front of him, then filled in the space, standing close behind me.

*I'll wait eight minutes,* I decided. *Arbitrary, but long enough.*

At six-oh-three, Agent Wills nudged my elbow and motioned me to follow him outside.

"It's too crowded," he said, voicing the obvious. "My mom is Italian. Her lasagna in my freezer is the best you've ever eaten. Let's go to my place."

"Are you going to make me stay outside again?"

He grinned. "Only if you insist." He took my arm and turned us toward the parking lot. The north wind cut through my clothing as we ran. I loved jogging beside him, matching stride for stride.

When we got to my car, he pulled me around to face him. "Ride with me."

I didn't see any hidden meaning in his expression, but a strange tension radiated from him that I didn't quite trust. "That's not necessary."

"I want you to go with me," he repeated.

"You won't mind getting out in the cold to bring me back later?"

"No." He lowered his voice. "If that's what you want later."

The hair on the back of my neck bristled a warning, but before I could voice my concerns, he wrapped an arm around my shoulders and was guiding me past a dozen cars to his drab brown SBI unit with the antennas. That car was stodgy enough to inspire trust.

His house was cold and dark when we arrived. We went from the garage, through the utility room, into a sterile, stainless steel kitchen with black and white accents.

Even after lights bathed the room, I wasn't ready to shed my coat. I wasn't sure if the source of my chill was the brisk weather or the warning that still crawled on the back of my neck.

He adjusted the thermostat in the dining room as he nudged me through to the den. I stood watching as he lit the gas jet under firewood already laid in the fireplace. Jim didn't say a word. The cozy blaze coaxed me forward. I eased onto the raised hearth, turned my chilled backside to the flames, and checked out the room.

An overstuffed sofa covered with a hard fabric in black and white geometrics faced the fireplace over a large glass and metal coffee table. A matching love seat flanked one side, two black accent chairs the other. The ceiling vaulted fifteen feet to skylights. I spotted a loft at the second level on one side of the room.

Shining black tiles made up the floor, accented by a black area rug that ran from the hearth beneath the coffee table and ended at the front edge of the sofa. The room wrapped around to a dining area and into the kitchen.

Jim watched me for a while before he said, "What do you think?"

"Very comfortable. Tasteful. Very tidy."

"And?"

I didn't know whether to continue with my actual impression or not.

"Come on. What?"

I cringed. "Seductive."

He grinned, nodded, and walked quickly to the kitchen as he muttered, "We can always hope." He obviously intended me to hear him.

I drew a deep breath and tried to ignore the butterflies filling my stomach. I seldom visited a bachelor's pad, particularly not without independent transportation. I felt uneasy and more than a little vulnerable.

But this was Jim Wills, I reminded myself. Cool, well disciplined and unemotional. What did a few kisses mean to a man like that? He would laugh if I said I was spooked. As a distraction, I continued my appraisal.

A built-in bookshelf and entertainment center, glistening white, monopolized the wall beneath the loft. The giant cabinet housed a TV, a collection of sound equipment and compartments for storing CDs, DVDs and books.

A profusion of black and white Ansel Adams prints in rimless frames adorned the white, white walls. The space looked immaculate, yet totally male.

The room temperature rose quickly as Jim made clattering noises in the kitchen. Finally warm enough to lose the coat, I called, "Need some help? I'm not much of a cook, but I can follow orders."

"No, thanks. Everything in here is under control."

Of course he would say that. Jim always had things under control.

I heard the swish of the door between the kitchen and the dining area as it swung closed, and the clattering in the kitchen became muffled.

Wandering around, looking for a place to hang my coat, I

found an entry closet tucked beneath the stairway. I figured the steps led to bedrooms above. The thought unsettled me. *I am such a dweeb.* I laughed lightly. *Most homes have bedrooms. That doesn't necessarily mean I will be seeing them or . . . whatever.* I briskly rubbed the back of my neck to quell the sinister vibes. Murders had brought Jim Wills into my life, but they had nothing to do with our relationship. The little hairs bristled again.

Returning to the cheery fire to shirk darker thoughts, I sank into the luxury of the sofa, kicked off my shoes and stretched my stockinged feet, pointing toes and then heels. Easing my head back, I stared into the flames over the end of my nose. The chopping sounds had stopped, so I called out, again offering assistance.

"I'm finished." Jim shouldered his way through the swinging door carrying two full wine glasses. He was in his shirtsleeves. "There will be a brief wait, but the bar here is nice and not nearly as crowded as that last place."

I sat up straight and avoided looking directly into his eyes. Except for the jogging, I had never seen him casual. He flashed a smile as he handed me a glass of wine. It was an unremarkable smile with no hidden meaning. He walked to the sound system. "What kind of music do you like?"

I shrugged and leaned back, feeling safe, at least for the moment. "I like everything." My wine glass tipped precariously and I righted it just before it spilled.

James Taylor's smooth tones filled the room. "Yes." I smiled without looking at Jim. "What else did you choose?"

"A mellow mix of vocal and instrumental." He closed the cabinet and walked over to ease onto the sofa beside me. Holding his wine glass with both hands, he leaned back and propped his feet on the coffee table.

"If you don't like it, don't drink it," he said, indicating the wine. "Would you prefer something else?"

I took a sip and sighed an uh-huh. It felt nice, being in this room. Cozy and warm. And friendly.

He smiled at his wine. "I met one of your housemates today. Angela Fires. In the court clerk's office."

I hummed a nonverbal acknowledgment to indicate I had heard. My eyes slits, I stared into the fire. "Do you think she's attractive?"

"Yes, she's a nice-looking girl."

"Had you noticed her before?"

"No." He, too, gazed into the fire, propping his wine glass on his leg. "About Steven Carruthers...."

"Oh no, you don't." Suddenly alert, I looked at him. "I get first questions tonight."

He laughed, signaling tacit consent.

"People talk about you, but I get the idea you're not much of a ladies' man," I said.

He chuckled while I took another sip of wine. His laughter softened to a grin. "Was that a question?"

"Not yet. In your office this morning, you said you'd dated your share of women." I rolled my head on the sofa's pillowback to look at him.

"Correction," he said, turning his face toward mine and arching his distinctive eyebrows. "I said I've liked a lot of ladies and they've had a fair share of my attention. I was referring to distractions in my work, clarifying the fact that they hadn't been but that you are."

"Okay, these ladies who've had a fair share of your attention, name one."

"Right this minute, looking at you, I can't remember any other name or face."

I studied his expression while contemplating his words.

"That's a very good line. You need to keep it as part of your repertoire. Is it new?"

He licked his lips. I stared at his mouth without intending to. "A lot of things on my mind these days are new since you turned up," he said softly. "For the last couple of weeks I've imagined you sitting right here." He paused, then pretended chagrin. "In my imaginings, of course, you were . . . quieter."

I feigned a pout, giving him credit for the cut. "Love, fifteen. Point, Wills."

His grin faded. "Did you ever figure out why me?"

"Yes." I had decided candor was best. "It's your thumbs."

He sputtered, half laugh, half cough. "Oh, yeah?"

"Everyone has body parts others admire. I'm kind of hung up on forearms and calves. Yours are always covered, but your hands fascinate me. They're unusually thick, which makes you seem capable. Muscular hands and forearms provide little space for veins, consequently yours have to ride along the surface, just under your skin. I particularly admire your veins."

"I see." He regarded his hands skeptically

"Then we come to your thumbs." Timidly, I tapped an index finger on one of his thumbs, which was braced on the bowl of his wineglass. "See how they mound up before they get to your wrists?"

He gave his thumbs a puzzled look.

"To a person who admires forearms, those thumbs are tantalizing."

Wills began laughing again, a low rumble welling up from deep inside.

"What?" Was he laughing at me? I didn't know whether to be offended or not.

"I never met a woman who got turned on by thumbs. I'm

laughing at you because I know you're kidding, and at myself for falling for it."

"I'm not kidding."

Urgency in my tone reignited his laughter. He studied my face closely as he sobered. "You've already seen most of me. At the pool and the other day at Jessup." We both smiled at our wine glasses for a long moment. "You like remembering that, do you?" he asked. "We almost got run down and you smile thinking about it."

I focused on my glass. "I didn't know that was you at the pool. But I remember exactly how those arms and shoulders looked. At Jessup, I was nervous about how you would react to my horning in on your morning ritual. Were you irritated when you saw me?"

His dark eyes were playful. "I thought, 'She's here for me. I'm going to get her. Be cool, man. Don't scare her off.' "

My mouth gaped and his smile broadened.

The bold statement and his smug smile pricked my temper. "No way are you going to *get me*."

"You're here."

"Not for the reason you're thinking."

"You don't have any idea what I'm thinking."

"Yeah, right." I oozed sarcasm.

His eyes narrowed and remained fixed on my face. "You aren't as subtle as you think, Dewhurst. Your amateur standing is obvious. In this context there are two kinds of women: those who have and those who haven't. I figure maybe you're ready to cross over and I happen to," he smiled and arched his brows, "have the best thumbs."

"Wrong." I straightened so abruptly, I nearly spilled my wine again. "If this is an example of your detecting skill, Wills, maybe you should consider another line of work."

"We'll see." His smile was an open taunt. Moving slowly,

he leaned forward and put his wine glass on the table in front of us. Deliberately, watching me closely, he unbuttoned the cuff of one of his sleeves and began folding it up.

Warmed by the wine and mesmerized by his movements, I scarcely breathed as he cuffed the sleeve to expose an impressive forearm.

Without thinking, I whispered, "Let me see the inside of your elbow."

Obediently, he bent his arm back and flexed. I stared, admiring him without a word. As if he knew what I was thinking, he began rolling up the other sleeve. His eyes never left mine as my glance flitted from his face to his marvelous forearms and back. I had never seen anything more beautiful, and I am a connoisseur of forearms.

He leaned to take my glass, which was again tipping dangerously close to a spill, and placed it on the table next to his own. He caught my upper arms and pulled me closer. I glared, hoping to ward him off, but I could not make myself struggle or complain.

Neither of us closed our eyes as he brushed his lips over mine. He grinned, teasing me again. I tossed my head and turned my face away from him. He took what I gave and nibbled little kisses from my temple down my jaw line, easing his way to my throat.

Oh, lord, but I liked being kissed that way . . . by him. I was usually very particular about intimacy, but this man did not wait for permission and obviously wasn't intimidated by my pretended lack of interest. In fact, he seemed to disregard my non-response entirely.

I sat stiffly erect for several seconds, letting him nibble, before I realized I was gulping air in short, quick spurts without exhaling. Then his lips crawled to my mouth.

More than anything, I wanted to touch the muscles flexing

in his upper arms. Almost angrily, I allowed my fingers to trace those bunching biceps to his shoulders. Slowly, moving as if they were independent of my will, my wandering fingers found their way around his neck. When they encountered warm flesh, he caught my waist in both hands, lifted and pressed my body to his.

His marvelous mouth worried my bottom lip and I seemed to stop breathing altogether, yet I couldn't make myself interrupt the kissing long enough to inhale. When, finally, my lungs filled, making my chest heave against his, his breath quickened.

"Somethin' in the way she moves . . ." James Taylor crooned in the background.

Jim withdrew his mouth a little distance as I again massaged his marvelous biceps. Our faces mere inches apart, he watched me gasp for air. I stared at his lips until he lowered them again, devouring mine. His tongue encroached and I yielded, tilting my head to maintain the seal with his mouth. I felt disoriented as I opened, welcoming his ruthless invasion. This bewitchment had never happened before, this debilitating desire to have a man closer . . . and closer . . . then closer still. What was happening? What had become of my usual reserve?

*No more wine,* I admonished silently, my mouth eagerly inviting his. Surely I couldn't blame my wild behavior on the wine. I'd only taken a few sips.

His upper arms bunched as he leaned away and pulled me along, positioning me across his lap. His taunting tongue came and went at will and I wrapped my arms more tightly around him. With no conscious permission, my body shifted, undulating against his. His hand at my waist caught a fistful of shirt and tugged it out of the waist of my slacks. Gasping, I pushed away from him.

"Wait." My voice was husky. I didn't want him to stop. What, then? "I want to watch your face when you . . . when you . . . look at me."

He looked puzzled. I got to my knees beside him, facing him, then rolled sideways onto one hip and leaned across his lap again.

Getting the idea, he smiled and propped one ankle on his other knee, providing a back for me to rest against. I had no idea what I was doing or why, but I felt happy that he grasped and even assisted my effort.

Face to face, we began kissing again. Slowly, as his tongue ran sorties into my eager mouth, he set a hand to unbuttoning my shirt. Aware of what was happening, I didn't object. With perverse curiosity, I leaned back to watch his face as he got his first view of the swell of my breasts above my bra.

"As you can see," he said, his voice husky, "you're not the only one who gets turned on by anatomical mounds." Both hands on my waist, he tugged me closer.

His mouth was warm, his skin feverish, as he kissed the swells, but I put my hands on his chest and pushed away as he fumbled with the closer on the back of my bra.

"Jim." My voice had an unfamiliar breathless quality. "I'm not going to have sex with you. Do you understand what I'm saying?"

"Yes." He sounded breathless, too. "This train's running full throttle. You say stop, we stop. You don't, we don't. Do you understand what I'm saying?"

Those wise little hairs on the back of my neck bristled another warning. I felt threatened, not so much by the man in my arms as by my own emerging passion. I kept my hands firmly planted at his chest, thinking. At that precise moment, the oven timer began its insistent buzz.

Jim smiled. "Good." Grasping my shoulders, he pushed

me off of his lap, then hesitated long enough to steady me before he stood. "Let's go fuel up."

Abandoned, I buttoned my shirt, feeling confused and curious and more than a little frustrated.

While he put dressing on the salad and served plates of lasagna, I set two places at the dining table. He was not at all self-conscious about what had just happened between us, and I marveled at his ease.

Moving on his command, I removed garlic bread from the oven and put it in a serving basket.

"Wine, tea or water?" he asked.

At his direction, I fixed us both ice water as he refilled the wine glasses.

He held my chair at the table but I didn't risk a look at his face as I took it.

"What's this preoccupation you have with muscles?" he asked as we began to eat. It was a semi-safe topic and I had finally gotten my thready breathing back to normal. I would be all right if I kept my eyes and mind focused on the food in front of me.

"In school, I could pretty much tell what sport an athlete played by his physique," I said. "It got so friends would bring people by to test me, to see if I could tell what a person did by looking at him . . . or her."

"Could you?"

"Usually."

"How?"

"By the development of their bodies. Their muscles. Tennis players often have one arm and shoulder bigger than the other. Swimmers are inclined to long, loose muscles that quiver. Basketball players have long, firm muscles. Baseball players have gorgeous forearms but they're frequently broad across the beam. It's from all the bench sitting, I guess."

He laughed, drawing my attention to his dark, shimmering eyes. "How about football players and wrestlers?" His gaze held mine even when I tried to break free.

"Linemen are easy. They've got big calves and are often pigeon-toed, like you. I figured you for an offensive lineman. A guard or center. You're substantially built but not gargantuan like a tackle or a defensive lineman. That toeing-in seems to give a guy more thrust."

His approving smile warmed my insides. "I played center and linebacker."

Hating my own eager responses to him, I began prattling to cover the renegade self-consciousness.

"Backs—defensive or offensive—frequently have legs like frogs with big thighs and smaller calves. Real fast guys usually have the frog legs and fragile-looking ankles." I drew a shuddering breath and hurried on, afraid to let him speak or to look at him again.

"Wrestlers are built like football players, except they're shorter. Gymnasts look a lot like wrestlers but with thinner necks." I stopped talking long enough to take another bite of lasagna. "You were right. Your mother's lasagna is terrific."

"Are you afraid you might be frigid?" Wills asked the question softly.

The lasagna hung in my throat. I slurped a quick drink of water. When I finally felt steady enough to respond, I shook my head. "No. Why? Do I seem cold to you?"

He laughed out loud, then looked down at his plate and shook his head. He seemed to want me to continue, so I did, trying not to sound defensive.

"Mom and I had our sex talk when I was eight years old. I've had a lot of time to get comfortable with the concept. Mom once said she'd never met a woman who liked sex her first time. She said sex for women was more of an acquired taste, like wine." I fingered the wine glass in front of me.

"Your mother told you that?"

I nodded without raising my eyes from the glass.

"And you bought it?"

"I didn't just take her word for it. I conducted surveys of my own."

I grinned sheepishly at the laughter in his voice as he said, "Oh yeah? Where was that?"

"I sort of polled friends in high school informally. Ones who knew. Later, girls in my freshman dorm, women in the sorority house, and finally, my housemates." I shot him a warning look. "My findings verified Mom's."

Jim's smile withered, so I hurried on, not allowing him an opportunity to probe any deeper into that sensitive subject.

"She also said having sex just once with someone wouldn't be satisfactory, that it was better for a woman to wait until she was going to sleep with the same person regularly before she indulged." I shrugged, again without looking at him. "It made sense to me."

"So, didn't you ever go steady?"

"Sure, but never with a guy who met my requirements or, really, anyone who made me curious."

"What do you mean?"

"I dated one guy because I couldn't beat him at tennis. We played for blood and we played all the time. I dated another one because he was funny. He had a great personality." I felt a little sad at that memory before I looked back at Wills. "But he was homely. I couldn't ever bring myself to kiss him.

"There was Larry, who was a great dancer, athletic and handsome, but dumb as a post."

Wills put his fork down but didn't interrupt.

"Steven is ambitious, athletic and nice-looking. He's real smart too." I didn't know why I hesitated.

"How about his thumbs?" Jim's teasing grin made me wince.

"Marginal. But it's Steven's attitude that's the real turnoff. He categorizes everything, including people—particularly women."

"But you've been dating him exclusively?"

"It's better that way. He's stodgy but polite, always has plenty of money and . . ."

"What?" Wills prodded when I faltered again.

I stared at the table. "Actually, the best thing about Steven is Riley Wedge. When Wedge calls next fall, I don't want any strings holding me here. I hadn't actually thought this through. I'd probably better patch things up with Steven."

Wills cleared his throat, interrupting my private contemplation and luring me back. "Didn't any of these steadies ever try to get you into the sack?"

"Sure. What do you think?" I knew that sounded defensive and I raised my eyebrows in mock surprise. "My celibacy, Wills, has *not* been a lack of opportunity. It has been—and continues to be—a conscious choice."

A mischievous grin stole across his face and I braced myself for whatever was coming.

"In this mix of men and attributes, Jancy, describe me."

The question lightened the moment and I gave him an intentionally sinister laugh as I considered it. I took a moment, jabbing a fork at my food, reluctant to look at him. "You," I emphasized the word, "could be dangerous."

"Go on."

I risked a look and grinned at him as I hatched a new idea. "You have good conformation. You're especially strong through the withers. . . ."

"Are you describing me or a horse?" His teasing tone made me feel even more light-hearted.

"Whatever." I waved a hand as if his question weren't worth serious consideration. "You've got a strong self-image, which borders on the excessive. When the subject is music or sports or women or anything, so far, you don't feel the need to lecture or wax eloquently, you just say what you think. In many ways, you are really quite refreshing."

I looked directly at him and frowned. "I thought you might be frugal. I cannot abide a stingy man." Entertaining a new thought, I eyed him critically. "Actually, you still haven't really bought me anything."

"Dinner at Cheeries."

"Okay." I nodded, conceding the point. "Walking is important to me. I have to walk off nerves and mads and sorrow. At the house the other night, when you asked if I wanted to go for a walk, that was a stroke of genius. I didn't even know it before, but I needed to walk off all that anxiety."

I paused to give him a chance to jump into the conversation, but he made no attempt to speak, so I continued, afraid of getting flustered if there were too much quiet. "But we're still new. You may be a tightwad or a liar or a ladies' man or an alcoholic or all of the above."

"And would any of those make a difference?"

I felt almost hopeful. "Yes. If you are any of those, I could afford to hang out with you without getting involved. So, are you?"

"Maybe, maybe not." He laughed, then grew serious again. "I haven't lied to you, but I have quibbled about something."

I regarded him curiously and felt my smile dwindling.

"Remember my asking you about Steven Carruthers?"

"Yes. You said the SBI does security checks on people who are taking the bar exam."

"Right. And that's true. But I don't do those. I wanted you to tell me about Carruthers so I could see how you looked and hear how you sounded when you talked about him."

Before I could pursue that subject, Wills stood abruptly and began clearing our dishes. It didn't look to me like either of us had finished, but I picked up the bread basket and salad bowl and followed him to the kitchen.

"You were right about your mother's lasagna." I gave him an uncertain smile when he looked pointedly at my plate, where most of my serving remained uneaten.

Covering another awkward moment, I went to the sink to rinse dishes for the dishwasher. After that, I scraped the leftover lasagna into a smaller container and slipped the crusted pan into soapy water to soak.

Jim wiped the counters, then eased up close behind me at the sink. He tossed the sponge into the water and put his hands on the small of my back. He rubbed my lower back a moment, which felt insanely good, before his thick fingers followed my waist from back to front. His arms surrounded me as he splayed his warm hands on my midriff and kissed the back of my neck. Chill bumps raked my arms and my breath came in little gasps.

I should leave and would have, if my hands hadn't been covered with suds. Then I got an idea.

Turning in his arms, I patted handfuls of bubbles on either side of his face.

Laughing, ignoring the bubbles, he lowered his mouth to mine. I wrapped my arms around his shoulders and pulled myself up tight against him, marvelously aware of his thighs against my thighs, his stomach and chest aligned with mine, his breath coming in short, heavy pulls.

I was genuinely surprised that his intensity again aroused passion in me I had not experienced before. I didn't think I could blame a few sips of wine before dinner for my feelings or my behavior. The excitement of his nearness effectively canceled my ability to think, yet I didn't feel at all frightened.

He held me tight, his mouth against my ear, and murmured. "I can't seem to get close enough to you. I can't breathe deeply enough to fill up on the scent of you."

"My perfume?"

"Your hair. It smells like outdoors, like clothes on the clothesline in the sunshine. Your body smells sweet, and look how we fit. Perfectly. Can you feel how well we fit?" I hummed unspoken agreement as he continued. "We talk easily. About everything. We laugh at the same things. I want to know you. I want to touch you and taste every inch of your warm, sweet body."

He stopped speaking and leaned his head back to study my face. "At the same time, I'm scared to death about you and for you. I've never felt this . . . this turbulence. It's like trying to hold onto your temper when you feel it slipping out of control. You don't want to let it go. You don't want to scare anyone."

Seeing the intensity in his face, I nodded. I did understand.

He plunged ahead. "This excitement, this emotional spike . . . it's new to me. I'm afraid to turn it loose, afraid I'll scare you. Hell, I'm afraid I'll scare me."

I nodded again almost imperceptibly. It felt as if we were working with dangerous explosives—delicate, volatile elements that must be handled very, very carefully.

He turned me, wrapped one arm around my waist and one behind my knees, lifted me easily and carried me to the living room. He placed me on the sofa, then turned his back and walked away.

My gaze followed, but he avoided looking at me.

Without allowing me to see his face, he stoked the fire and added logs. Then, drawing a deep breath, he pivoted to face me again, his expression pleasant but controlled. "Would you like a tour of the house? Do you want to see the upstairs?"

Looking him in the eye, I shook my head no.

"You don't want to see my bedroom?"

I shook my head again and gave him a wordless, apologetic smile. The imagined explosives might be more unstable, detonate more readily in a bedroom.

"Jancy, you don't have to be afraid to go to bed with me." His words were like a caress, reassuring and coaxing. "We'll take it slow. I won't hurt you. I promise. You'll be safe. No communicable diseases. No bedbugs."

"No, thanks."

"What are you afraid of?"

I frowned at him for a minute, contemplating. "I'm not afraid of the physical part. I've waited mostly because I just wasn't interested enough to go to the trouble to learn."

"What then?"

"What I am afraid of is getting trapped. Emotionally. Psychologically. What if it turns out I'm not a 'wham, bam, thank you ma'am' kind of woman? What if I can't walk away and be me anymore?

"I'm not going to sleep with someone I don't love, and psychologically, I'm afraid to sleep with someone I could."

He remained on his feet in front of the fire, gazing down across the coffee table at me as I stayed on the sofa. "Someone you could *love?*"

I gave an awkward half-laugh. I had already said more

than I had intended. "Are you trying to confuse the already complex?"

He snorted an answering half laugh. "We've got a dilemma here." He hesitated, as if thinking. Then his uncertain look became resolve. "I've lost it all with you, Jancy—my dignity, my self-esteem, my intellect. It's all gone. I feel like I've been run over by a truck. And, woman, I didn't even see it coming."

"It sounds painful."

He cringed. "You have no idea." He looked at me, then at my reflection in the glass coffee table. "Benedict knew. He had the same problem. He tried to tell me."

My heart felt as if it had dropped into my stomach. "No, Jim. Ansel and I had nothing like this."

"You could have, if you'd given in, even a little."

"Why are you saying that? I loved Ansel, but there wasn't any romance."

Wills regarded me critically. "You owned the man's soul and I think you damn well knew it."

I had never admitted anything of the kind, even to myself. I sighed and frowned at the floor. "Maybe I suspected something." I glanced at him. "But you know what a coward I am." He started to protest but I hurried on to prevent it. "Ansel was cowardly, too. That made me mad. I cannot abide cowardice in others because I'm such a chicken myself."

Jim regarded me with disbelief. "You proved your courage when you went after the intruder with the broom."

"That was no intruder." I hesitated, wondering if I should tell him about my afternoon's activities, then decided I probably should. "But . . . but today I was brave. I'm learning about courage. I think maybe I'm learning it from you."

He smiled at me, then looked curious. "Brave about what?"

"I wanted to help with your investigation, but I felt intimidated by my own fear. Today I overcame that—a little of it, at least. I went to see Jason Trout. I even nosed around their house. Then I went to see his sister, Maggie."

The idle curiosity on Wills' face changed to concern, then to thinly veiled anger. "How did you happen to see them?" He asked the question as he paced to one of the accent chairs and sank onto its edge. He leaned forward, elbows on his knees, hands clasped tightly.

"I called on Jason at his house." I watched Jim carefully, wondering at his suddenly calm facade.

Slowly, thoroughly, with his prompting, I recounted the afternoon's conversations, first with Jason Trout, then with Maggie. I included details, particularly the part about Thom Leek.

Wills debriefed me impersonally, as I realized he had been trained to do, wringing every detail out of my memory.

"Don't do that again," he said finally.

"But what they said confirms your theory, if it's Patsy, doesn't it?"

"Don't go off on your own like that again."

"How does my talking to those two kids injure you?"

He stood and glared down at me. "Jancy, this is not a game." He enunciated each word, his eyes hard on my face. "People have died, murdered by someone who kills with bare hands. This killer is emotionally or mentally unstable. Success is feeding that insanity. You have to understand. If you pry into the killer's lair, if you threaten exposure, this maniac may come after you. This person is prowling around now, deciding who has offended. Whom to destroy next."

Moving so quickly he startled me, he took both my hands, pulled me up from the sofa and wrapped my body roughly against his own. "This is the only place I feel like you're safe." His whispered words were as intense as his grip. "Right here, while I'm holding you. Don't scare me. Don't take chances. Go to work. Go home. Lock your doors, in your car and in the house.

"I can get this killer, honey. I can get the evidence we need, but I can't do it if I'm distracted. I can't be worrying about you." He backed off a step, caught my face between his thick hands and stared at me. "I don't expect you to know what I'm talking about, but you have to trust me."

He sounded like he was apologizing. I returned his intense gaze, my heart pounding. "But I do know, Jim. I can feel your heart. It feels like an echo of all the commotion going on inside me. Feel." Without thinking, I guided his hand to my midriff and placed it in front of my ribs, where I knew he could feel my heart thrumming to the same rhythm as his own.

"Beat for beat." He laughed, still gripping my chin with one hand. He pressed his forehead against mine. "I can get this killer," he repeated, "but I have to have all my faculties. I have to be able to focus. To do that, Jancy, I have to know you're safe. I have a solid theory, but it takes time to prove it, to track down the evidence we need. You have to give me that time. Do you understand?"

I nodded but didn't attempt to speak.

He had teased about the dog and the car attack and the gunshots, made light of things normally taken seriously. Those things had frightened him, not out of fear for his own safety, but for mine. I did understand. Finally.

I patted his cheek, traced his features with my fingertips, then ran those fingers around my own mouth. "Did you shave before you went to Bailey's?"

He regarded me oddly, and I could see the tension leach

from his face in advance of the slow, familiar smile. "I went from the office. I didn't have time. Why?"

"I've got a little whisker burn."

"Sorry."

"I like it. It'll give me something to remember you by."

He grinned. "Well now, I think we can do a whole lot better than that." Locking his arms around my shoulders, he rubbed his stubbly chin round and round my mouth. He kissed me once, then again, and again, each kiss more intense than the last. When he worked his tongue into my mouth, he lifted me off my feet and kissed me breathless.

Locked in his arms, I held still long enough to be sure my voice was steady before I said, "Will you take me back to my car now?"

"Now?" He looked surprised, but continued to hold onto me.

I nodded, trying to look more resolute than I felt, but I needed to get out of there. Take a step back to reconnoiter.

"Am I scaring you?" he asked.

I laughed and shook my head before paraphrasing. "I say stop, we stop."

He nodded and lowered my feet to the floor, then playfully pushed me onto the sofa. He picked up my shoes, sat on the coffee table facing me, carefully placed each of my feet in its respective shoe and tied the laces. When he finished, he held the last foot a moment with both hands, then smiled, patted my ankle and went to get our coats.

Relief and sharp disappointment warred inside me.

# *Chapter Thirteen*

Tuesday afternoon, as I read over an assault report in the sheriff's office, Patsy cooed sarcastically, "I hear you're dating Jim Wills."

I acknowledged I'd heard without confirming or denying the statement. I glanced up to see Pat watching me. Clearly the dispatcher was fishing for more of a response. Also, she didn't mention my visit to her home. Apparently Jason hadn't had a chance to tell her, or maybe he chose not to.

Patsy prodded my silence. "He's a real piece of work, isn't he? Wills?"

I hummed another non-answer.

"I've thought about taking him up on his offers a time or two myself."

That surprised me.

"Aren't those skylights fascinating? And the way he loves a roaring fire in that fireplace. He sure knows how to stoke those fires in a girl, too, doesn't he?" Not to be ignored this time, she repeated, "Doesn't he?"

Caught off-balance by the thought of Jim hustling Patsy, I mumbled, "I . . . wouldn't know." I laid the report back on the bar.

"She's just funnin' you." I hadn't seen Gary, who strode to the counter. He looked concerned by the exchange. I gave him a patient smile, certain that he meant well.

The phone rang. Pat answered, listened and became animated as she asked several questions. "When and how did you get this information?" There was a brief pause as she listened to the caller. "Where is he now?" Another delay. "Tell him to stay put. I'll send someone, quick as I can. Wait. Hold a minute, will you?"

Putting the telephone on hold, Pat turned to the radio and tried to raise the sheriff in his unit. There was no response.

"Unit Two." Her voice rose a third as she tried Wheeler, again and again. The undersheriff wasn't answering, either. "Damn."

Gary fairly danced with excitement. "What is it?"

"A witness in the Crook case." Pat's words tumbled over each other as she spoke, her voice shrill. "A long-haul trucker, just got home. He saw a vehicle out on the Effinger place early the Friday Senator Crook died. We need to follow up."

She sounded genuinely excited about this possible breakthrough. No killer would be that enthusiastic about information that might lead to her. I felt washed with relief.

Gary's intensity burst. "Let me go, Pat. Let me take the call."

Regarding him as if he'd asked to do open-heart surgery, she shook her head. "No, Spence. Not with that bad leg."

"Pat, this is fate. It's an opportunity to get me out of this office and into some real police work. You've got to let me take this."

"You'd have to meet him at Legends Truck Stop, all the way out by Spires."

"My pickup's back and in good shape." His limp scarcely noticeable, he paced to the outer door. "I'm practically gone already."

"I don't know what the sheriff will say, my sending you all the way out there in your condition. Alone."

The deputy's eyes darted to the only other person in the room. "Jancy! Jancy, you'll go with me, right?"

I couldn't resist his excitement. My work was done for the day. What danger could there be in interviewing a witness? This could be a break in the case and a page one story. Plus, I'd be safe with Gary, particularly now that Patsy was no longer a suspect.

"Why not?"

Spence darted back to the counter and grabbed my arm. We bolted to the exit before Pat could change her mind.

"What's his name?" Spence yelled back over his shoulder.

"Gypson. David Gypson."

When they'd gone, clattering down the stairs, Patsy turned back to the switchboard and reopened the line to the caller on hold.

"Thanks, Sam. You're timing is perfect. I had a little problem, but you helped me solve it. You Legends folks are great people for helping a girl out of a bind."

Sheriff Roundtree brought Agent Wills to his office about four o'clock to discuss which evidence and what testimony might be ready to take to the D.A. in the ribbon killings.

"Bring us some coffee, will you, Pat?" He glanced around. "Where's Spence?"

"On a call."

Roundtree hesitated in the doorway and turned back to face her. "What call?"

"Someone with a lead on the Crook thing."

"And you sent Spence?"

"I couldn't raise you or Wheeler, and everyone else was doing one thing or another."

Wills, who had preceded Roundtree into the inner office, reappeared, regarding Patsy curiously. She flashed him a haughty smile, then turned solemn as she again faced the sheriff.

"They left twenty-, twenty-five minutes ago." She emphasized "they."

"They who?" Wills asked before the sheriff could speak.

"He and Jancy, of course." She tossed the words out lightly, but her eyes fastened on Wills' face.

Roundtree's voice boomed. "What is this, amateur night? Is he in his unit?"

Pat nodded meekly as if ashamed of herself.

"Call the S.O.B."

She attempted the call. When she got no response, she looked back at the sheriff.

"He probably forgot to turn it on. Sheriff, you don't let Spence out of here often enough to get him properly trained." She hesitated, giving her next words emphasis. "I'm almost sure he's trainable."

Wills glared at her. "Where are they going?"

"Let me see." Patsy stalled, flipping through a notebook at her desk, pretending to search for the afternoon's lone call. As Wills walked around the counter to assist, she found it. "Legends Truck Stop."

"Out at Spires?" Roundtree bellowed with disbelief. "Damn it, Pat."

Wills continued glaring at the seemingly contrite dispatcher. "Does Spence have a beeper?"

Roundtree brightened. "Give him a buzz."

Patsy flipped a switch. A beeper whined from the coffee room.

"Hell," the sheriff shouted.

"Sheriff Roundtree," Pat kept her voice calm, apparently meant to placate him, "Jancy's got a lot of savvy. She'll watch out for him. Those two have been spoiling for a little time alone together." She shot a meaningful look at Wills.

Roundtree stormed into his office and slammed the door. Patsy swiveled around in her chair to look straight at Jim and gave him a wicked little smile.

He set his mouth in a grim line and was halfway down the stairs when he turned and trotted back up. "Let me see the call box."

Patsy handed him the box, which reflected a call from Legends at three forty-three. "Satisfied, lover?"

Wordlessly, he hurried out and down the stairs.

"I'd love to give you a hand, sweetheart, if I could." Patsy whispered under her breath, opening and closing her hands as if kneading something. "Maybe I'll catch up with you later, you handsome devil."

Wills stopped at the courthouse door to scan the *Clarion* lot. Jancy's car sat in its usual place. He called the newspaper from his car as he drove toward the highway.

"Ms. Dewhurst is out," the operator said. "Can I take a message?"

He asked for Melchoir.

"If Jancy calls in, have her call the SBI office and tell them to relay the call to Agent Wills."

"Is Jance in trouble?" Melchoir sounded curious but not alarmed.

"I sure as hell hope not."

Wills didn't like to run code three, but he used lights and siren as he raced out the old highway and crossed the line into deeply wooded Lowrimore County.

Legends was far enough away to give him time to think. What would he say to her? What could he say? He had explained how things were. He thought she understood. He'd look foolish racing all the way over here.

He didn't care.

He was a professional law enforcement officer who was supposed to be prepping a murder case, not chasing around like some lovesick bovine.

Remembering the shotgun rigged in the Leopolds' cabin, he floor-boarded the accelerator.

He knew Patsy's implication about Spence and Jancy wanting time alone was a lie, but the words tormented him as he drove.

Forty minutes later, Wills felt an overwhelming surge of relief when he spotted Spence's pickup truck in Legends' lot. He wheeled his car in near the deputy's vehicle.

He took his time walking to the restaurant, searching for the right words. He had no excuse. He was there, all the way out at Spires, for one reason: he had to see her face, to assure himself she was safe. He couldn't think beyond that.

He stepped inside the sprawling cafe, looked around and nodded to a trucker he recognized. He didn't see Deputy Spence or Dewhurst. He went into the men's room. No sign of Spence.

Back in the restaurant, a waitress sauntered up to him. "Help you?"

"I'm looking for a couple who came in here a little while ago. A deputy sheriff and a young woman."

"From Bishop County? Nice looking? Smiled a lot?"

Wills nodded, defeated.

"They met Davy Gypson. They loaded up and left in his tractor."

"Where were they going?"

She shrugged and regarded him oddly. "They didn't say."

"Does Gypson make short runs or long ones?"

"A couple of hours or a week. He wasn't hauling no trailer. He'll likely be back this evenin'. Can I get something for ya?"

Wills shook his head, took a deep breath and swiped both hands through his short-cropped hair, front to back.

One of several young thugs bumped him, then hackled as if spoiling for a fight. Wills clenched his jaw, then his fists at his sides. He wasn't in a forgiving frame of mind. The young man glared at him for a heartbeat, then wilted and stood clear as the angry agent strode forward.

"Is all this interest personal or professional?" The familiar voice boomed as Wills paced back from the far windows, staring at the floor, clenching and unclenching his jaw and fists.

He looked up at Sheriff Roundtree and exhaled, shaking his head. "Both."

Roundtree indicated they should sit and called to the waitress. "Two coffees."

Reluctantly, Wills slid into the booth.

"She's all right." Roundtree's voice was soothing. "Gary'll watch out for her."

Jim gave him a weary look. "He's too stupid to watch out for her."

"Maybe, but Jancy's not stupid."

"No," Wills agreed, shaking his head, "she's just naive."

Roundtree cleared his throat and tried again. "Wills, he's probably carrying a weapon. He's a damn good shot. He'd defend her with his life."

Wills snorted and looked pained. "That's probably so, but it's not a lot of comfort to think if one of them turns up dead, the other one will too."

The ragtag bunch of thugs caught Wills' attention again. They stood at a pinball machine, talking loud and tough and eyeballing him. He squinted at them. "What're those punks looking at? Do you know them?"

Roundtree glanced at the cluster of kids. "Just some local hooligans. Wills, what's happened to you? You've got a reputation for being cool under fire, the hotter the better."

Wills slumped in the booth. "That was before Dewhurst busted into my life. It's her. She's turning me upside-down and wrong-side out." He looked up, his eyes pleading. "I want to know where she is. I want to know now." He let his gaze slide to his fists braced on top of the table. His voice dropped as he lowered his head. "I need to know she's all right."

"She is all right, Jimbo."

Wills' eyes flashed. "What makes you think so? You've seen what this killer is capable of doing."

"But we haven't had a single woman victim."

"Not yet."

"Why do you think the killer would change now?"

"Because Jancy's been asking too many questions, talking to too many people."

Roundtree chuckled. "It may have put her in jeopardy a time or two, Jim, but it hasn't got her dead yet and Sis has always asked way too many questions."

"She's nosing too close this time."

Roundtree's smile dissolved to a frown. "What do you mean? Does Jancy have a suspect?"

"Yes. And so do I. And, as it turns out, our suspects are the same person."

The sheriff folded his arms over his chest. "I figured if you were zeroing in on someone, you'd talk to me. You usually do."

"It's never been someone this close to you before."

"You suspect one of my people?" Roundtree attempted a

smile. "Don't be simple-minded, son. It isn't." There was a long silence. Roundtree muttered again, more to himself than to Wills. "It isn't." He looked thoughtful. "Do you think it's Spence? Is that what's got you in such a flap? Wills, it isn't Spence. I give you my word it's not."

"You're right. It's not."

"Tell me who you think it is, then."

"If I do, you might tip my hand before I'm ready."

"Son, I've had the highest national security clearance they give—during wartime."

Staring at the floor, Wills shook his head. "I'm going to call in, let the office know where I am, just in case."

Roundtree growled, "You're puttin' yourself through all this for nothing. I know you've seen people get crazy like you're doin' with grief or frustration. Maybe you ought to wonder more about why you've been pulled off the scent, following this red herring all the way out here."

Jim slid out of the booth, then paused to eye the sheriff. "You're right. I need to get my concentration back." He took a deep breath. "And I will, just as soon as Dewhurst is where I can see her."

There was no word at the SBI office. Wills called in at twenty minutes before and twenty minutes after the hour, every hour. Nothing.

Shortly after nine p.m., a tractor without a trailer pulled into the parking lot.

Spence opened the passenger side door and climbed awkwardly to the ground, then waited to help me down.

"Hi," I said, surprised to see Wills and Roundtree emerge from the truck stop. Wills was clenching his fists as if trying to get himself under control. Seeing their faces, I got serious in a hurry. "What's wrong?"

Wills stepped in front of me. He looked like he was making a supreme effort not to explode. "Ms. Dewhurst," he said coldly, "you are interfering with a police investigation. You will cease and desist or I will arrest you for obstruction of justice."

"You're going to arrest me?" I stared at him.

"That's right. I can file the obstruction charge or haul you into protective custody if I feel the situation warrants it. You, Ms. Dewhurst, obviously have problems with authority."

The hair on the back of my neck bristled. "And you, Agent Wills, are having identity problems if you think you have any authority over me."

"Am I going to have to arrest you, then?"

"You wouldn't dare."

"Don't bet on it."

Suddenly I was incensed. "What, so Pat can entertain the guys with lurid tales of my strip search? I guarantee arresting me will be your last official act, hot shot."

Wills' eyes narrowed. "The governor's given me full authority to take any steps I deem necessary in this matter. Am I going to have to lock you up?" His face was chiseled in anger as we glowered at one another.

"Wills, it wasn't her fault," Spence stammered.

Wills turned his fury on the deputy. "And you!" His eyes shot daggers. "If you ever hope to become a legitimate law enforcement officer, Deputy, you'd damn well better learn how to conduct yourself and an investigation by the book."

"Don't you want to know what we found out?" I interrupted in an effort to keep things from escalating. It occurred to me that eventually we might all be embarrassed about this big public scene.

"Sheriff Roundtree will debrief you both." Wills set a hard stare on Spence. "Deputy, I'll expect your written report on my desk first thing in the morning. That's eight a.m., mister."

Without another look at anyone else, including me, Agent Wills turned on his heel, stormed to his car, got in and peeled out of the lot.

# Chapter Fourteen

"What's going on?" Ron Melchoir nailed me with an accusing look when I walked into the office Wednesday morning. "The governor's office called Bryce DeWitt early. Asked him to take you off the ribbon thing. Said you'd interfered with the investigation."

I hadn't slept well, furious with Jim one moment, forgiving him the next, then vowing never to see or speak to him again. After tossing and turning all night, this new little glitch so early in the day galled me to the core.

"Since when do politicians dictate who covers what story?" I spat the words. Melchoir leaned back in his chair, putting a little more distance between us. I pressed my advantage. "Is the *Clarion* going with managed news now?"

He looked embarrassed. "It's just that I thought you had Wills under your thumb."

"Obviously not." Dismissing him, I marched to my desk. Then I sat there and brooded. When that didn't seem to get me anywhere, I tried to think of a more productive activity that would at least get my mind off Wills and that ugly exchange in the parking lot. I phoned the university health sciences center, where I spoke with the director about mono on campus. By pursuing that story, I could divert my attention without getting completely off the subject, and flesh out my feature for Sunday.

I made notes of people I needed to call later to follow up

on my idea of tracing dollars from one taxpayer to the university. I had mentioned the idea to Maggie Trout as a ruse, but later decided the idea might make a story.

About nine-thirty, calmed and resolute, I walked over to the courthouse to run my regular beat.

In the election board office, John Denman grinned at me. "My nephew Lance, the Hollywood stunt man, is going to be in town for homecoming November sixth. I'm reserving you a full hour for an interview."

I gave him a quick buss on the cheek and thanked him. Not just for the story lead. He had brightened my day. At least I hadn't screwed up all my sources.

I bypassed the second floor, going on up to the third to touch base with the judges. Finally, sluggishly, I plodded to the D.A.'s office on two.

Assistant District Attorney Reese Mabry looked glad to see me. "How's the ribbon investigation coming along?"

The question hit me like a bucket of cold water, but I tried not to let my angst show. "Is it your case?"

He grunted affirmatively. "I've been waiting to hear from Wills all morning. I called, but they said he's in a conference." Mabry frowned at me, which set my neck bristling again.

"What?" I demanded. "Do you think he's using a rubber hose on someone?"

Reese lowered his voice. "How well do you know him, Dewhurst?"

"I recognize him when I see him." That was closer to the truth than I had realized. The bottom line I'd reached was that I didn't know the man nearly as well as I thought.

Reese got up and strolled around me to look out at the vacant receptionist's desk before he looked at me again, still sporting the frown. "The guy's always been kind of a cold fish, but lately he smiles and speaks. Tuesday, he called me by name."

"Maybe he was preoccupied before, or worried about doing well at his job."

"Yeah, right." The prosecutor grinned. "By the time Wills brings a case in here, it's bound so tight all we have to decide is how much time we want the bad guy to serve. Jim Wills' name on an investigator's sheet means a conviction. My win-loss record has skyrocketed in the last six months. Want to know why? I sign up for cases coming off his desk."

He winked. Usually when Mabry felt playful, which wasn't often, I smiled or winked back. This time I turned around and stalked out. I could hear him mutter as I left.

"Get one hard-nose straightened out and a friendly goes sour. It's a damn shame."

Patsy was alone in the sheriff's reception room when I finally dragged myself in there. Roundtree's door was open, his office dark. The dispatcher regarded me with practiced indifference. "People are looking for you."

"For me? Who?"

"Roundtree. Spence. Wills, I suppose." Patsy's bottom lip protruded and she shrugged.

Every ragged ending in my nervous system went on red alert. "Should I wait here?"

"You can if you want to, but they're over at Wills' office. They have questions for you, Missy."

"Are they mad?"

"They will be by the time you get there. They've been trying to track you down for an hour."

I raced down the stairs and across the narrow green belt to the annex. In trouble with all those guys at once was no small deal.

Mrs. Teeman peered over her reading glasses as I trotted

up the stairs to the SBI offices. When she saw me, the older woman smiled, nodded and buzzed the intercom. She didn't look mad. That was a relief. I patted my flyaway hair.

A young man in soiled clothes sat in the waiting area. He looked up and glowered as I walked to a chair. I tried a smile. He lowered his eyes without acknowledging it.

Having received no instructions from Mrs. Teeman, I sat, leaving an empty chair between myself and the young man. He kept glancing at me, but didn't say anything.

"What are you in for?" I asked, trying to sound pleasant.

He sized me up, then ducked his head again. I figured he wasn't going to answer when he mumbled something.

"What?" I asked.

"Nothin'."

"Good. I'm glad you're not in any trouble. I'm afraid maybe I am."

"Oh, yeah?" He shot me a quick glance. "What for?"

"Trying to help a friend."

He gave me a curious look. "That's funny, that's exactly what I was doin'."

I allowed a little silence to see if he would continue. He folded his hands together and leaned forward, bracing his elbows on his knees. "This friend of mine got himself hired to do a job." His voice was barely audible. "He needed some help. We was gonna get fifty bucks apiece for doin' not an hour's worth of work."

In an effort to demonstrate some interest, I gave him a subdued smile. "Doesn't sound legal, unless you're a doctor or a lawyer."

"Or maybe a plumber." He gave me a self-satisfied grin. "It wasn't exactly illegal. Guys do this kind of stuff all the time for free."

"What's that?"

"This woman he knows got dumped in some love triangle deal. She hired my buddy to beat up her lover boy and then unload him over at her place in Bishop."

"Did you know her name?"

"Nah. My bud had the details."

"She didn't want you to kill him or anything, did she?" I picked up a magazine, acting like I was only half paying attention.

"No. Nothing like that."

"So, what did you do with the fifty bucks?"

The man's eyes rounded. "No, no. I never got it. See, me and my bud and this other guy was supposed to be at Legends, that's a truck stop over in Lowrimore County. This old gal was going to make sure this dude showed up over there. She said he'd be wearing a suit and tie. A guy dressed up like that'd be easy to spot at Legends." He leaned back in his chair. "Well, we was there all afternoon. You might remember it. You come in with that deputy. Ain't that so?"

I nodded. "Yes, I was there."

"Anyway," he shrugged, getting back to his story, "no one who looked like the guy she described showed until late. You was gone by then. About quitting time, this guy in a suit comes in looking around. You could tell he was barely keeping a lid on it. When he don't find who he's looking for, he looks like he's gonna blow for sure.

"Now, looking at him, I knew this easy fifty bucks wasn't going to be all that easy. The suit didn't fool me. I mean, this guy had muscles on top of muscles. And he's pacing around there like he's in no mood to be messed with.

"My bud and me, we decide we could split the dough a little thinner and he calls a couple more guys we know to come help out. We're not pusses, but with five, some can

240

pound and some can rest and we can work him over longer that way."

Fascinated, I realized I was staring at the guy. He interrupted himself. "Say, you're not a cop or anything, are you?"

I shook my head, feeling a little queasy as I got a niggling suspicion about who might have orchestrated the scene at the truck stop. Had Patsy sent Gary and me to lure Wills and the sheriff? If so, why? My companion looked puzzled. He was waiting for an answer.

"No," I said. "Just because I'm not wearing handcuffs doesn't mean I've got friends here."

He seemed to breathe easier. "Good."

"So you only got part of the fifty dollars?"

"You're pretty interested in my money. I can't help you out myself, but I know a guy who makes bonds. He's high dollar, but he's there when you need 'im. Do you want me to give you his name?"

"I'm hoping I won't get that far." I glanced toward Mrs. Teeman, wondering if she was picking up on our conversation, but she appeared to be engrossed in her word processor. As I turned my attention back to the man in the waiting area, I noticed a shadow on the underside of the shade on the table lamp between us. I didn't see any need to mention it.

The guy hunched his shoulders. "Anyway, like I was sayin', this dude was fumin', walking around, spoiling to tear somebody's head off. He'd just been there a little while when this lawman, I think he might be sheriff over here, he comes strolling in. I'm figuring I'm lucky to be there 'cause if these two mix it up, that fight'll be worth seein'."

His eager look changed to sorrow. "But that ain't the way it played. Instead of a standoff, the lawman tried to calm the dude down.

"Now you can tell by this lawman's face, he's been in a

fight or two in his time. He's old but crusty and lookin' like he's a little nervous, too, peerin' all around. I can tell you right now, five of us wasn't going to be enough for them two, even at fifty bucks apiece. I don't have no health insurance and it looked to me like anyone taking on those two was going to be needin' serious coverage.

"I told my bud, get on the horn and call this thing off. He wasn't liking the looks of it neither, so he called and canceled.

"Today they sent a deputy out to my mom's house saying they was needin' to talk to me friendly, unless I don't want to come. Will I come? Here I am. My bud got here at nine o'clock. I come in at ten. This lady's the only one I seen so far, until you."

I nodded and tried to give him a reassuring smile. "Are you going to tell them everything?"

"Sure. I don't want no trouble with the law. I didn't do nothin' wrong. They don't come after you for listenin' about a job or for thinkin' it over."

"No, you're right." I needed time to think this through and figure out exactly what Jim was so mad about. "I don't think you did anything wrong either."

We fell silent for several minutes, listening to the muted clattering of the word processor. Patsy had set us all up—Wills, Roundtree, Davy Gypson, Spence and me—every one of us. But why? As far as I knew, there were no new corpses. If Patsy were the killer, what was she trying to prove with the truck stop scenario?

"Okay." The young man's voice in the silence made me jump. "Sorry."

I waved off his apology.

"So why're you here?" he asked.

"I think they want to ask me some questions about a truck

driver I know." Was Gypson in on the ruse? I didn't think so. He seemed like a down-home, good old country boy.

"Are you going to tell it?"

Good question. "Yes. Just like you. I didn't do anything wrong either."

The door to Wills' office opened. Gary Spence looked at me and couldn't bite back a smile. "Ms. Dewhurst, will you come in?" He spoke in his best radio voice.

The young guy beside me nodded, bolstering my confidence a little. "It don't look like they're too mad at you. Least that one ain't."

"Thanks." I smiled, but my stomach flipped into my throat.

Eight people filled Wills' office. A court reporter had his machine on a corner of the library table by the window. Wills, in the chair behind his desk, stood as I walked into the room.

"Ms. Dewhurst, I think you know everyone," he said. "You know Jerry, of course, who is making a record of this meeting. Agents Brown and Foxworthy—" I recognized the SBI agents from the adjoining offices, "—David Gypson, Deputy Spence, Sheriff Roundtree and, of course, Bryce DeWitt, who is here looking out for your interest and the *Clarion*'s."

I couldn't bring myself to look at Jim, but I glanced at and acknowledged everyone else.

"Sit here." Jim motioned me to sit in his chair behind the desk. He sauntered around it to lean against the window sill before he resumed speaking. "Do you know the man in the reception room?"

Jerry began pounding his machine, recording question and answer.

"No."

"You've never seen him before?"

"No, sir, I don't think so."

"You and he were having quite a conversation out there. What was your conversation about?"

"About being at Legends. You remember. You were there." I set a firm gaze on him. "By the way, how did you happen to be at Legends last night, Agent Wills?"

"I'll ask the questions, Ms. Dewhurst. You just answer them as concisely and accurately as you can. Do you understand what I'm saying?"

The familiar question shook my resolve and I looked at my hands folded in my lap. Did he remember saying those same words in a very different context the night we necked on his sofa? Was he repeating them to be cruel, or as a reminder? When I raised my eyes to his, I knew. He did remember. He had chosen those words intentionally.

"Yes. I do understand, Agent Wills. Perfectly."

"So?"

"Is that a question?" Somehow I felt like I'd get a little of my self-respect back by mocking him.

Wills glared, but I sat quietly. As the silence yawned through the room, I shifted my gaze to the carpet near the exit and waited. For what seemed like a full minute, no one spoke. Jerry had stopped clattering on his machine by the time Jim broke the silence.

"What exactly did Mr. Nichols—that's Mr. Nichols outside there—say to you?"

"Wills, I saw the bug on the lamp." I looked straight into his face, defying him. "Listen to your tape or whatever. You're wasting our time here. I have a noon deadline to make. Either ask me about something you need to know or I'm out of here."

Wills turned to look out the window. Muscles corded in his neck.

"Jancy?" The quiet voice came from David Gypson, the truck driver Spence and I had ridden with the night before.

Turning toward him, I bristled again, newly annoyed by Wills' self-centeredness. "Davy, I guess the Gestapo chief here made you give up your Missouri run, huh? The police probably don't realize it's costing you money to be a good citizen." I looked at Wills, who appeared to ignore the jab. "Have you told them what you saw the night Crook died?"

Gypson shook his head. "They had that other kid in here before. They haven't got to me yet."

"Well, if they ever do," I sniped, casting another dark look at Jim, "Wills can get on with his original read on this mess and we can all go home."

Wills turned an angry glower on Spence.

"I don't know what she's talking about," the deputy said. "I don't know what *read* she's talking about."

Wills drew a visual bead on the trucker. "Okay, Gypson, we're to you."

Gypson cleared his throat. "Sam at Legends called me the other night when I got in." He looked around the room at the various faces, then settled his gaze on me. I guess I was the least threatening target. "He wanted me to help him pull a guy's leg. He wanted me to tell this friend of his that I saw a particular car out by Effinger's before I left on my last run. He knew I'd been gone. I live out that way and the guy'd believe me.

"The funny thing was, I had seen one.

"I had to leave by three-thirty that Friday morning. While I was loading my stuff, a fine-looking black car comes sliding out of the dark up our road. We don't get much traffic out there during the daytime, much less at night. Lately, there's been some drug deals going down out our direction, so we've all been keeping our eyes open. Nice cars cruisin' around there have 'drug deal' written all over them, so I looked that car over pretty good until I saw the personal plate: 'Senate Seat 78.' Everybody knows that's Senator Crook's plate.

"I couldn't tell if the driver was a man or a woman, but it was a little person, just barely peepin' over the steering wheel. A guy was slumped over on the passenger side. I thought he was sleepin'. You know what everyone says about Crook and his drinkin' and these two didn't look like trouble. I figured 'em for lost, but they didn't stop and I wasn't goin' to flag 'em down to see if they needed help."

Scarcely able to conceal his excitement, Wills looked at me. When our eyes met, I looked away.

Roundtree stood, a formidable presence. "Why didn't you come forward when you heard we found Crook's body in Effinger's pond that next day?" His stance and demeanor made the question sound like an accusation.

"I didn't know it." Gypson's tone was matter-of-fact. "When I'm on the road, I only call home every two or three nights. My boy's fourteen years old. He got a front tooth knocked out at school while I was gone. Nobody thought to tell me about it until I got back." He spoke to Roundtree. "I considered my boy losing a tooth was news. Well, same thing about the killing. It just didn't come up."

Roundtree eased back down onto the edge of his chair, frowning but looking convinced. Spence flared. "It was in the papers and on the television."

Gypson turned his focus on the deputy. "Not in Vicksburg, it wasn't. Besides that, I don't see much TV when I'm on the road."

Wills said, "You didn't recognize anyone in the car?"

"Either one, the driver or the passenger, could've been Senator Crook. I couldn't see all that good, but they both looked to be short."

"Is this the information you gave Deputy Spence and Ms. Dewhurst yesterday?"

"That and I took them out and showed them where I saw the car."

"Will you show me?"

"Be glad to."

Suddenly Wills got moving. He glanced at the court reporter. "That's all, Jerry. Thanks." He looked at me. "Do you want to go?"

Pursing my lips, I smoothed the front of my skirt and shook my head without bothering to return his look. "No."

Jim turned to the deputy. "Spence, how about you?"

Roundtree stood, fidgeting. "I'll take the van. We can all go. How about that, Jance?"

"Thanks, Sheriff, I still have a deadline *and* a job, no thanks to the bureaucrats." I turned on Wills. "May I be excused now, your lordship?"

Every movement in the room stopped for a brief, awkward moment. Then Bryce DeWitt stepped over to shake the sheriff's hand. The others stood too and began shuffling toward the door.

"Jancy . . ." Jim began, then glanced around at the others, who were filing into the reception room as they talked quietly together.

Looking at him, my anger wavered. I fought the attraction as I pushed myself out of his chair. "See ya around, Wills." With that, I walked stiffly to the door and out.

# Chapter Fifteen

The bureau lab was processing plaster casts of tire tread, fibers collected from the back of Crook's trousers and pieces of blue ribbon, and comparing paint on a tree with a scrape on the side of Mrs. Crook's Cadillac.

Wills subpoenaed telephone records from several phones, including the pay phone at Legends.

With the investigation coming to a head, Mrs. Teeman watched Agent Wills closely.

"Are you staying late again?" she asked, shutting down machines and preparing to leave the office Friday evening.

He nodded.

"You were here early this morning."

He grunted agreement.

"Usually when you smell the kill, you relax a little."

"This case is different."

He was at his desk again Saturday when Mrs. Teeman stopped by the office to drop off the mail. She had expected to find him there. His eyes looked sunken, his olive skin sallow. She wanted to help. "Are you sleeping at all?"

"Not much."

"Do you have a date tonight?"

Wills looked up at her, surprised. "No, why?"

"It's Saturday. I thought you might."

"No," he muttered, "I don't."

By nine o'clock Saturday night, Wills was ready for a

break. On impulse, he drove to Cherry Street. He cruised by Jancy's house, parked a block away and got out of the car.

The crisp air tingled as he breathed in deep draughts. The case was coming to an end, the pieces of the puzzle finally spinning into place, but the victory felt hollow.

He strolled down Cherry, away from her house, then back toward his car before he noticed the tree. Their tree. He stepped under the branches and put his hand on the bark, patted it and smiled.

As he started to leave, he noticed a figure approaching from the other direction. With some consternation, he recognized her stride. He would have to pass in front of her to get to his car. He withdrew into the shadows of the massive tree.

I walked down Cherry Street and looked at the big old tree. I had gone that direction on purpose. Wallowing in happy memories could make a person sad sometimes, but I already felt miserable. Maybe happy memories would help.

Something didn't look right about the trunk. I did a double-take and stopped.

Jim stepped from under the branches into the diffused light from the street. Startled, wondering if I had somehow conjured this illusion by wishing him there, I stared for a long moment until I was convinced he was real.

Neither of us said anything. We just stood there looking at each other and breathing the brisk night air.

I shifted from one foot to the other, which moved me half a step forward. Apparently taking that as some kind of signal, Jim opened his arms and beckoned me forward.

I shivered, resisting. Was that all it took? All he had to do was whistle and I'd come? What a sad commentary on my character. But I was cold and tired and knew I'd have a terrible time sleeping again that night, even after I gave up the good fight and went to bed.

My shoulders rose and fell with a deep sigh. As I walked toward him, he didn't look so much victorious as relieved. His looking contrite helped. Then he did the nicest thing of all. He unbuttoned his overcoat and his suit coat and opened them, a wordless invitation to share his warmth.

My hands brushed the front of his shirt. Before I realized what I was doing, I gathered handfuls of the fabric and crushed it. His arms came around me and his body heat drew me like a cheery fire on the hearth lures a weary traveler. Clutching at him, I pulled myself into the shelter and shivered again at his warmth.

Gently, he cocooned us both in his coats. When I was securely in his arms, folded tightly against his body, he drew a deep, deep breath.

We stood there without a word. Minutes ticked by, yet neither of us moved. He seemed to enjoy sharing the quiet as much as I did. When he finally moved, it was to kiss my forehead, then my face. Maybe too eagerly, I raised my mouth. He gathered me closer and seemed to rise up over me. Our lips sealed, joining us in an intimacy that eliminated all thought or sound, every other person or event.

Without intending to, I began rubbing against him until I became aware of mutual sounds of want.

He kissed me again and again, pushing deeper with each thrust, pulling me so close it felt like our bodies would join in spite of our clothing, flesh to flesh.

Scarcely able to breathe enough air to feed my pounding heart that sent blood coursing crazily through my veins from tip to toe, I couldn't get enough of him.

He was the one, finally, who made a decision. He stood

taller, pulling his mouth from mine. When I opened my eyes, he was studying my face. His expression was not triumphant—which would have sent me running—but sober. He held us like that for several moments, I suppose, to allow our ardor to cool.

Gradually the intensity ebbed and I was content simply to stand locked in his arms. Still, neither of us risked a word. I was deathly afraid of ruining the amnesty and reawakening the discord.

When I squirmed a little, Jim eased his vise-like hold. I shivered as I shrugged out of his wraps. When I sprang free, he caught my shoulders, steadying me. Then he turned me and clasped my hand as we walked back toward my house.

When we reached his parked car, Jim stopped and pulled me around to face him before breaking our silence. "Go home with me." The huskiness in his voice revealed pent-up passion, which served as wake-up and fair warning.

I did the last thing I wanted to do at that moment. I shook my head. "Not tonight."

"Why not tonight?"

"Because tonight I might not say stop."

We stood looking at each other for a long minute before I rose onto my tiptoes and kissed his cheek. He caught me up under the arms and pivoted, pressing me against his car, and leaning his lower body into me. "Can you sleep?" His voice was hoarse.

"No."

"You could beside me."

"I know."

"Please. I need you, Jancy. Now. Tonight. Please."

I was amazed that my voice sounded so firm when my resolve was so liquid. "No."

★ ★ ★ ★ ★

The phone in my room was ringing by the time I got there. "Hello?"

"You are wise beyond your years."

I smiled, caressed by the resonance of Jim's voice, which seemed to wash me clean with forgiveness.

"Finally you have detected a bit of truth," I said. "And all by yourself."

"If you had come home with me tonight, I wouldn't have let you escape. I would have locked you up and kept you my prisoner forever."

My laugh sounded nervous, even to me. "I'm glad I don't have a clue about what you mean."

He became quiet, apparently content to hear me breathing on the other end of the line.

"Jim, how's the case shaping up?"

He snorted a caustic laugh. "Fine, thanks in no small part to your meddling."

"That's your reward for getting smitten with a nosy woman."

"It's only a small flaw." He hesitated. "Like a feather in an almost perfect diamond."

"I see."

"Would you like to have an almost perfect diamond?"

"Nah, I'd probably lose it. I have trouble keeping up with small objects. I even misplaced my car one time—at the Jessup Y. That little oversight has caused me all kinds of grief."

"You don't want to talk about diamonds?"

"No. We have a lot of more immediate things to talk about."

"But you might want to think about a diamond someday?"

"Maybe, maybe not. One thing is certain, I'm enjoying

this conversation. In fact, this may be my all-time favorite discussion." I paused, struggling to make my voice business-like. "Now, quit changing the subject and tell me how your evidence is coming together."

It was his turn to heave a sigh. "Okay. Right now I'm scrambling. Imagine the murders are spokes running from the hub of a wheel. I've located the hub. The villain. But I need some hard evidence. It may be right in front of me, but I can't put my finger on it. I have to find the key to this thing."

I gasped.

"What's wrong?"

"Wills." I wanted to measure my words and stay calm. "I know where we might find a piece of your evidence. Agent Wills, the key might be a key."

"What are you talking about?"

"Remember when you found Crook's car, his keys were in the seat but the ignition key wasn't on the key ring?"

"Right."

"A Cadillac key is distinctive, isn't it?"

"Yes, gold-plated, one-of-a-kind. We had to wait until Mrs. Crook got back from her daughter's to move the car. Even Emery's dealership didn't have a key that would drive it."

"Wills, if you were an avid collector of keys, had been since childhood, and you happened upon a one-of-a-kind keepsake—actually had it in your hand—and you had reason to believe no one would come looking for that item, would never guess it was in your possession, you might decide to hang onto that little trinket, mightn't you?"

"I guess. What are you talking about?"

"Jim, Patsy Leek has a collection of keys."

"How do you know that?"

"I hesitate to remind you of my visit with Jason Trout." I

paused a moment to let him assimilate that. When he didn't speak, I hurried on. "Remember, I told you, while I was there Jason asked me to make him some soup. Above the cabinets in Patsy's kitchen she had three collections. Baseball caps, fishing lures and a glass display case with a key collection. It was impressive. I commented on it, thinking it was Jason's. He said it was hers.

"He also told me she has hundreds of keys in the box below the case, but the best ones are on display, in front of God and everybody. Not only that, I think I remember a shiny new gold-colored car key."

Jim's words came in a rush. "I need to check it out. I may be able to get a warrant."

In my excitement, I interrupted. "I could drop by, tell them I wanted to check details of my mono feature with Jason."

"No!" His voice had that familiar edge. "We're not going through another session like the one at Legends the other night."

"Don't start talking tough with me, Wills, ordering me around, threatening to arrest me and all that junk. Just say, 'Jancy, I don't want you to go.' "

"Jancy, I don't want you to go." He gave a self-effacing laugh. "Jason's not there, anyway. We've had people on her and the house for several days. The kid's at his dad's in Dominion. I, however, might be able to wangle an invitation. If she invites me over socially, we circumvent the warrant. She might do it. She might even do it tomorrow."

"Are you shutting me out? This was my idea, remember?"

The timbre of his voice changed and I could practically hear him grinning. "You be the brains, I'll be the muscle."

"Muscle trimmed in rubber bands and ribbons isn't all that attractive."

He chuckled darkly. "I hear that. Stop by the office in the morning. We'll devise and implement Plan A."

"Your office? On Sunday?"

"Unless I can talk you into a return trip to my parlor, little fly."

"Right. You are absolutely right."

"About ten? You'll be safe enough at the office. Several people are in and out, even on weekends. See you there."

# Chapter Sixteen

"Well, hello, tall, dark and handsome," Patsy Leek said as Agent Wills arrived at the sheriff's office Monday. "It's been lonesome around here lately, what with you keeping my staff holed up at your place every day. When are you going to invite me over to play your little games?"

"I guess I've been waiting for you to invite me first." Wills smiled, noting that the light was on in the sheriff's private office and the door stood ajar.

"Actually," Pat lowered her voice to an intimate tone, "I've been having a little trouble with my kid. A guy like you might be able to help straighten him out. I'll cook you a steak. We can tell him we're in love. That'll be half true, anyway."

"I'm pretty busy right now," Wills hedged. He didn't want to appear too eager.

"Honey, you have to eat. Come around about eight. I'll have everything ready. We won't waste any time, baby. We'll get right to it." She winked and pulled her skirt up to show a little more leg.

Wills smiled. It had been easier than he thought, but the words of a nursery rhyme rolled through his mind. "Come into my parlor, said the spider. . . ."

"Oh, baby," Pat said, interrupting his thought, "don't tell anyone you're coming. You know how people around here love to gossip about the least little impropriety."

"You mean the *appearance* of impropriety, don't you?"

She gave him a suggestive shrug and another wink.

Wills returned the smile. "Thanks, Patsy. I appreciate the invite." He stepped to Roundtree's door and poked his head in to speak to the sheriff. "We're having a little meeting at the office this afternoon. Can you come by around three-thirty or four?"

Standing next to his desk thumbing through his mail, the sheriff glanced up. "I'll be there. When're you going to let me in on your theory?"

"This afternoon. We may have a new development. I'll tell you about it then."

"You seem calmer. You and Jancy patch it up?"

"No." Wills fought the urge to look for Patsy's reaction.

Roundtree shook his head. "She's aces, Jimbo. Really. The best there is."

Wills nodded solemnly. "I'm sure she is. Thanks, Sheriff. See you this afternoon."

After Wills had gone, Roundtree walked into the front office. "Patsy, I didn't know you were having trouble with the boy."

She looked surprised.

"I overheard you talking to Wills. Honey, you know I'm crazy about both your kids. I'd be more than glad to help. I'll run by this afternoon after work and see if Jason wants to go fishing Saturday, have a little man-to-man outing."

"I appreciate your interest, Sheriff, but Jason's coming around. I just thought seeing a hard-nosed career type like Wills might motivate him."

Roundtree was reading a letter open in his hand. He didn't appear to have heard. "I'll probably be stuck at Wills' office 'til five or after. I'll swing by your place on my way home and ask the kid about Saturday."

Patsy studied the empty doorway for a long while after Roundtree settled back at his desk. Then she smiled and turned back to her switchboard.

"Sheriff, it's three-thirty," she reminded him later. Roundtree gathered papers into a file folder on his desk, put it under his arm and was almost out of the office when she spoke again. "I'll have you a bourbon and branch water ready and waiting at the house about five. Maybe you shouldn't mention to anyone that you're stopping by my place. No use having word leak back to the little woman, huh?"

He raised his eyebrows and nodded.

Patsy poured bourbon into a glass as soon as she got home from work. She dropped in four small white tablets and stirred. She would add the ice and a shot of water later.

Hurriedly she changed into her jeans, a button-up shirt and ladies' hunting boots, unconcerned about the mismatched laces. She took two steaks out of the freezer and laid them on the drainer to thaw before she threw together a quick salad. Glancing at the clock, she fumbled through her purse, snagged the car keys and ran outside.

She drove to the next street and down a block to the small church, parked in the empty lot, then jogged home. "Schedule's a little tight," she muttered.

She had just caught her breath when Roundtree's cruiser pulled up. She opened the front door to call to him. "My car's in the shop. Pull to the carport 'round back."

Roundtree frowned.

She pointed around the corner, went back inside and closed the door, then stepped to the window to make sure he did as he was told.

"Yes." She made a fist in the air as the cruiser moved.

Running through the house, Pat turned on the shower in the front bathroom, closed the door and hesitated. The running water was clearly audible. Good. She grabbed the beginning of the sheriff's drink and added ice and water. Stirring the highball, she smiled as her visitor came through the back door.

"Hi. Jason's in the shower. Your drink's ready."

"Where's yours?"

"I'm fixing it next."

"Here, you take this one and I'll make my own." He tried to hand her his glass.

"Not a chance. You're the man just in from a hard day at the office. You get served first. Besides, I like mine with cola." Roundtree looked at her as if he intended to argue, but she nudged him toward the living room and he appeared to forget it.

She poured Coke and a dash of bourbon into a glass and hurried to join Roundtree on the sofa.

They sat sipping, listening to the shower in the other room and making small talk about new carpeting for his office and how much it would cost to update the communications system. Pat was chatty and Roundtree began to relax.

"Boy, I'm beat," he said. "I'll be glad to get home. Good idea, pulling around into the carport. It's a hell of a lot closer."

She simpered at the compliment. "Are you ready for a refill? It may be a couple of minutes yet. That kid loves a good soak in the shower. I imagine he'll be along pretty quick now."

Roundtree finished off his drink and leaned his head back. "Wills is wrong." The sheriff's words were slurred.

Pat perked up.

"Dead wrong. She's fine, just like I told him. Good as

259

ever." Roundtree tried a hapless grin before his mouth flopped open. His drinking glass dropped out of his hand and sent ice skittering across the rug.

She picked up the glass, disregarding the spilled contents. She assumed he was talking about Jancy again. The girl was going to be devastated, losing two of her greatest admirers in a single day. Patsy snorted. It was for the best. A woman needed to get used to disappointments where men were concerned. Besides, killing them ultimately would save Jancy's life. Unless she kept nosing around asking questions.

Patsy gave him five minutes on the clock, enough time for her to turn off the shower and thaw the steaks in the microwave. She hoped she'd remember to put the potatoes in to bake at six forty-five. She'd be back by then.

"I always did love two-for-one sales. A cruder person might call this an honest-to-goodness, life and death doubleheader." She snickered as she raced to her bedroom and fumbled at the back of her closet to retrieve the little girl's eyelet nightgown laced through with baby blue satin ribbon. She cut a length of the ragged ribbon, smiling, then hung the gown back behind the other clothing, smoothing it so it didn't wrinkle.

From the weekender bag on the overhead shelf, she picked out a stack of hundred-dollar bills bound with sturdy rubber bands from the office. She slipped one rubber band free, hesitated, then took a second one. Might as well. It would save her the trouble of getting the suitcase down again later.

"Waste not, want not." She slipped one rubber band over her hand to dangle from her wrist and hung the second one on the doorknob, wishing she had thought to clip two pieces of ribbon from the nightgown when it was out.

She picked up the sheriff's glass, washed it and put it away.

Back in the living room, she shook Roundtree's shoulder, then pushed his eyelids with her index finger. He didn't stir. Pleased, she knelt beside him on the sofa, slipped on the latex gloves from her pocket and began struggling with his big brass belt buckle.

Perspiring, she glanced at the clock. *Six o'clock. Straight up. How appropriate.*

Tugging at his clothing, she laid open Roundtree's trousers, ran her hand into the fly of his under shorts and pulled out the prize. She balanced it in her hand, looking it over critically, before she began stroking it.

It didn't take long to induce her willing subject to a cooperative stance. Her fingers nimble, she wound the rubber band round and round Roundtree's penis, cutting off all circulation.

"Die, you little son of a bitch." She hissed the words, breathing through her mouth in her excitement. She pulled the end of the ribbon from her pocket and tied it neatly, redoing it twice to make sure it was perfect.

Carefully, she placed the strangling member back inside Roundtree's shorts and zipped his uniform trousers, snapped off the gloves and stuffed them in her jeans pocket.

"There," she said, patting the package. "Don't ever let it be said that Patsy Leek can't still turn a man's head." Then she covered her mouth with both hands and giggled.

Six-ten.

She moved two chairs, clearing a path, then pulled Roundtree forward, leaning him over his own knees. His head bobbed forward and his arms dangled to the floor beside his legs. She backed up to him on her knees and wrapped his arms one at a time across the front of her. She clasped the arms tightly, then struggled to her feet.

She had not anticipated he would be so heavy. Neither

Benunda nor Speir was as large as Roundtree. They had been easy to transport. Crook was shorter, and of course she hadn't had to lift Benedict at all.

Roundtree's dead weight was almost more than she could manage. She could drag him only a few feet at a time between rests. The extra effort he required made her angry.

The clock seemed to be running faster.

She tried to hurry. She was sweating profusely. The more anxious she became, the more she perspired.

Patsy was halfway across the kitchen, nearly to the back door, when Roundtree's toes caught on the threshold from the living room. The added resistance, together with her perspiring palms, ripped him from her grasp.

Lurching, struggling to balance her load and maintain her footing, she fell forward onto her knees. Roundtree slid silently down her back and into a heap on the floor.

The clock. Damn it. It was six-thirty. She'd better put the potatoes in to bake. She turned on the oven, got two potatoes from the bin under the sink, scrubbed them quickly and shoved them into the oven, stepping over Roundtree's bulk in the middle of the room.

She didn't have time to transport him now.

She couldn't leave him where he was, she thought frantically, then giggled at her ridiculous dilemma.

She would have to hide him until Wills was ready.

With Roundtree and Wills dead, she would be home free. No one else even suspected. She'd thought Dewhurst would have to be her first female victim, but Jancy was no longer a threat now that Wills had lost interest in her.

Pat thought about Wills. Now there was a prize. She looked forward to getting her hands on him. She wondered, icily, if she might give him a little less of the Ambien, then coax him into *doing her* before she *did him*. Sometimes he seemed interested. Dare she take such a chance? It would be quite a coup. Later she might get a chance to tell Dewhurst about it, in detail—making her story hypothetical, of course.

She stared at Roundtree's crumpled body, then scanned the room. Her utility room had no door. No place to hide him there, unless she stuffed him inside an appliance. She eyeballed him again. The sheriff was definitely too big to squeeze into her dryer tub.

She could stand him in the pantry, but he would have to remain upright and he'd gone completely limp. She'd have to come up with something better than that. Not enough time left to transport him to the back of the house. Her mind raced. She turned round and round in the kitchen. Her eyes fell to the cabinet door that concealed the yawning area under the sink. She had left it ajar when she got the potatoes.

Quickly, she opened both doors and eyed the space. She had always wanted a shelf to give her more storage, but never put one in. Lucky for her. And he'd probably fit. She pulled out the potato bin, the cleaning products and the trash can. Perfect.

She got on her hands and knees and started to shove Roundtree's body toward the opening. Inch by inch, he slid over the linoleum. When she'd got him close, she sat down, braced herself with her arms, put her feet on him for better leverage and pushed. Nearly there. She glanced at the clock. Lordy, it was seven-fifteen.

Deftly she rolled him up over the sill and pushed his legs in first, wrapping him around the pea trap that looped down from the sink.

He was nearly inside when she closed the doors to see if she could finish pushing him with those. Something crunched.

Pat threw the doors open. She had mashed his pinkie between a door and the sill. Blood spurted from his torn fingernail.

"Damn."

Squeezing, shoving, pinching and smashing, finally she got Roundtree's massive body inside. She closed the doors and sat back on the floor, leaning on her arms, looking down at herself, then up at the clock. Seven-thirty.

She had to move his cruiser. But she'd forgotten to get his keys.

Her chin fell forward onto her chest. So much trouble. So many complications. Roundtree was more work than he was worth. After all, he'd been relatively harmless, sometimes even helpful promoting her schemes. But it was too late to change her mind.

Carefully she reopened the doors and peered inside. He was breathing evenly, almost snoring. She grimaced.

Patting his trousers, she located the keys. The clock continued moving at record speed. Quelling a rising panic, she snaked her hand around the top of his pocket, touched the keys, grasped them and pulled. They wouldn't budge.

She tried smoothing his trousers. No deal.

Finally, she pulled his thigh and straightened his leg enough to free the keys. When she had them in her hand, she bent his leg back into its original position and shut the doors. One kept popping open a little. She couldn't make herself look at the clock.

Nearly out of time, she allowed the stubborn cupboard door to remain ajar. She darted out the back door, hopped into the sheriff's cruiser and backed it into the alley.

A shade-tree mechanic in the next block always had cars lining the alleyway. She parked the sheriff's unit among the vehicles awaiting attention.

Pulling up her shirttail, she used it to wipe the steering

wheel and the keys and the door handle, then stuck the keys back in the ignition.

Again using the shirttail, she closed the car door. Then she ran all the way back to her house and darted in the back door just as the doorbell sounded.

She caught her breath, tousled her hair with her fingers, jammed her shirttail into her jeans, glanced around the kitchen, then ran to the front door.

"I thought you might have forgotten." Wills looked her up and down, obviously surprised by her appearance.

"I had a little trouble with the plumbing." She tried to speak slowly enough to hide her breathlessness. "Everything's under control now. Come on in."

Any other time, Wills would have left, but plan A was underway.

"What will you have to drink?" She was still trying to tidy her clothing and maintain an air of calm.

"Nothing, thanks."

"Oh, come on. How about a fresh cup of coffee?"

"That sounds good."

"You just sit right down here." She fluffed the pillows on the back of the couch.

"Is Jason here?"

"No," she said, then glanced at Wills' face with some surprise. "He's. . . ." She hesitated. Oh, yeah, Wills was there to see Jason. "He ran to the store for me, but he'll be back any minute." Wills followed her as she turned and hurried toward the kitchen.

"Go on," she insisted, turning back to nudge him toward the couch. He seemed determined to stay with her. She tried again. "Take a load off. Let me get you that coffee." She hurried from the room and swung the door closed behind her quickly enough to discourage his following her.

Wills did not sit down, however. Instead, he paced the living area, wondering at its condition.

Jancy had said the house was tidy. This room was not. The braided rug in the center of the floor was rumpled, one edge flipped up, and there was a big wet spot in front of the couch. Could that be from the plumbing problems?

Walking around, Wills smoothed the rug and kicked the edge back. He caught a whiff of bourbon. Maybe Patsy had been drinking. Something was odd. That much was obvious. Several pieces of furniture had been hurriedly rearranged, judging by the marks in the rug.

After two or three minutes, Jim walked to the kitchen door, pushed it open and peered into the room.

The coffee pot sputtered and hissed. Pat was absent. Wills frowned, wondering about the trash can and the potato bin abandoned in the middle of the floor. He noticed that the door to the area under the sink had been left ajar. Likely the plumber had left the mess.

Easing into the room, he nudged the cabinet door closed as he looked up to the lighted area above the cupboards. There were the baseball caps and the printer's cases containing the fishing lures, just as Jancy had described, but no key collection.

Had Jancy been mistaken?

She had accurately described the other items. What then?

As he pondered, a spot of red liquid caught his eye. It was on the floor in front of the sink and seemed to be getting bigger as he watched. His curiosity piqued, he reached down to reopen the cabinet door he had just closed.

Wills saw what he first thought was a trash bag. He touched it. It was firm and warm. Beside the bag was what appeared to be a large, bloody, human finger. Wills frowned as he touched the finger. It was attached to a hand, and the hand to an arm. He stooped and peered into the darkened space under the sink.

Gently lifting and pulling, Wills gradually eased Sheriff Dudley Roundtree from beneath Patsy Leek's kitchen sink.

Just as he rolled Roundtree free from the enclosure and was unwinding the sheriff on the kitchen floor, a tiny gasp drew Wills' attention to the door behind him.

Pat stood in the doorway, a toothbrush hanging from her mouth, both hands wrapped around a .38-caliber Police Special pointed at his head.

"Tell the truth, Pat," Wills said calmly, "aren't you a little bit glad it's over?"

She looked puzzled. "It isn't over." She shook her head, barely able to enunciate around the toothbrush. "You haven't had your coffee yet. Things will look entirely different after you've had some of my coffee. All the boys like my coffee."

He smiled and nodded slowly. "It smells good." Cautiously, benignly, he stood. His motions deliberate, he reached for the cup waiting on the counter by the coffee maker. As he picked it up, he heard something slide across the bottom. Without looking inside, he turned the cup in his hands.

"It's ready," Patsy urged. "Go ahead. Pour some. You'll love my coffee. All the boys do."

He gave her his best, most encouraging smile. "Would you get it for me?"

She looked at him oddly just as he lobbed the cup high into the air.

Her eyes followed the airborne missile sailing toward her head. Patsy took one hand off the gun and grabbed at the flying cup. In that split second, the gun barrel dipped toward the floor.

"Let me help you with that." Wills moved with catlike quickness. "Your hands are full." He grabbed the gun, barrel first, and pushed it to one side.

Both hands free, toothbrush clenched between her teeth, Patsy triumphantly presented the cup.

Wills secured the special, placed Patsy on the kitchen stool and watched her as he telephoned for an ambulance and the police.

Roundtree's bloody pinkie seemed the least of the slumbering sheriff's troubles. Wills checked his pupils and asked Pat what she had given him.

"I suppose he's on drugs. I wouldn't know what kind. I'm drug-free myself."

"Right."

As the ambulance arrived, Wills unzipped Roundtree's fly.

"Keep her on that stool," he ordered when the medics rushed in. They stood astonished as the SBI agent produced a small pocketknife, then opened the sheriff's trousers and underwear to reveal the bow and the rubber band. He wielded the pocketknife carefully, cutting away both of the grim decorations.

"Have you ever treated anything like that before?" the younger medic asked his older partner.

Eyes wide, his companion shook his head.

# Chapter Seventeen

I got to Patsy's house with Undersheriff Raymond Wheeler moments behind the ambulance and police.

Patsy, her hands cuffed in front of her and carrying a toothbrush, called hello and waved to me as officers led her to a city police cruiser.

The two medics needed assistance wheeling Sheriff Roundtree's stretcher to the waiting ambulance. The undersheriff signaled them to stop.

"Don't stop," I pleaded, but they did anyway.

Roundtree looked up at me and tried to focus glassy eyes. "He was right, Sis." The sheriff's words came out slurred. "Wills was right the whole time. Let him take care of you, little girl. Let him watch after you until I get better."

I smiled, blinking to clear the sudden, unexpected tears. "I will, Sheriff. I'll do exactly what you say, until you're well enough to put up a decent fight."

He looked pleased at my gentle teasing. "Good." He wheezed and closed his eyes.

One of the medics gave me a reassuring look. "She gave him enough of that stuff to stop a bull. And it did, too." The man grinned. "But it didn't stop him long."

Wills had sent three patrolmen through the neighborhood to find the sheriff's car. Inside the house, he had others searching for evidence. When one produced the ancient child's nightgown partially laced with the familiar blue trim,

Wills examined it carefully before he bagged it and sent it to the lab. "See if they can match this trim with the ribbons found on or with the victims."

Another policeman digging through Patsy's closet turned up the suitcase containing packets of cash.

Wills used a pencil to move the money packets, which were tied with thick, familiar rubber bands. At the bottom of the suitcase, he uncovered a yellowed, laminated hospital nursery card that read, "Baby Boy Leek, 8 lbs. 4 oz., 21-1/2 inches." A blue ribbon threaded through a hole in one corner of the card was looped into a neat bow, eerily similar to the blue bows found at the scenes of each of the four murders and the one newly removed from Sheriff Roundtree.

"Well, look here at this," Undersheriff Wheeler called from another room. Wills followed the sound of Wheeler's voice to Jason Trout's bedroom. There, on the boy's bedside table, was the box containing Pat's extensive collection of keys. Apparently Jancy's comments had piqued his curiosity and Jason had been checking it out.

Again using a pencil to keep from marring fingerprints, Wills riffled through the contents until he uncovered the lone, distinctive Cadillac key.

"Have the lab check this for prints." He bagged the key in a small brown sack. "Then get it back to Foxworthy. Have him see if it fits Senator Crook's car."

Still searching the bedroom, Wills looked up and grinned when I stepped into the doorway. I tried to return the smile, but mine was a little shaky. "Is the sheriff going to be all right?"

He nodded. "Yes. Except for a bruise and a scrape here and there, he's fine."

"Did he . . . ?"

"Yes. If it hadn't been for you, the sheriff might have been our perp's fifth victim."

I swallowed hard and my eyes stung. "Plan A was a little riskier than I realized."

"I was ready, but Roundtree heard her invite me over. I told him this afternoon that she was my prime suspect and why. Even faced with the circumstantial evidence, he thought I was wrong. He's a loyal friend. He had to find out for himself."

"I hope he's convinced."

"He's got some very solid, very personal physical evidence this time."

"How about Patsy?"

Wills frowned at the floor. "I can't tell about her. She's seen people beat raps. Insanity is a pretty iffy defense. I don't think the toothbrush is a prop. If the judge buys her act, he'll send her to a mental health facility for evaluation. If she can fool them, she stays until the medical staff declares she's regained her sanity. Then, maybe, she's back on the street."

"Do you think she's crazy?"

"Like a fox."

As Jim moved toward me, I stepped away from the door to allow him to pass, then I fell into step behind him. "Jim, did you notice she was wearing lace-up boots?"

He turned and squinted at me.

I shrugged. "I just happened to notice. The laces don't match. One's newer. Remember the thong around Benunda's neck?"

"Wheeler," Wills shouted. The undersheriff reared his head from the far side of Pat's bed. "Call the jail. If he hasn't done it already, have the jailer go get Patsy Leek's boots. She knows procedure, knows how dangerous it is to allow emotionally unstable inmates to have shoelaces in a cell. Get the boots to the lab. Tell them to compare the laces, see if either one of them matches the thong from Benunda's neck."

He fixed me with an admiring gaze. "You are good."

I gave him a modestly triumphant smile as I pulled out the old reliable spiral notebook. Wills' rigid posture wilted slightly as he pivoted to walk toward the front of the house.

"Come on," I said, trailing him. "I let you run Plan A. Stick to our deal."

He shook his head, sighed and paused as he reached the front door. He stood against one jamb and pushed me to the other to allow the police a clear path in and out. "Where do you want to start?"

"At the beginning. Why Benunda and Speir?"

Patiently, he repeated his interviews with Spence and Angela Fires, their eyewitness accounts of the pizza delivery at the sheriff's office.

"Speir saw Patsy put office money in her purse. He teased her about it. He could probably tell he'd struck a nerve.

"Telephone records show someone called the sheriff's office twice a week from Benunda and Speir's apartment from then until their deaths.

"The Jessup apartments are student housing. The university keeps records of outgoing calls. But the phone records Patsy kept in the sheriff's office didn't show their calls incoming, not from either one of those guys or anyone else at the times indicated."

"So what?"

"Why do you think one or both of those guys would call the sheriff's office twice a week and she didn't bother to log those calls?"

"They were shaking her down?"

"That's my theory. Actually, you bolstered it with Maggie Trout's comments about her mother having some new financial crisis. We got a statement from Maggie which amounts to basically what she told you." He gave me a grudging look. "Because of what you found out, we knew the questions to ask.

"Anyway, Patsy was embezzling from the sheriff's coffers with both hands. We found a suitcase of cash in her closet. Apparently she's been trying to recoup the money she had to pay out to the blackmailer."

"Were both Benunda and Speir involved?"

"I don't think so. Benunda had a whole different agenda. A higher mission. No, I think the blackmail was strictly Speir's game. I think Benunda was an innocent bystander whom Patsy mistakenly assumed knew too much. She didn't want to take chances with her golden goose setup.

"Anyway, following that trail, I asked the sheriff to give us duplicates of his office financial records on the Q.T.

"Cash receipts indicated someone was stealing big time. Cash flows through his office, thousands of dollars at a whack. Patsy handled all the money. There were no safeguards. She wrote all the checks, did all the bookkeeping. Roundtree liked it that way. He refused to think she would steal from him.

"Even when I showed him enough evidence to convince him of the embezzlement, he thought she had a major financial crisis, did it for her kids or some other noble reason. He wouldn't buy the murder theory with her as sole perpetrator at all."

Wills stepped out onto the front porch, into the fresh air. I followed.

"It looked to me like Speir's ridicule and the blackmail triggered some kind of breakdown," Wills continued, moving to one side so as not to impede officers still moving briskly in and out of the house. "Speir may have come on to her sexually. Our conversations with her daughter indicated sexual pressure was a dangerous road to take with Patsy. She may have felt physically vulnerable with Speir, fearful that she couldn't afford to refuse his advances and risk getting in trouble with authority figures. It may have been too close a parallel to her situation with her older brother when she was a kid. Anyway, something inside her snapped.

"The deaths of Benunda and Speir started me following the gay rights theory, which was a red herring. Of course, my main problem was you."

I glanced up from my notebook and he gave me a lopsided smile.

"After I met you, my usually reliable ability to concentrate went on the fritz. It began the first minute I saw you . . . startled you . . . standing by Roundtree's cruiser out on the highway.

"You turned around, all big-eyed wonderment. I liked you in a heartbeat—your face, your body, your excitement. The rush caught me flat-footed." He looked a little surprised at his own choice of words. "Save the cute comments about flat feet and cops."

I smiled indulgently but didn't speak. He eased into a metal lawn chair on the porch, and indicated I should take the other one. I did, still scribbling in my notebook, as he continued.

"I was back on task when I ran into you in the morgue two days later. Your hair was fried, your clothes rumpled and you weren't wearing any makeup, but something about you knifed straight to my heart." He hesitated. "Besides that, you smelled terrific.

"When you and I stood there looking at the old man's body, I was aware of only one thing—you breathing in and out next to me. I would have been content to stand there, gazing into that guy's wrinkled old face for a long time, if it meant keeping you beside me." He paused and I looked up to find him staring at me.

"Then we saw Speir," I reminded him. I didn't want either one of us to get distracted, and his comments were pulling me far afield.

Wills nodded. "Yeah. That scared you. When you recognized him, you took off like a shot. You flew up those stairs, only hitting about every third one.

"I went back to the office and had a serious session with myself about solving the crime first and investigating you later.

"A couple of days went by and I got back on track about the time we turned up Crook's body.

"Sunrise Plaza Nursing Home records showed they wrote monthly checks to Patsy Leek, whom they paid as an adviser. They refused to take county referrals after the last day of July, on Crook's order. He had flagged the ledger. The checks to Patsy dwindled as the people she had referred died. The checks stopped altogether in September with the death of her last referral. For Pat, that well had gone dry right at the time she desperately needed money to pay off a blackmailer. Like I said, under the pressure, something inside her snapped.

"Later, when you told me about your interviews with Jason and Maggie Trout, we dug a little deeper and found Pat had many, many reasons to be angry with Crook. First he dumped her, then he bailed out on their kickback scheme. She had already murdered the two boys and had gotten away with it, as far as she knew.

"She was keeping close tabs on our investigation. She knew we were stymied. Plus, I think she genuinely enjoyed killing men, especially if it meant torturing them first."

Wills paused to allow me to catch up with my notes. When

I finally looked up, he was watching me. Diverting his eyes, he returned to the recap. "She loved all the publicity her little signature got after we found Crook's body and you ran the ribbons story." He paused again.

"You don't think my stories aided and abetted her, do you?" I hated to think I had contributed to the murders in any way.

"No, but they gave her ego a boost. Of course, at that point, I couldn't make heads or tails of anything. I couldn't tell what was happening to me. I couldn't get you out of my mind.

"I thought I must be getting completely paranoid when I couldn't shake the idea that Gary's close call at the Leopolds' hunting cabin was somehow tied to the murders. Later, when I checked the phone logs from the sheriff's office, I thought of that and looked. There was no call from the Leopolds to the sheriff's office the afternoon Patsy sent Gary out there. That led me straight back to Pat. Her successes were making her overconfident. Apparently she decided if she could dispose of threats and enemies so easily, she might as well take out a nuisance while she was at it.

"When I asked Brewer Leopold why he had rigged the shotgun to fire at anyone opening the front door of the cabin, he said Pat had suggested the idea the Thursday before. Obviously, she hadn't forgotten her own advice in that short length a time. Just as obviously, she had some motive for sending Gary out there without having gotten a call from them."

One of the investigators stepped between us, interrupting to ask Jim about the box of fishing lures. Jim looked at me. I shrugged.

"I don't think they have anything to do with the case," he told the officer. "Leave them."

The telephone rang in the house. An officer stuck his head out the door to tell Jim that Ms. Leek's son, Jason, was on the phone.

Jim became somber. "Is he at his dad's?"

"I'm not sure."

"Get a number. Tell him to stay put. I'll call him back."

The officer left and Jim turned his full attention back to me. "I didn't know until later that Gary had nosed into the office deposit book the Sunday before. I don't know if Pat thought Gary was a genuine threat to her or if sending him out there was punishment for meddling in her business. In either event, she apparently decided Gary should die, and she had already set it up if Brewer had followed her advice. She may have run out there and checked on it to make sure he had.

"After Spence got injured, while we were loading him into my car to transport him, someone in a car like Pat's cruised by on the scenic highway. Later, I realized it was probably her. If he had been alone, dying or already dead at the cabin, all she'd have had to do was finish it and sign off on the body. No one would have suspected her.

"By then I pretty well knew who we were after, but I didn't know how she selected her victims. And, of course, we didn't have any hard evidence."

Jim stood and paced down the steps into the front yard. As usual, I hopped up and followed, juggling my purse while jotting in my notebook. Wills stopped and turned to watch me. When I glanced up, a slight smile played at the corners of his mouth.

"Anyway, after the close call with Gary, I really got concerned," he continued.

I didn't know what that scrutinizing look was about.

"I had to get focused. Our little killer was damned efficient and seemed to be enjoying her work. I thought Ansel might be able to help me.

"When I went to see him that afternoon, it was like a nightmare. I wanted him to help get my head on straight, and he walked out of his office with his arm around you. You were dogging me at every turn."

I laughed. "I thought you looked annoyed."

"I was. At myself. Just about the time I'd get back on track with the investigation, you'd pop up and set me daydreaming again.

"That next morning, I was running to clear my head for the day, and lo and behold. . . ."

"There I was again." I giggled, trying not to look too smug. "I didn't know. Everyone had been ordered to refer questions about the investigation to you. Ron Melchoir said we had to get close to you."

"Well, you did that. You were tromping in and out of my mind every waking minute and most of the time in my sleep."

I couldn't help smiling. There's a lot of satisfaction in knowing you appeal to someone who appeals to you. When our eyes locked, his blatant admiration became a little overwhelming, and I quickly turned my attention to my notes. "Go on."

He snorted with amusement before he continued. "So, there we were, jogging, getting acquainted, when up roars Mrs. Crook's Cadillac. That little incident was a warning for me and it worked. The killer figured I had an eye for you. She was showing me you were an easy target."

"What about the Rottweiler?"

This time his laugh was genuine. "Actually, the pup's attack was comic relief. Even as paranoid as I'd gotten, I couldn't believe someone had trained that pup to come after you. It was funny, but that's when I realized I had some abilities you lacked."

I shot him a warning glance. We'd already had the conversation covering his courage and my cowardice. I didn't want to go over old ground. He took the hint. "Later, I realized you observed things I didn't see. You had abilities I lacked. We complemented each other."

I exhaled relief. It was a nice thing for him to notice, much less to say. But that brought our review to the next murder. "Then there was Ansel," I said softly.

We both went quiet for a long moment, remembering that awful scene at Ansel's office.

Wills bowed his head as he shook it. "That's the one I understood least."

I couldn't bear to watch the hurt in his face. "I figure Jason was the reason for that one," I said. "I hope he never knows it."

Jim nodded. "All he did was try to solve that age-old mystery about his own sexuality."

"But when he told his mother he thought he was gay, she assumed Ansel was encouraging him."

Jim looked as if he wanted to challenge my statement. "But that wasn't true."

"We know that," I granted, "but Patsy jumped to her own conclusions based on what little she let Jason tell her. He said he thought he was gay and had a long talk with Benedict about homosexuality, came home with beer on his breath and told her he felt relieved. You don't have to be a cop to see how she reached her conclusion.

"By the way," I interrupted myself, determined not to let him see that I was offended, "Patsy told me she thought about taking you up on your offers. She described your condo. She said she'd been there under intimate circumstances."

Jim's dark expression lifted to a broad grin.

I didn't really intend to pry but, darn it, I wanted to know. "Had she?"

"Had she what?" He went all wide-eyed, pretending innocence.

I grimaced but plodded on. "Been there? Had she been in your condo?"

"Yes."

I felt defeated. But I had to play it out. "Under intimate circumstances?"

"No." He eyed me playfully.

"Last fall when the governor and the attorney general were campaigning, they asked me to have some people over. I invited some county Democratic office holders and their employees. Pat showed up, along with thirty or forty other people. It was hardly what you would call intimate."

"She talked about a roaring fire in the fireplace."

"It rained and got cool that night. I like fires in the fireplace. You know that." Our eyes met and held. We just stood there, oblivious to the police busily scurrying around us. I had to get myself together and get to the office and write this story while no one else had it. But I suddenly had another question.

"You're a Democrat?" I asked, barely able to endure his penetrating gaze.

"Yellow dog."

"Oh." I couldn't seem to get beyond that. "Ansel was a big Republican. We were always arguing about it."

"I know." Jim's voice was consoling. "It was part of his charming facade."

I nodded, then took a breath and tried to kick-start my brain again. "One thing I didn't understand. What was she thinking when she sent Spence and me all the way out to Legends?"

"That's easy," he said gently, as if he were speaking to a child. "By then, Pat knew she was my prime suspect. She realized I had cut Roundtree out of the loop on the investigation. She also had you pegged as my Achilles heel. It was a grandstand play to make a point. She wanted to show me she could put you out of the reach of my protection any time she wanted to, at least temporarily."

"But I wasn't in any danger with Spence and Davy Gypson."

"I warned you to be careful, to stay locked in safe places. You agreed, but you were too naive to know safe from unsafe. You wandered off on her say-so. It was a game to her and you were my pawn. She wanted to see if I was willing to sacrifice you." He looked like he was getting agitated again. "I was angry for a lot of reasons. I wanted you to respect my wishes, which you did not. I wanted you safe, which it appeared you were not. And I wanted to put her on notice: harm to you would mean, not just prison, but harm to her."

"But she hired those thugs to beat you up."

He chuckled. "Not to sound immodest, but yeah, right. She knew those kids would only wind up making me mad. But she also knew they would get my attention, especially if you were missing in the mix."

"So did she think you were going to let her go on killing people?"

"She probably hoped to neutralize me, to allow her some wiggle room to dodge the bullet, or in this case, a lethal injection."

"Did it work?"

He gave me a jaundiced look and shook his head. "It was like any hostage situation. At the state prison, there are standing orders. A guard does not open the gates for inmates with hostages. Experience has taught that an inmate who escapes with a hostage gets out and kills the hostage anyway. If the hostage is going to get injured or die, let it happen inside where the convict is still confined."

Jim began walking toward his car. I stayed close at his side, trying to walk and write at the same time as he continued speaking.

"For all intents and purposes, you were Patsy's hostage. If she went free, you were still in danger. I sure as hell wasn't going to take a chance like that. Hence, Plan A."

"I was worried about you with Plan A." I glanced at him as we stopped at the curb. "You were the one she addressed using terms of endearment. Maggie had said that was a sure sign she was after you. I figured you were her target. I didn't know it had anything to do with me or Roundtree. Weren't you in any danger at all?"

He grinned. I hoped he knew I didn't mean that the way it sounded, like I was disappointed that he hadn't been in jeopardy. "No," he said, "because I saw her coming. She and I were the ones, finally, who squared off against each other. I told the sheriff. Roundtree's a pro, but he wanted to give her every benefit of the doubt. She just blindsided him."

"You mean you were never in any danger?" There, I'd done it again, but Jim seemed to take it well. His rolling chuckle simmered a moment, then boiled into an outright laugh.

"I wasn't in nearly as much danger with her as I am with you. Analyzing it, I'm probably the one who ought to cop the insanity plea."

I blushed, not sure what he meant, but I wasn't inclined to ask. Eventually, I stopped writing to peer up at him. "But this case was unusual," I said, trying to let him off the hook. "Maybe without all the pressure you'll realize you don't even like me."

He smiled into my face. "I didn't like you several times already, but it didn't seem to make any difference . . . to the other."

I drew a deep breath. No way was I going to pursue that. "Well, now I can get back to my routine life," I said, "and you can get back to yours. When our paths cross, we'll collaborate."

"Collaborate?" His eyebrows arched. "Does that mean midnight meetings under our tree? Two-stepping some night at Ropers? Regulation-type dating? An occasional sleepover?"

I suddenly grew very serious. "Wills, I told you about my plan. I have a career waiting. I'm going to work for a wire service overseas. I'm going to be in the middle of hot breaking news all over the world. I can't afford to get involved with someone like you."

Not looking the least bit discouraged, he flashed a taunting grin. "How about if you define *involved* and *someone like you*."

I puzzled over that a minute. "Let's put it this way: Any time you need help with a case, I'm your man." His smile broadened, which made me stammer and my blush burn more brightly. "Okay, you know what I mean."

He cocked an eyebrow, leaned toward me and whispered, "Then there's something I need to tell you."

I stood unmoving and silent, waiting for him to continue.

"There's some funny business going on aboard the *Choctaw Gambler* riverboat. They called from the attorney general's office, after they got word we were mopping up here. They asked me to run down there, see if I could help. Would you care to tag along?"

Every instinct told me to refuse or at least shake my head no, but I hesitated as I looked into Wills' hypnotic eyes.

Finally, a little sheepishly, I smiled. "Why not? I'm going to be around another year anyway. I might as well make myself useful."

Wills chuckled and eased closer. I just stood there as he snaked an arm around my waist and brushed his lips over mine. "Yeah, right."

"Wills, you are not going to *get me*." I turned my face to avoid the next whispering little kiss but I didn't try to escape from his hold.

Flashing the familiar Cheshire Cat grin, he squared himself and kissed me again, this time seriously.

I didn't object as he proprietarily pulled my body tightly against his. "We'll see," he said.

Coming up for air, I swayed, glad that he was holding onto me.

He leaned away from me a little, smiled into my eyes for a heartbeat, then, arching a lone eyebrow, he repeated the taunt. "We'll just see."

# *About the Author*

A former newspaper reporter, Sharon Ervin has a journalism degree from the University of Oklahoma. She has written four earlier novels: *Jusu and Mother Earth*, *Bodacious*, *Counterfeit Cowboy*, and *Weekend Wife*. Her short work has appeared in national magazines. She is married, lives in McAlester, Oklahoma, and has four grown children. Visit Sharon's Web site: sharonervin.com.